T0304868

A Good Place to Hide a Body

Also by Laura Marshall

Friend Request

Three Little Lies

The Anniversary

My Husband's Killer

Laura Marshall

A Good Place
to Hide a Body

HODDER &
STOUGHTON

First published in Great Britain in 2024 by Hodder & Stoughton Limited
An Hachette UK company

1

Copyright © Laura Marshall 2024

A CIP catalogue record for this title is available from the British Library

Hardback ISBN 978 1 399 72962 8
Paperback ISBN 978 1 399 72963 5
ebook ISBN 978 1 399 72965 9

Typeset in Sabon MT by Hewer Text UK Ltd, Edinburgh
Printed and bound in Great Britain by Clays Ltd, Elcograf S.p.A.

Hodder & Stoughton policy is to use papers that are natural, renewable
and recyclable products and made from wood grown in sustainable
forests. The logging and manufacturing processes are expected to
conform to the environmental regulations of the country of origin.

Hodder & Stoughton Limited
Carmelite House
50 Victoria Embankment
London EC4Y 0DZ

www.hodder.co.uk

For Jon, of course

Prologue

I scrub frantically at a smear of blood on my hand. The scene I've just fled from flashes before me, over and over, my parents' garden stark in the moonlight. I rub my eyes as if I can wipe away the stain of it, but it's no good. I can still see the silver glint of the scythe, the scarlet petals scattered everywhere and . . . I shudder. I can't bear to think of it.

I shouldn't have run. I should have stayed and tried to clear up the mess, but I panicked, drove back to my flat and here I am, motionless with shock on the sofa, body immobilised, brain scrambling furiously to catch up with the events of the last hour.

I don't want my parents to see it. I want to protect them at all costs, but it's beyond that now. There is no tidying this away, no neat resolution.

Should I call the police? What would I say? How could I begin to explain what has happened over the past few months between my parents and their tenant? How can I possibly unpick the chain of events that has led to the awful scene I've left behind me in their garden?

My mobile rings and I jump. It's flashing 'M & D'. It takes me a second for the significance of this to hit me but when it does, it's like a punch to the head. It's their landline. Mum and Dad are home. They're supposed to be in Norfolk visiting their friend

Marie, but they're not, they're not. They're home. Oh God, have they been into the garden? Please, please, no.

I pick up. At first, whichever of them it is says nothing. For a second, I think we've been cut off and I'm about to call them back when there's a faint cry on the other end of the line.

'Dad?'

'Oh, darling . . .' He tries to go on but the words spill into tears followed by a hysterical intake of breath. To hear my beloved father reduced to this is almost more than I can bear.

'I know,' I say. 'I'm so, so sorry. I didn't want you to see it. I wanted to clear up before you got back, but I panicked. You should have told me you were coming home.'

'Can you come round?' he says tremulously. 'Can you come round *now*?'

'Of course.' My body finally gets the message that action is required and I jump up, gathering purse, coat, keys, shoving my feet into laced-up trainers. 'Are you OK? Is Mum? Shall I . . . do you want me to . . . call the police?'

'No!' He almost shouts it. 'Just come quickly. The garden . . . the . . . body. We need you, Penny.'

THREE MONTHS EARLIER

Chapter 1

Zach sighs as I root around in my bag for the front door key I've had for my parents' home since I was a teenager.

'No wonder you can never find anything in there, what *is* all that crap?' he says.

'That's rich coming from you. You only got back from uni yesterday and your room's already a tip.' I know only too well that parent/child roles always reverse in the end (me and my parents being a case in point) but Zach's only nineteen, I'm not having him telling me off.

'Grandma and Grandpa need to get this doorknob fixed,' he remarks.

'Good luck telling them that,' I say. He's right, it's hanging by a thread, but it's a drop in the ocean compared to everything else that needs doing in the house. Nevertheless, I add it to my mental list.

I finally locate the key and we go into the hall. The house is Victorian, all high ceilings and cornices, and packed with that favourite of every estate agent, original features. If it wasn't so dilapidated it would be beautiful. The familiar scent of dog assaults our nostrils, along with a delicious, savoury, garlicky smell wafting from the kitchen.

'Hello!' I call, hanging my coat on one of the only pegs that hasn't come loose from its moorings and made its way hopelessly to the floor. Zach shrugs out of his enormous parka and does the same.

'Through here!' Mum calls. We make our way down the hall and into the kitchen, where she presides over a vast, bubbling vat of soup on the stove. Dad is doing the *Guardian* cryptic crossword at the battered pine table, its surface scored with scratches and burn marks. His long legs are stretched out and their elderly Westmoreland Terrier, Dottie, lies adoringly across his feet. As ever, he looks slightly too big for his surroundings, a Ken doll in a house built for miniature Sylvanian families.

'Here's my favourite grandson!' Mum says, waving the wooden spoon cheerfully, silver bangles clanking together, splattering thick orange liquid across the worktop. She is tall too, with long, wild grey hair that defies any attempt to tame it, and still wiry and strong at seventy-five. She used to joke that she chose Dad because he was the only man who could make her feel dainty.

'I mean, I'm your only grandson, but yeah hi, Grandma.'

Zach lopes over and gives her a hug and then bends to give Dad one too, plonking himself down at the table next to him. 'What's cooking?'

'Everything soup!' she says. 'All the stuff that needed using up from the allotment. We've struggled to get through everything without you and your appetite. I've got some home-grown raspberries from last summer out of the freezer for pudding too.'

This kitchen has always been the heart of the home and, for a moment, all is as it should be, as it used to be. Even when I was fighting with my parents as a teenager, or Mum was embarrassing me with her tie-dye tops and flares when everyone else's mum was in straight jeans and neat little cardigans, there was comfort to be found here. I find it still in the chipped, earthenware mugs hanging from the dresser, the shelf of well-thumbed cookbooks, spines broken and pages stained with the remnants of meals past, the shelf of tall glass jars each containing a different kind of pasta.

Today that shelf is looped, as always at this time of year, with strands of threadbare tinsel and a string of tattered paper chains with a red and green crayon design scribbled by a long-ago, five-year-old Zach.

'What do you think about nine across?' Dad holds out the paper to Zach, who studies it intently for a few seconds.

'Album,' he says and passes it back. Thanks to the hours he spent here when he was younger, he's a whizz at the insanely difficult crosswords his grandparents favour. It must have skipped a generation as they make absolutely no sense to me whatsoever.

'So, how was your first term?' Mum says.

'Good, thanks,' Zach says. That's about as much as I've got out of him since he got back from Winchester for the Christmas holidays yesterday. I want to press for details – in some ways I wish it was like nursery school where they'd give you a detailed rundown of your child's day when you picked them up. Realistically, I probably wouldn't want to know.

'Ah, I remember those days,' Mum says, misty-eyed. 'I met your grandpa on the very first day at UCL, can you believe it? I'd led ever such a sheltered life, really, up until then. Hardly any of the girls from my school even went to university. Even though it was the late sixties, it wasn't the free love kind of sixties you hear about now. The teachers were working on the assumption that we'd work as secretaries for a few years and then find nice husbands and settle down and have babies.'

'You did do that,' I point out unkindly. Mum and Dad were married almost as soon as they left university and I was born three years after that.

'Well, I got married and had . . . you, yes.' She looks hurt and I feel instantly guilty. 'But I certainly wasn't a secretary, and I worked on and off throughout your whole childhood. Anyway, meeting Heath when I was eighteen changed everything.'

'I know, I know. He took you on an anti-Vietnam protest. I've heard the story a million times.'

'I haven't,' Zach says. 'What was it like?'

'You must have not been listening then,' I say. 'She's always banging on about how she was arrested.'

'You were arrested?' Zach's eyes are like saucers. 'Blimey, Grandma. Sounds like you were living your best life. How on earth did you end up here?'

'There's nothing wrong with here,' I say. They moved from London to this quiet, residential road in a small town in Sussex because they thought it would be a good place to raise children. And they were right, it was great growing up here. I could walk to school, to friends' houses, into the town centre which although not exactly cosmopolitan, boasts a thriving high street. It was why I was so keen for Martin and I to move back here when I was pregnant with Zach.

'What's going on with the scaffolding next door?' I say, to prevent having to hear the arrest story for the million and first time.

'What an eyesore!' Dad says. 'What on earth do Philip and Sue need all that scaffolding for just to get a few roof tiles fixed?'

'I don't suppose they'd have it if it wasn't necessary,' I say.

'Nonsense!' Mum says. 'When we had some loose tiles, Bob's

nephew shinned up there – all done in a couple of hours and at a fraction of the cost of scaffolding.'

'Why don't you ask them?' I say.

'Ha!' Dad says. 'We'd never get a straight answer out of them. We've been trying to get them to take those hideous leylandii down for the last fifty years.'

The huge, admittedly ugly trees that form the boundary between their garden and next door have been a thorn in my parents' side for as long as I can remember. When they bought the house, they were head height and my parents didn't realise they would quickly come to tower over everything, blocking out much of the natural light.

'At least it means your garden is lovely and private, especially given Sue can be a bit of a busybody,' I say. 'You're not over-looked at all, with those on Philip and Sue's side and the road on the other.'

'We weren't overlooked when they were only six feet tall,' Mum says. 'There's absolutely no need for them to be so ridicu-lously high.'

In trying to get out of one oft-repeated conversation I've acci-dentally strayed into another, so I cast around for a distraction. Unfortunately it comes in the form of Dad's spectacles, one lens cracked, the frames held together by a piece of Sellotape wrapped around the bridge.

'What happened to your glasses?'

'I dropped them.'

'Dropped them? From what height? How did they get so mangled up?'

His eyes flicker nervously to Mum at the stove. She stirs the soup intently as if her life depends on it.

'Mum?' I say.

'Oh well . . . somebody left a trowel lying about at the allotment and your father tripped and twisted his ankle. If you ask me, Val Peters left it there on purpose – her and Clive have always been jealous of our cauliflower harvest. We should put up a camera and catch them at it next time.'

I ignore this ludicrous accusation and focus on Dad.

'Why didn't you tell me you'd had a fall?'

'Why have I "had a fall"?' he says testily. 'If the same thing had happened to you, you wouldn't describe it that way – you'd say you tripped and fell. I'm fitter than you are – I ran a half marathon six months ago.'

'You're definitely fitter than me,' Zach says. 'I wouldn't have a hope in hell of running even a quarter of a marathon.'

'You would if you didn't spend all your time gaming and . . .' I was going to say smoking weed, but even though my parents are liberal lefties, I'm not sure how they'd feel about that, so I hold back. 'Oh, Dad, look at that.' I step closer to examine his right hand, which is bruised and swollen. 'Have you been to the doctor?'

'Of course not!' he says, yanking the sleeve of his jumper down which is, as ever, too short for his mighty arms. 'It's just a scratch.'

'You should get it looked at. You probably need to call them anyway to renew your prescriptions.' I rifle through the bowl of tablets on the dresser.

'That's a joke,' Dad says. 'It's impossible to get through to them on the phone. I called at 8am on the dot the other day and it was engaged already.'

'You need to keep redialling, you'll get through eventually.'

'Can't you do the online booking thing for us?' he says. Since the Covid pandemic made my boss Janine realise accountants could very well work from home, and it would be a good deal cheaper for her if they did, I no longer work in an office. Unfortunately my parents have taken this to mean I no longer have to work at all and can be at their constant beck and call.

'You can do it yourself . . . hang on, isn't it Wednesday?'

'Yes.'

'You haven't taken Monday or Tuesday of these ones – what are they for again?' The last question is more to myself than either of them.

'I expect he has,' Mum says. 'It's just sometimes he takes them out of one of the other packs, so the days get out of sync.'

'But that's the whole point of having the days on them, so you don't get confused about what you've taken! No wonder you had a fall, it's probably side effects from not taking the tablets correctly.'

You'd never think he'd spent his working life running a wildly successful History department at the local secondary school. Under his leadership, the students achieved more As at A level than the posh school at the top of town that charges thousands of pounds a term. Now he's messing up a simple medication regime.

'I didn't have a fall. I tripped over a trowel.' He twitches angrily and Dottie stirs, growling in her sleep. It's only then that I notice the walking stick leaning against the wall near him, an elegant, heavy oak cane with a silver fox head for a handle that he inherited from his own father.

'If you're feeling unsteady on your feet, you could always use that second-hand wheelchair I got you last time you fell. I know it's a bit rusty, but it does the job.'

'A wheelchair? For God's sake, I'm not totally decrepit. I'm absolutely fine with my stick. I've put myself in for the Blackhawk Point 10k in September.'

'The notoriously punishing clifftop run?'

'Awesome,' Zach says, looking up from his phone.

'That's the one,' he says firmly, filling in a crossword clue.

'He's fine,' Mum says briskly. 'Once it's healed, he can come to Pilates with me – it's brilliant for building strength. Now, let's all have some soup.' She pulls open a cupboard door to get the bowls out and it swings perilously off its hinges.

'You need to get someone in to fix that.'

'I'll get Bob to have a look at it next time he's here,' she says evasively.

'No, not Bob, he'll stick it back on with superglue.' Bob is an ancient retired handyman who's been repairing anything that's gone wrong in this house since the dawn of time. 'Get someone proper in – or I can try and find someone.'

'Bob's fine – and, more importantly, he's cheap.'

'Alright, but that's the tip of the iceberg, Mum. Fixing it would be like flinging a small cup of water onto a burning building. What about all the other kitchen cupboards, the cracked window frames, the radiators that have to be bled every day or they don't heat up? The downstairs loo has been blocked for six months!'

'That's not a huge problem, we can use the upstairs one,' Dad protests.

'What about your ankle, though? It's ridiculous when you've got a perfectly good loo down here. I wish I could help more, but . . .'

The truth is that since the divorce I'm almost as skint as they are. Martin and I sold the house but the equity was minimal as we'd borrowed against it over the years to do home improvements that I'd thought were a long-term investment. Martin's OK – his salary is much higher than mine plus he's moved straight in with Elaine who earns a decent wage herself. Whereas I only just managed to get a mortgage on a two-bedroom flat by the skin of my teeth, and am killing myself to make the payments every month, as well as supporting Zach at university as much as I'm able.

'It's alright, love, we wouldn't want you to anyway,' Mum says. 'Can you get the butter out?'

I open the fridge door and have to bite my tongue when I see a lump of cheese that hasn't been covered, the edges cracked and crusting like the dry heels in a Dr Scholl treatment commercial. It sits alongside an open packet of ham, the slices spilling out of it, curling and crispy.

'If you'd moved into the basement when Martin left like we suggested, we'd be able to afford to get someone in properly,' says Dad, obviously wanting to punish me for making him feel like an old person.

'We discussed why that wasn't a good idea.'

The basement, converted many years ago into a teenage den for me and my friends, has fallen into disrepair much like the rest of the house. 'There was no room for Zach, for a start.' It's no more than a studio flat with a kitchenette and a tiny, flat-roofed bathroom tacked onto the back. It does at least have its own entrance. The house is built on a slope, so although the basement annexe is underground at the front, at the rear it's on ground level, with an external door and two small windows on the side of the house.

'He's in Winchester most of the time now, though. And he

could have stayed in the house with us in the holidays – we'd have loved to have you, darling. You could help us in the garden like you used to. Remember that little set we bought you – a dinky trowel and fork with those shiny red handles?'

'Oh yeah, I do remember that!' Zach grins, and I realise with a little spike of worry that it's the first time I've seen him look properly happy since he got back from university.

'I'll lay the table,' I say, changing the subject to avoid admitting the real reasons I didn't want to move back in with my parents – the implicit failure of my own independent life, and the fact that they'd have driven me mad in the time it took to unpack my belongings. I reach to open the drawer where they keep the placemats.

'No, not in there,' Mum says quickly. 'They're already out – look.'

So they are, neatly piled on the table. I open the drawer anyway, the air thick with something I don't understand. Red capital letters leap out at me, screaming FINAL DEMAND. I lift the top sheet of paper and there's another underneath threatening debt collectors, hinting at repossession.

'What are all these?' I pick up a fistful and wave them at my parents, but it's a redundant question. Their red faces say it all.

'Why didn't you tell me things were so bad?'

'We didn't want to worry you, love,' Dad says, putting down his pen. 'You've had enough on your plate.'

'I could have helped.' The words come out automatically but although I would do anything to protect them from stress and pain, in reality there is little I could have done. I've don't have anything left at the end of each month myself. 'How have you got to this point?'

'Dad's pension only goes so far,' Mum says. 'And mine's so negligible I may as well not bother collecting it.' Mum worked sporadically when I was younger, often switching jobs. She's a qualified social worker who did a lot of work with victims of domestic violence – 'battered women' as they were known back in the eighties. 'The house is expensive to heat,' she goes on. 'We're both fit as fiddles but we can't be cold, not at our age.'

Funny how the moment there's a whiff of turning the heating down, they're no longer hale and hearty marathon runners, but poor old dears who can't be cold. Anyway, the heating bills are only part of the story. As pensioners their income is limited, but those open packs in the fridge were from Waitrose, not Lidl. They're not spendthrifts but they do like the finer things in life.

'Maybe it's time to think about downsizing.' I'm not sure why I bother to say it. I know what the response will be. I've suggested it in the past and they always react as if I'd suggested one of them kills and eats the other to save on the food bill.

'No,' Dad says firmly. 'This is our home.'

'And the garden. I could never leave the garden.' Mum's voice trembles with emotion. 'I know you don't understand, not being a gardener, but that garden is our life's work. It's a labour of love. You might as well ask me to cut off my own head as leave that garden.'

'Yes – and we've just planted some new roses. We couldn't leave them now.'

Their rose garden is the pièce de résistance, the apple of their eye – possibly dearer to them than me or even Zach. If they spent half as much time and money maintaining the house as they do the garden, it'd be a show home. The rose garden has grown over the years with the existing bushes trailing ever further along the trellises and more varieties being added. That's why they got their allotment a few years ago – there was no room in the garden for vegetables. The one thing they had neglected out there was the ancient patio, cracked and broken, but they're currently in the throes of having that redone. The tiles have been removed and the area dug out ready for it to be replaced with smart new charcoal slate. I dread to think how they're paying for that – stuck it on one of their many credit cards, I dare say.

'What about getting a tenant in to rent the annexe?'

I'm expecting the usual push back on this as well, but it doesn't come. They exchange a meaningful look.

'We have discussed that,' Dad admits. Blimey, things must be really bad.

'Great. I can help with sorting that. You'll need to do a few repairs first though, you can't expect someone to live in it as it is.'

'We don't,' Mum says, affronted. 'We'll get Bob round. Now, let's have this soup.'

Two hours later, having taken a thorough inventory of what needs doing in the annexe before they could let it, plus submitted to the obligatory tour of the rose garden to admire their latest acquisition, Zach and I make our way back down the front steps. The sky was a deep, glowering grey when we were out in the garden and as I open my car door, the first fat drops of rain begin to fall. One splashes onto the back of my neck and trickles down between my shoulder blades. I shiver.

Chapter 2

A few weeks later, with Christmas out of the way and Zach installed back at university, I arrive early at Mum and Dad's. I want to make sure they've done everything they said they would before this prospective tenant comes to look round. As I get out of the car, I catch my skirt on the door and it rides up, exposing a few inches of thigh. I hear wolf whistles from Philip and Sue's scaffold and turn in fury to give them a piece of my mind – how DARE they make me feel uncomfortable by demonstrating their patriarchal power over me? I close my mouth when I realise they're not whistling at me, but at a much younger woman dressed for a night out in a sequined minidress. She tugs it down and gathers her jacket more closely around her, eyes on the ground. I'm incensed on her behalf, but don't say anything. There's a vain, internally misogynistic part of me that is, shamefully, disappointed they weren't whistling at me. Of course they weren't. I'm not unattractive. I'm average-sized and I have decent skin due to never having been a sun worshipper. I'm still vain enough to dye my greying hair and shell out for a decent cut, but the fact is I am fifty years old. It doesn't matter how much effort I put in to maintaining my appearance, I can walk through life without anyone giving me a second look. I might as well be invisible and often it feels as though I am. This ought to be a relief and sometimes it is – but not always. When I was still married the lack of attention didn't bother me, but since I've been single it cuts more deeply. I don't particularly want to meet anyone else, but I can't deny that Martin leaving me for someone fifteen years my junior stung. And while he's having a high old time with his new girlfriend, my life is slowly but surely becoming as invisible as me.

I let myself in the side door which goes straight into the basement annexe, to give myself a chance to check it out without my parents hovering. It definitely looks better in here. In the bathroom, Bob has worked some magic on the damp patches on the ceiling, although there's a strong possibility he's simply covered them up as opposed to fixing the root of the problem. The mould has been cleaned from the tiles and they've been regrouted. It's plain and old fashioned, but perfectly serviceable.

The main room is clean, and there's a fresh coat of magnolia paint on the walls. They've moved the old double bed from the spare room down here with what looks like the original mattress, stained but not too saggy. There's a small two-seater sofa, also repurposed from the main house. A fringed purple throw I wore as a teenage goth covers the threadbare upholstery. It points at a bulky television squatting on an old pine sideboard. Next to the bed there's a small wardrobe. The kitchen units, stove and fridge are clean, if worn. It's not a luxury five-star hotel, but it's OK for the reasonable price they're charging. The guy the agency is bringing is around my age, so I'm guessing he's seeking reprieve from a marriage breakdown, a temporary refuge until the family home is sold.

I hear a car drawing up outside, and then a ring on the main doorbell. There's a flurry of voices and a rumble of footsteps as they come down the stairs and through the door that leads from the main house. Mum and Dad lead the way, twittery and on edge, followed by the estate agent, an acne-ridden young man with an excessive amount of product in his hair and a too-tight shiny suit. He looks younger than Zach. There's a pause before the potential tenant follows them into the room as if to heighten the drama of his entrance, and then he fills the doorway. He's not tall but he has an imposing presence, slim but muscular in a natural rather than narcissistic, gym bunny way. He's got a full, tousled head of mid-brown hair and he's wearing well-fitted, worn-in jeans, a checked shirt and thick-soled brown brogues. I stifle a preposterous urge to lay my cheek against the soft brushed cotton of his shirt. Instead, I reach out my hand.

'Hi, I'm Penny, Sissy and Heath's daughter.'

'Cooper Brownlow.' He shakes it with a broad smile. 'Nice to meet you.' He's well-spoken with a hint of Estuary.

'I'm Dean Rendall, from Woodford Peters,' Shiny Suit says, thrusting a damp hand into my palm in which the warm, dry imprint of Cooper's handshake still lingers. 'What a great little place, madam.'

'Yes, it's nice. I used to use it as a teenage den back when I lived here.'

'Whew, bet it's seen a few things, eh?' Cooper says.

I redden.

'Parties and things, I meant,' he says quickly. 'Sorry, I wasn't being . . . inappropriate.'

'It's fine.' I laugh. 'You're right, there may have been a few get-togethers, but not in front of my mum and dad, OK?'

'Right, of course.' He taps the side of his nose.

'Don't worry, we knew what she was up to, didn't we, Heath?'

'Oh, yes. Nothing much gets past us!'

They've obviously taken to him already. They're right, I never had to hide what I was doing from them – they always said they'd prefer to know and be available to help if needed, than have me sneaking around behind their backs and lying to them. My best friend from school, Caitlin, loved them and was envious of how permissive they were. Conversely, I sometimes wished Mum was a 'proper' mother like Caitlin's. Her dad was a bank manager and her mum didn't work. Their house was tidy and smelled of pine trees. It was free from chaos and didn't have bruised and battered women turning up at all hours, wanting my mother's help. She wasn't supposed to give them her address of course, but she often did. Thinking of Caitlin gives me the stab of pain it always does. I wonder if I'll ever stop missing her.

'So, it won't take long to show you the place.' I wave an arm around the room. 'This is pretty much it, and then the bathroom's at the back there.'

'May I?'

'Ah, yes, let me show you,' says Dean eagerly. I'm getting strong work experience trainee vibes from him. Cooper, however, is already on his way, swooping across the room in a few strides and poking his head into the bathroom. With the five of us in here, the annexe feels smaller than ever. I should have told Mum and Dad to stay upstairs.

'Seems fine,' Cooper says.

'So . . . how long a lease are you looking for?' I ask.

'Six months initially,' he says, 'but it may end up being longer.'

'That's no problem,' says Dean, trying to assert his authority. 'We're happy to set the lease for six months for yourself, with an option to renew.'

'And it's . . . just you?' I try to keep my interest sounding entirely professional.

'Just me,' he says, looking right into my eyes. Something pings inside me.

'Ha ha that's good, wouldn't be much room in here for anyone else,' I witter. 'You'd have to keep them under the bed!' Oh God. I will myself to stop talking but I feel my mouth opening and I genuinely fear what's going to come out next. Thankfully, at that very moment Dottie starts barking from upstairs.

'I'll go,' Dad says. 'Make a bit more room in here.' He ducks through the internal door into the main part of the house, but there's a kerfuffle and Dottie comes barrelling into the room, little pink tongue hanging out, white fluffy hair sticking up around her face, closely followed by Dad puffing along as fast as he can with his walking stick.

'Sorry, Dottie made a break for it through my legs. Wanted to know what was going on down here.'

'Hello, you!' Cooper crouches down and runs his hand over her head. She instantly rolls onto her back, legs waving madly. He laughs and gently tickles her tummy and she growls in ecstasy.

'Someone likes you,' I say.

'Hopefully not only Dottie,' he says, looking up at the four of us, eyes crinkling appealingly. I almost simper and have to give myself a mental shake. If this is how I'm going to behave around every vaguely attractive man I encounter, I'll have to stop leaving the house. Mind you, I can't remember the last time I met an attractive man of my own age, let alone an apparently single one.

'So, what do you do, Cooper?' I ask in an attempt to calm myself down.

'I'm in property – self-employed at the moment, but I can provide tax returns, references and all that.' He looks at Dean for confirmation.

'Yes, that's all in order,' he says, tapping his clipboard.

'You didn't have any properties lying empty you could have stayed in?' I say, fishing.

'No, I'm . . . between properties, you might say.' For the first time since he arrived, Cooper looks uneasy. As I thought, he's mid (or post) divorce.

'Yes, I've been there,' I say in an undignified attempt to let him know that I too am 'just me'. His eyes sweep across the fourth finger of my left hand and back up again so quickly I don't know if I imagined it. I haven't thought of meeting anyone else in the year since Martin left me. If anything, I've assumed I'd be alone for the rest of my life. Middle-aged dating felt so . . . undignified, so foolish. I'd forgotten what it felt like, this little zing, the thrill of possibility, slight as it is, that there could be something between me and this handsome, self-assured man.

'Do you have any questions at all yourself, Mr Brownlow?' Dean asks.

'You said the rent includes council tax and all utilities, that's right?' he asks.

'Yes, as it's essentially all one house there's no other obvious way to do it,' I say. 'And speaking of, you would need to be mindful that whilst the annexe has its own entrance and is completely self-contained, the walls are thin and any noise will travel. We would ask that you respect that.'

'You'll hardly know I'm here,' Cooper says with a wink. I try to pretend to myself that it hasn't, but my stomach gives a little flip. Maybe Cooper can see me. Maybe I'm not as invisible as I thought.

Chapter 3

'How are you getting on?' I ask Cooper stiffly, cursing my dog-walking attire of wellies, old jeans and a motheaten rollneck jumper, topped off with a sensible cagoule.

He moved in two weeks ago and the first few times I came round to Mum and Dad's, I found excuses to dress up a little and take care over my hair and makeup. Of course he was never anywhere to be seen until today, when I bumped into him on the driveway on my way back from walking Dottie.

'Not bad, thanks. Nice walk?' he asks.

Dottie capers around his feet and he stoops to ruffle her fur. I take the opportunity to run a surreptitious finger over my chin to check for the hairs that spring up near-daily, and pull my rollneck up a little higher.

'It was fine. She's pretty old, so we don't go too far. Mum and Dad are out so they asked me to come over and take her for a quick spin.'

'That was kind.'

'Ah, not really, I was glad of an excuse to get out of my flat.'

'I know what you mean,' he says. 'I'm off for an exciting trip to buy milk. You must have lots of friends around here though?'

'Not really. I work from home now, so that doesn't help. I used to have a lot of mum friends when my son was younger, but that's tailed off a bit. And then there was . . . oh, never mind.'

I'm embarrassing myself, blathering on when he just wants to get to the corner shop.

'No, it's OK,' he says, moving infinitesimally closer. 'What were you going to say?'

'I did have a friend, a very close one, from school. Caitlin. She died a year ago.'

'I'm so sorry.'

'Thanks.' I almost call it a day there and make my excuses, but I can't resist the feeling of her name in my mouth. I so rarely get the chance to talk about her.

'She lived round here her whole life. Before she got ill, if I was ever at a loose end, I'd call her up and we'd hang out like we did when we were teenagers – go for clifftop walks out at Blackhawk Point, lie around watching movies, mooch around the shops.'

'Sounds great,' he says. 'Must have left a big hole.'

'It has.'

I've got other friends, of course, but we all have busy lives and it's all too easy for three months to pass without any contact. But Caitlin was different. As well as being my closest friend, with whom I could talk about the big stuff, she was also an everyday friend. When you only speak to someone a few times a year, the conversation is very much big picture – you catch up on news: jobs, health, children, partners, parents, house renovations, holidays. Everyday friends know the little details – that tooth filling you're dreading, which six of the seven tops you ordered online you're sending back, how the rude woman who fitted you for a bra poked your boob into a too-small cup. That's what I miss. Actually, I miss all of it. I miss her.

'Sorry,' I say, my voice cracking. Oh God, I need to wrap this up, I don't want him to think I'm completely neurotic.

'That's OK,' he says, although he looks a little alarmed.

I'm not sure either of us know where the conversation is going to go next, but at that moment my phone begins to ring.

'I'd better get that,' I say, grateful even when I see that it's Martin calling.

Cooper nods and gives a little wave as he heads off out of the drive.

'Hello?' I say to Martin as I open the front door and let Dottie off the lead, the phone tucked under my chin and a question apparent in my voice.

'Hi, Pen, how are you?'

'I'm fine.' Our exchanges are civil now – always have been, really, once the initial shock and resentment wore off. I slowly came to realise that Martin and I hadn't been happy for a long time. I'd been so mired in the bog of our marriage that I hadn't been able to see it – or didn't want to. There are even times now when I think he did me a favour.

'Are you at home?'

'No, I'm at Mum and Dad's. They asked me to walk Dottie while they're out.'

'Even better – I'm really close to you. Can I pop in?'

'What for?'

'Oh, just a chat – I'll see you in about five minutes.'

'What the hell does he want?' I say out loud as I unzip my cagoule. I don't believe in heaven. I don't think Caitlin is looking down on me. But I can't believe that all our conversations, all the things we went through together, all the love we had for each other, have disappeared into thin air. She's still here in my memories, in the ways she changed me. I've got into the habit of talking to her at odd moments and her responses always pop into my head as if she's here. I know she isn't – I don't believe in ghosts either – but I knew her so well that I know what her reaction would be in any given situation.

God knows, she says, *but it's unlikely to be anything good.*

I scroll aimlessly through my phone while I wait for Martin to arrive. I hear the slam of the door downstairs as Cooper returns from the shop and allow myself to drift into a fantasy where he comes up to borrow a cup of sugar (although what he'd want sugar for I don't know – or why it should be in a cup). We've found ourselves in a compromising position in the larder when I'm rudely interrupted by the doorbell. All thoughts of illicit kitchen trysts are banished by the sight of Martin, puffing at the door dressed head to toe in fluorescent Lycra.

'Blimey, did you run here?'

'No . . .' He takes a gulp of air and gestures behind him at an expensive-looking, sleek racing bike. 'Cycled.'

'Since when were you a cyclist?'

'Elaine thought I should do more exercise. I've been all the way to Blackhawk Point and back today.'

'I hope you weren't tempted to fling yourself off the edge.' We're about ten miles from the south coast here, and Blackhawk Point, as well as being a local landmark, is a notorious suicide spot.

'Ha ha, no. Elaine wanted me to go to yoga with her, but I didn't fancy that – and this gets me out of the house.'

I don't ask him whose benefit that's for.

'Come in.'

In the kitchen, I make him a cup of coffee without asking – old habits die hard, I guess.

'How is Elaine?' I ask, my teeth only slightly gritted. Seeing him in this outlandish costume I feel mainly gratitude that this obvious midlife crisis is not my responsibility.

'Oh, well . . . she's fine, but . . .'

I take a sip of my tea and wait. I'm not going to beg for information, although I can't deny there will be a certain satisfaction if not everything in his new life is rosy.

'She wants us to have a baby, Pen.'

'Oh, Martin!' I can't hold back a snigger.

'Don't laugh,' he says, injured.

'Sorry, but what did you expect? She's thirty-five years old, of course she wants children. Had you not discussed this before?'

'Yes, but she's always said she wasn't sure if she wanted them, said she'd never felt hugely maternal or experienced that overwhelming instinct that some women talk about.'

'I bet she did.'

'What d'you mean by that?'

'She would say that while she was trying to reel you in. She might have even believed it. But now her clock's ticking. You really should have seen this coming.' I cannot hide my glee.

'I can't go through all that again, Penny. I'm fifty-five! The sleepless nights, the potty training. I'll be retirement age before they leave school! Everyone at the school gate will think I'm the grandad!'

The desire to say *You should have thought of that before you hightailed off with a woman twenty years younger than you* is strong, but I resist.

'Have you said any of this to her? Does she know you're not keen?'

'How can I? If I won't give her a baby, she might leave me for someone who will.'

'That's the risk you've taken, Martin. I'm not being funny, but I'm not the best person to talk to about this.'

'I haven't got anyone else,' he says. 'You were always the one I wanted to talk to about my problems. You still are. Sometimes I think . . . Oh, never mind.'

He cannot be serious. Has he actually come here, to my parents' house, to tell me he's made a mistake, that he wants to come back? I'm formulating my response to this when there's a gentle knocking sound. It takes me a second to place it before I realise it's coming from the internal door to the basement annexe, which is down a small flight of steps in the hall.

'What's that?' Martin says, frowning.

'Mum and Dad have got a tenant in the annexe. I'd better go down and see what he wants.'

Martin regards me suspiciously as my hand reflexively moves to fluff up my hair.

I trot down the stairs and open the annexe door, noticing that although Mum and Dad got Bob to fit a bolt on this side, they haven't bothered to lock it.

'Hello again!' Cooper says. 'This sounds a bit weird, like you're a small child who's answered the door, but are your parents home?'

'I'm afraid not. Do you want to come in?'

He steps towards me, close enough for me to smell him – a heady scent of woodsmoke and spice and fresh sweat. Longing swells inside me and a breath catches in my throat. I can't recall the last time I felt anything like this. I don't remember ever feeling it with Martin, even at the start, this heat that's building inside me at the mere whiff of the man. I thought menopause was meant to lower your libido. That's certainly the excuse I used with

Martin when I experienced my first peri-menopausal symptoms. Maybe that's one of the great myths of middle-aged woman-hood – we haven't gone off sex. We've gone off our husbands.

'Is everything OK?' I ask.

Martin coughs loudly behind me and Cooper and I turn to look at him standing at the top of the stairs, the curve of his Lycra-encased belly highlighted by the light spilling through the glass panels in the front door.

'Oh sorry – this is Martin, my ex-husband. Martin, this is Cooper.'

'Cooper? How very American,' Martin says, walking down the stairs and holding out his hand for Cooper to shake. The space at the bottom of the steps is barely a metre square and we're now all uncomfortably close.

'Nice to meet you,' Cooper says, giving Martin's hand a brief shake and taking half a step back into the basement to give us all some breathing space. 'I'm having a bit of trouble with the window at the back. I opened it and now I can't get it closed again.'

'There's a knack to that, mate,' Martin chips in. 'Let me show you.' He breezes past Cooper, who follows with me trailing behind. It doesn't look much different down here to how it did when we showed Cooper around. The bed is made and there are a few bits and pieces spread around the place but he doesn't seem to have many belongings. I dare say all his stuff from the marital home is temporarily in storage.

'Whew, Sis and the Heathster have spruced it up a bit down here, haven't they?'

Nobody, least of all Martin, calls my parents by those nick-names. It's a blatant display of willy-waving which in a way is hilarious, but also concerning. Has Martin divined my attraction to Cooper? In which case, can Cooper sense it too? Am I making a total fool of myself?

'It's simply a matter of turning it in a specific way.' Martin strides over to the window and twists at the catch. It comes off in his hand.

'Ah. Sorry.'

'Oh dear. You seem to have lost the knack,' Cooper says, smiling at me behind Martin's back.

'Hmm, yes I think it needs screwing back on.'

'Leave it, Martin. I'll call Bob, my parents' handyman,' I say to Cooper. 'I'm sure he can fix it.'

'Thanks, I'd appreciate that.'

'Come on, Martin, let's leave Cooper in peace. Can I . . . do you want to give me your number so I can let you know when Bob can fix the window?'

'Sure.'

We exchange numbers under Martin's watchful and somewhat baleful eye, and Martin and I return upstairs.

'I'm not sure about him,' Martin says darkly when we're back in the kitchen. 'There's something not right there.'

'Don't be ridiculous. He's very kind, actually.' I think of his warmth, his sympathy about Caitlin.

'Hmph. It all happened very quickly.'

'Yes, well, we were lucky he was able to move in pretty much straight away.'

'What's a middle-aged man like him doing renting a room in someone's basement?'

'Don't be ridiculous. He's recently divorced and it's a temporary base.' I don't know this for sure of course, but Martin doesn't need to know that. 'Not everyone walks straight out of one relationship into another.'

He has the good grace to redden.

'And while we're on the subject,' I say tartly, 'please don't use me as your therapist. If you want to moan about Elaine, find another shoulder to cry on.'

His face falls.

'You're right. Sorry, Pen. I'd better go.'

'Yes, I think you had.'

I see him to the door and watch as he wobbles away on his bike, feeling a mixture of exasperation and a reluctant affection that even his infidelity hasn't managed to wash away. I'm about to close the door when a small, rusty car roars into the drive, music thumping, and disgorges a couple of scrawny, late teenage boys in baggy jeans hanging perilously low on their hips.

'Can I help you?' I say faux-politely. They've clearly got the wrong address.

'Is Cooper in?' the driver of the car says.

'Oh! Yes, he's ... the entrance is round the side,' I say, wrongfooted.

'Ta.'

They troop round and bang on the door. I hear it open and the boys go inside. A couple of minutes later, they emerge looking pleased with themselves. One of them gives me a cheery wave and they bundle into the car. The driver pulls out without check-ing for traffic and they narrowly avoid being ploughed into by a hatchet-faced woman driving an outsize four-by-four. She hoots furiously but they speed off without a care. What was that about? Who were those boys? The warmth I felt earlier in Cooper's presence withers, and Martin's words about what

Cooper is doing renting a one-room apartment echo through my mind. I try to recapture the excitement I felt when Cooper was inches from me and focus on being angry with Martin for planting doubt in my mind. This is all his fault. He's trying to drag me down because he's unhappy with his own situation – a situation that is entirely of his own making, let's not forget. It's got nothing to do with Cooper. Nothing at all.

Chapter 4

'There's been an awful lot of banging around,' Dad says a few days later, putting my cup of tea down in front of me on the kitchen table. 'What the blazes is he doing down there?'

'You're used to having the place to yourselves – you have to accept that there's going to be some noise. You can't expect him to sit there in silence.' I'm pretty sure he's exaggerating – there's no noise at all coming from the basement now although Cooper's car is here so I think he's in.

'He's very rude,' Mum chips in. 'I passed him in town the other day and he didn't so much as acknowledge me.'

'He probably didn't see you.'

'I very much doubt it. He got back the same time as me the other day and I was struggling to get all these shopping bags up the steps and he didn't offer to help.'

'He's your tenant, not your carer. Why should he have to help?'

It is a bit crap if that's true, but now I've taken up the position of defending him I feel I can't abandon it.

'There's unsavoury people coming and going at all hours of the day and night,' Dad says.

'What do you mean?' The seed of unease that was planted by those boy racers the other day sprouts a little higher.

'Somebody pulled up in a car at three in the morning last night, didn't they, Sissy?'

'Did they? I didn't hear anything.'

'Yes you did! I'm sure you were awake.'

'I certainly was not. You were probably dreaming.'

'I wasn't dreaming. It took me ages to go back to sleep after.'

I have to admit he does look tired. There are shadowy pouches under his eyes that I'm sure weren't there before and his eyeballs are spidered with red. He's still using the walking stick, even though I'm sure he's recovered from the fall.

'I dare say it was one of those funny hallucinations you get in the night,' says Mum. 'He woke me up the other night trying to stop a black dog from savaging me – nearly crushed me to death.'

'What hallucinations? Dad?'

'She's exaggerating. They're not hallucinations, just sort of . . . waking dreams, where I think there's someone in the room. Then I wake up properly and snap out of it. It's fine.'

I'm beginning to think they've got bigger problems than a noisy tenant.

'Do you want me to talk to him?' I say. It's the last thing I want to do, but if there is going to be a problem, I'd rather it was me that had to deal with it than them. They drive me crazy, but I feel as protective of them as I do Zach.

'Yes please.' Dad's gratitude is plain. This is seriously bothering them.

'Right, no time like the present.'

In the hall, I hesitate. The quickest route would be to knock on the internal door to the basement, but would that be intrusive, an invasion of Cooper's privacy? I don't live here, after all. After deliberating for a minute, I go outside and knock at the external door. He takes a while to answer and I shiver as a cool breeze whips down the side of the house.

'Hello.' Cooper is pulling a faded grey T-shirt over his head and I make an unsuccessful attempt not to look at his bare chest. I try to swallow but my mouth is dry. He ruffles his hair and yawns.

'Sorry, were you asleep?' I manage to get some words out.

'I'm afraid so,' he says. 'Bit embarrassing in the middle of the day, but I guess that's middle age for you!'

'I think that's one of the good things about middle age – we can do whatever the hell we want. Mind you, I say that but they're by no means words I live by. Unless whatever the hell I want is in fact endless nights in front of the telly or having Marmite on toast for dinner because I can't be bothered to cook.'

Oh God, I'm spewing words again.

'Good point!' Thankfully he doesn't seem fazed. 'Would you like to come in?'

'No, it's OK, I won't stay long.' I gather my cardigan tighter and wrap my arms around me.

'Don't be silly, you're freezing. Come in for a minute.'

The room is fuller and more cluttered than the last time I was here.

'What can I do for you?' It's an innocent question. I think. I'm so out of practice I can't tell if I'm imagining a hint of something more salacious.

'It's a bit awkward. Dad said there's been a bit of noise – he described it as banging around. I appreciate that they're not used to having another person in their space, and I'm sure it wasn't unacceptable noise, but I said I'd come and talk to you.'

'I'm sorry. I bought some flatpack furniture – I expect what they heard was me putting it together. They may have heard a few choice swear words too! This chest of drawers was a particular bastard.'

'We've all been there.' I'm hugely relieved, but I need to broach the other subject too. 'They also mentioned that you've been having a lot of visitors – Dad said he was woken up by some very late ones last night, although to be fair Mum didn't think that had actually happened, so I don't know . . .' I trail off. It seems a very paltry complaint now I'm down here. Banging some nails in and having a few visitors? He's renting an apartment, not living in a silent monastery.

'That'll die down soon, I promise. The truth is I have had quite a few friends visit me, but my circumstances in my last place were a bit tricky for visitors. The person I lived with didn't like me having anyone round. My mates supported me through a tough time and I'm showing my gratitude by hosting them.'

We hear a lot about coercively controlling men these days who isolate their partners from friends and family, but of course it can happen the other way round too. Poor Cooper.

'It's fine – goodness, I don't want you to feel you can't have visitors. My parents are getting on and they can be set in their ways. They're just getting used to having you in the house. I'm sure it'll all settle down once everyone's used to the situation.' I want to say more but I'm nervous of taking things to a more personal level. I teeter on the edge for a few seconds, then close my eyes and jump. 'I'm recently divorced myself, so I know how it can be.'

'Ah yes, the man in Lycra. I'm sorry you've been through that.' He doesn't sound or look very sorry. 'Was that your decision or . . .?' I know I'm out of practice, but he's definitely flirting now. I feel ungainly, out of place in my own body. What could he see in me? He's so attractive and I'm . . . ordinary. I'm not ugly. Mothers don't cover their children's eyes as I pass to shield them from my hideousness. I'm an average-looking, averagely well-preserved woman who looks every inch of her fifty years.

'Martin thought life would be better with a woman fifteen years younger than me – and twenty years younger than him.' Might as well get it all out in the open.

'I can't think of anything worse than being with someone twenty years younger – we wouldn't have anything in common.'

'That's what I said when he told me! All those shared reference points from your youth – the TV shows, the chocolate bars, the alcopops – they don't have any of that. She was born in the late 1980s!' She also has a flat stomach and no cellulite and she can bounce happily away on a trampoline without fear of wetting herself. Mind you, those things will all be over if she gets her way and has a baby. That thought cheers me up a bit.

'So . . .' Cooper says, looking at me so directly that heat prickles on my chest and blooms up my neck. 'Would you fancy going for a drink with someone who hears "Doctor Who" and thinks "Tom Baker"?'

'Are we going to spend the evening reminiscing about when there were only three TV channels?' It's the first thing that tumbles out of my mouth and is a neat, if unconscious, way of avoiding the question. My heart is skittering away in my chest. Does he really want to go out with me? Do I want to go out with him? I never seriously thought he'd be interested. It was a flirtation, a fantasy. Now I'm faced with the prospect of a real date, my first in over twenty years. Even then, Martin and I didn't 'date', as such. We shared a drunken snog at some post-work drinks and moved instantly and seamlessly into coupledom.

'We can spend the evening however you like,' he says with another one of those piercing stares that send vibrations flooding through my body.

'OK,' I say feebly.

'I'll give you a text later in the week to arrange details.'

'OK.' Is that all I can say? 'I'd . . . like that.' Better, but still pathetic. 'I should get back up to Mum and Dad. Thanks.'

'Thank *you*,' he says with a little bow. 'Why don't you go back up the other way, save you going out in the cold again?'

I scan the room as I cross it, taking in the new chest of drawers he mentioned. The top drawer is open and I can't help sneaking a peek. Sitting on top of the socks is a small plastic bag containing some dried leaves – clearly marijuana. I quickly look away. We say goodbye at the internal door and when he's closed it, I stand there for a minute at the bottom of the stairs to the hall. My hands are trembling, and I'm not sure if it's from the shock of being asked on a date or seeing Cooper's weed. I'm being foolish I know – weed is so common most people wouldn't even consider it transgressive. I know Zach indulges – it's par for the course for someone his age, a rite of passage. I'm just not used to being around people of my age who use it. I give myself a shake for being such an old fart. It shouldn't – in fact, doesn't – bother me in the slightest if Cooper enjoys the odd spliff. Hell, maybe I'll join him. I could do with loosening up a bit.

As I go back into the kitchen, my parents raise their hopeful, expectant faces towards me. They have total trust that I will have solved any problems they have, or imagine they have, with Cooper. I hope to God I'm not about to let them down.

Chapter 5

It's been four days since Cooper suggested a date, and not a peep out of him. I pretend to myself that I'm looking to see if Martin's messaged me – he is twenty minutes late, after all – but in reality I'm checking if Cooper's texted. I haven't heard anything from Mum and Dad either, which is a good sign. Hopefully things have settled down as Cooper said they would. I shove my phone back into the depths of my handbag. A watched pot never boils.

I shift uncomfortably on the high bar stool and take a sip of my wine. It's a new bar, recently opened, that sells itself as an upmarket Mediterranean-style place. The young couple on the next table are picking at a few small pieces of cheese and a hunk of dense, dark bread served on a thick wooden board. When Martin asked if we could meet for a drink, my instinct was to say no. Partly because – as I told him – I have no interest in listening to his woes and also because I wanted to keep myself free in case Cooper set a date for our drink. But when Martin said he wanted to discuss Zach I could hardly turn him down, so here I am. My phone beeps and I rummage frantically in my bag, hoping desperately to see Cooper's name, but it's a special offer from my mobile phone provider. My disappointment must have made its way to my face, because the waitress, who is passing with yet another board, this one sparsely populated with anaemic cured meats, gives me a sympathetic smile.

'Been stood up?'

'No! Good heavens, no. My friend's just a bit late.' Martin's not exactly a friend, but she doesn't need to know that.

'Oh, sorry.' She shuffles off to deliver her board of meat, leaving me hot with humiliation at her pity. What have I been thinking, embarking on dating at my age? It's embarrassing. Zach would die if he knew. I pick up my phone and start composing a message to Cooper. I'll tell him I've changed my mind, got too much on, not in the right headspace for dating. As I'm trying to get the wording right – I don't want to leave any room for argument but I'm also keen not to imply that I thought he was in any way serious about me – Martin arrives in a flurry of apologies, shaking his umbrella all over the table.

'Martin! You're soaking me!'

'Sorry, sorry. And sorry for being late, I . . . got caught up at home.'

He looks strained and anxious.

'Don't worry,' I say, softening. 'It's not as if I'm not used to you being late. You're here now. Sit down. You don't need to go to the bar – the incredibly nosy waitress will come and take your order.'

He finally divests himself of all his outerwear and climbs onto the bar stool opposite me. He's wearing skinny jeans and a shirt patterned with violet flowers that he wouldn't have been seen dead in when we were together. Whilst I abhor the ageism and misogyny inherent in the phrase 'mutton dressed as lamb' when deployed against a woman, it's hard to stop it forming in my mind.

'So what's all this about Zach?' I say once the waitress has brought his fancy European beer.

'You haven't spoken to him?'

'Not for a week or so, but he's been texting me and I thought he sounded OK.' Part of me suspects this whole thing is a plot for Martin to talk to me about Elaine again.

'I spoke to him the night before last – frankly, I'm worried about him.'

'What d'you mean? Is he alright?'

The stupid, poncy bar and the insensitive waitress melt into the background and everything goes into slow motion. What is wrong with my boy?

'I don't know. He said he's having a hard time, struggling to make friends. That his flatmates have started making plans without him, and he thinks he's done something wrong, or they don't like him. But I'm not so sure, Pen. He sounded really spaced out. I'm worried he's smoking too much . . . you know . . . weed.'

'Don't be ridiculous. He has the odd joint, like most kids his age do.'

Martin's such an old stick-in-the-mud about this. He hit the roof the first time he found marijuana and Rizlas in Zach's room when he was sixteen. It was the latest in a long line of things about his son that made Martin angry and frustrated. I spent a lot of time in his early teenage years negotiating between the two of them, forever trying to protect Zach from Martin's unrealistic sense of the behaviour you could reasonably expect from a teenage boy.

'It's a bit more than that,' he says. 'I tried to talk to him about it but, quite honestly, he was too out of it. I wondered if you could have a try?'

'I'll talk to him, the poor darling, but I'm not sure having a go at him about drugs is the way to do it. I'm more concerned about these flatmates.'

This was what I worried about all the way through primary and secondary school. Zach is funny and caring and unique, but he's not one of those popular, golden children. It takes time to get to know him – but when you do, the rewards are huge. He only had one close friend at secondary school, a boy called Saul. He never wanted to go out and do anything, which I always felt would have done Zach – and him – the world of good. They would spend hours playing games online together, or hanging out at one or the other's house watching movies. I'd hoped that university would mean a fresh start and the chance to make some decent friends. To hear this news from Martin is one of my worst fears realised.

'Yes, I'm worried about that too,' Martin says, injured. 'But I don't know if we're getting the full story. If he's locking himself away in his room, smoking, they're not going to invite him out. My fear is that he's isolating himself. That the drugs are more important than anything else.'

'You're talking about him as if he's some kind of addict!'

'And you seem to be forgetting that he's our child, as usual. You've always been so keen to be his friend, Penny, that's your trouble. He needs boundaries, not another mate.'

'He's an adult. It's a bit late for that. It's good that I have a close relationship with him.'

'I'm close to him too,' Martin protests, but we both know it's not the same. Martin doesn't understand Zach like I do, never has. When Zach was younger, Martin used to joke that he felt like a gooseberry in our presence. I think he was joking, anyway.

'He needs time to find his tribe, make more of an effort to widen his social circle, join a few clubs or societies,' I say.

'Yes, those would all be good things. But we can't make him do them, can we? Shall we suggest he comes home for the week-end so we can talk about it properly?'

'Great idea. He just needs a bit of looking after, a few home comforts.'

My mind skips ahead to the supermarket, planning a trolley full of Zach's favourite snacks.

'Although,' Martin says doubtfully. 'I'm worried that if he comes home, he won't go back.'

'Is it really that bad?'

'I think so.'

'Maybe it wouldn't be so bad if he did leave. He could reapply – not everyone gets it right first time.' I don't voice the treacherous thought that it would be lovely to have him back home with me, but Martin can read me like a book.

'Oh no you don't. He needs to stick it out – we're bloody paying for it, for a start.'

'I'm not going to sacrifice my son's happiness for the sake of money! He may be an adult but it's never easy on a child when their parents split up.' This is a low blow, but I can't help myself. 'He's not had the easiest time in the last year.'

'Ouch.'

'Sorry.' I'm not remotely sorry.

We sit without speaking for a minute or two.

'What held you up at home?' I ask, more to fill the silence than out of any genuine curiosity.

'Oh . . . well . . .' Martin suddenly finds his beer very interesting. 'You know what we talked about last time I saw you? About Elaine wanting a baby?'

'Yes . . . Oh, Martin, she's not pregnant, is she?'

'Four months.'

'Four months! So she was actually already pregnant when we spoke about it last time?'

'Yes, but she didn't know it then. We weren't trying, as such, so she only thought to test this month.'

'For God's sake.'

'I know, but it's done now. We are where we are. I'll have to make the best of it.'

'Poor kid.'

We fall into silence again. I can't believe he's been so stupid, so irresponsible.

What the hell? I say silently to Caitlin.

I know, right? she says. *Could he be any more of a preposterous midlife cliché?*

Exactly. So why does it hurt?

Because you loved him, Caitlin says. *You probably still do in a weird sort of way. And you were the only person he'd been through this with until now – the finding out, the birth, the overwhelming love. He's going to share it with someone else. And you never will.*

'Do you know where the loos are?' Martin says, bringing me back to reality.

'Other side of the bar.'

'It's not one of those ones with the symbols, is it? I can never remember which is which.'

'I don't know!'

'Sorry. Back in a mo.'

My phone beeps. I'm so distracted by Martin's news and my worry about Zach that my heart doesn't give the stupid leap it's been doing since Cooper suggested a date. So naturally, this time, it's him. I was right about that watched pot.

In town now – do you fancy that drink?

I can still see the unsent message I was drafting to tell him I didn't want to go out with him. Ten minutes ago I was determined to send it. But now?

What do you think? I ask Caitlin.

Why not, darl? He's hot, and life's short, she says.

I look up and see Martin making his way back from the loo in clothes chosen by the woman with whom he replaced me. He stops to ask the waitress something and she answers him patiently but with obvious condescension. A thought strikes me: she wouldn't look at Cooper like that. They might be of a similar age, but Cooper is better-looking and cooler and commands more respect. Suddenly I don't want to spend the rest of the evening sitting across from Martin, with his face that's as familiar to me as my own, listening to him moaning about the child that is going to replace our darling son.

As he approaches, I rapidly delete my earlier draft message declining Cooper's offer and replace it with a thumbs up emoji and the word *Where?*

I tell Martin I'm not feeling well, down the remains of my wine in one gulp, thrust my arms into my coat and hurry out into the rain. Martin sits alone at the table, thoroughly confused at my speedy exit. A message comes through from Cooper suggesting a pub in the town centre. I wipe all thoughts of the past, put my head down against the rain and head off to meet my future.

Chapter 6

Cooper is sitting at a small, round table near a roaring fire. There are two heavy crystal tumblers in front of him each containing a good inch of amber liquid.

'I took the liberty of getting you a whisky,' he says by way of hello. 'It's that sort of weather.'

'Thanks.'

I hate whisky but although I know it makes me a bad feminist, I find it rather thrilling that Cooper has chosen my drink for me. I sit down and we clink glasses. I try not to grimace as the whisky burns my throat, and am surprised to find I don't mind the warm sensation as it slides down. I should try new things more often. It's easy to think that once you get to middle age you know what you like and what you don't, but perhaps that's reductive. My life isn't what I thought it would be at fifty, but it might be time to reframe that as a good thing.

'How was your day?' he says. How nice to be asked. My parents are always so keen to bring me their problems they don't have time for mine, and close as Zach and I are, he's as insular and self-involved as all teenagers. My instinct is to say it was fine, but I check myself. Might as well be real.

'Mixed. I just abandoned my ex-husband in another pub.'

'What did the MAMIL want?'

'The what?'

'MAMIL – you know, Middle-Aged Man In Lycra.'

I splutter into my whisky.

'Have you never heard that before?' he says once my coughing fit has subsided. 'They're a menace on the roads on a Sunday, tearing round country lanes in a desperate attempt to escape the living death of their home lives.'

'Ouch. Sounds like you may have experienced something like that.'

'I've never owned a bike,' he says faux-solemnly, neatly avoiding my real question. 'So what did he want?'

'Oof. Well . . . you know I mentioned he left me for a younger woman?'

'So predictable. Where's the originality?'

'Funny you should say that. What do you think would be the next piece of news from a middle-aged man who's married a woman in her thirties?'

'Hmm, let me think . . . she's up the duff?'

'Got it in one!'

We clink again and I feel lighter than I have in months.

'And he thought it was a good idea to tell you this . . . why?'

'To be fair, he wanted to meet to discuss our son. He's nineteen, away at uni. Apparently he called Martin the other night to say he's not happy there, so he wanted to talk to me about that.'

'I'm sorry to hear that – but sounds like that was an excuse to get you there so he could tell you about the baby.'

'Maybe,' I say although that's a bit of a leap. I guess Cooper's trying, clumsily, to be supportive. After all, I'm not painting Martin in the most flattering light. 'He's not happy about it – starting again with the sleepless nights and the nappies and all that at his age.'

48

'I'm not surprised, sounds like hell – but I'm not sure what it's got to do with you.'

'He's so used to me being his confidante it's hard for him to let go. Thinking about it, he doesn't really have any close friends that he'd talk to about this kind of stuff. It was always me.'

'He needs to find someone else – it's not fair on you. Sorry if this sounds weird – I hardly know you. But sometimes it's helpful to get an outsider's perspective.'

'Is that what you are, an outsider?' I raise my eyebrows as if I'd made a salacious remark. I am so out of practice at flirting.

'That's me, the Lone Ranger.' Thankfully he's not falling off his chair laughing. In fact he moves closer, so our knees are almost touching. I don't know if it's him or the fire or the menopause, but my body feels like it's going up in flames.

'Do you have kids?' I feel the need to move away from the danger zone back to something more prosaic. I'm not sure I'm ready for this to move to the next level – whatever that is these days.

'No,' he says, leaning back. 'Not deliberately as such, it just never happened. Timing, circumstance, all that.'

'So how long had you been with your ex-wife?'

'I don't have an ex-wife,' he says, puzzled.

'Oh.' There's a beat of silence, during which I remember I made up a whole back story for him, whereby he'd gone through a painful divorce and was using my parents' basement as a temporary home while the finances were sorted. 'Sorry, I think I assumed . . . I don't know why . . . sorry.'

'That's OK.' He doesn't seem offended, merely mildly nonplussed. 'Again, it wasn't a conscious decision, I just never met the right person.'

'I'm not sure I did either.' In my eagerness to distract him from the fact that I invented a whole imaginary life for him, I've overshared again.

'How did you and Martin meet?'

'We worked together in London. Martin's in finance – well, so was I, back then. We'd chat over the water cooler every now and then, but I didn't know him all that well. Then, one night, we went to a colleague's leaving drinks and got horrendously pissed and snogged in the disabled loos at the pub, and then . . . that was it, we were together.'

'That doesn't sound very romantic.'

'No, it wasn't really. But I suppose we had shared values and he did make me laugh.'

'He'd make anyone laugh in that get-up.'

I snort, feeling disloyal.

'You must have had some relationships, even if you haven't been married?' I say, trying to draw the conversation back to him. 'Have you ever lived with anyone?'

'No.'

'Really?' I try not to sound shocked, and as if I don't automatically see this as a red flag.

'I guess up until now I've just enjoyed my own space. Does that seem odd to you?'

'No, no, not at all!'

Cooper grins.

'You're a terrible liar.'

'Sorry. It's unusual, I suppose.'

'There's no big sinister reason,' he says. 'Growing up, my household was pretty full-on, you could say. My dad left when I was five, and then it was just me and my mum. We didn't have a lot, but it was OK. Then my mum met someone when I was twelve and they had another kid. They wanted to play happy families but a teenager wasn't part of that picture, so at sixteen I was out on my ear. Obviously I couldn't afford to live on my own, so I ended up in some not great situations. I guess it had always been the dream for me – to walk out of the house in the morning and come back to find it exactly as I left it. So I was loath to give that up once I'd got it, even when I've been in good relationships. Does that make sense?'

'It makes perfect sense. I miss Zach since he went to uni, but it is utter bliss to have everything exactly as I want it. Talking of living arrangements, how are you finding the annexe?'

'It's fine.'

I detect hesitation.

'Is there a problem? You must tell me if there is. I know my parents can be . . . they haven't looked after the basement as they should over the years, so if there's anything not right, please say.'

'No honestly, everything's fine. I don't want to talk about that tonight anyway.' He shifts closer still. His foot is pressing up against mine, his knee nudging between my legs, making my sensible knee-length skirt ride up my thighs. The buzz of chatter around us dies away and everything goes hazy.

'What do you want to talk about?' I say breathlessly.

'Nothing.' He leans towards me and this is actually happening, he's getting closer and closer, he's going to kiss me. Here, in the pub. The first man who's not Martin to do so for over twenty years. Blood thrums in my head and I'm shaking all over. His lips meet mine, soft and wet. It's been a long time but my mouth knows what to do, my response taking me by surprise. He kisses me harder, his tongue probing my mouth and at the same time his hand slides up my inner thigh. A jolt of desire shoots through me like an electric current and I push him away.

'Too much?' he laughs, trailing his hand slowly back down, my skin tingling everywhere he touches it.

'Yes, a bit,' I say, tugging my skirt down and surreptitiously looking around to see if anyone has noticed the utter filth that's occurring at our table.

'Sorry-not-sorry. I can't help it if I find you irresistible.'

'You'll have to give me a bit of time to get my head around that,' I say, my breathing slowly returning to normal. 'It's been a long time since anyone found me irresistible. I'm not entirely sure anyone ever has.'

'I don't believe that for a moment. What about Martin the MAMIL?'

'It was never really like that, between us. I mean, he wasn't . . . like . . . bad in bed or anything, but it was never that real rip-your-clothes-off thing.'

'That's because he's a good boy. Good boys are no fun.'

'Talking of which . . .' I need to get this off my chest and now seems a good time, him having cued me up. 'I saw something in your flat – in the drawer. I think it was . . . marijuana.' God, that sounds so prissy. I was going to say hash or weed, but that would have been so 'tragic old person trying to be hip'.

'Oh, right. Yeah, I smoke the odd joint – is that a problem?'

'No, of course not. No. Absolutely. Of course. Right.'

'Have you finished?' He takes my hand. 'It's just every now and then – it helps me relax. No different to having a beer – better, in my opinion. Do you never partake?'

'Not since I was at university, and very rarely then. Do you think I'm a total square?'

'That remains to be seen.' He tosses back the last of his whisky. 'Shall we go and find out?'

'I'd . . . I should be getting home.' I am definitely not ready for things to go any further.

'I understand. Walk you to the taxi rank?'

'Thanks, that'd be lovely.'

We huddle together under my umbrella as we walk down the street. Just before we get to the taxi rank, Cooper puts a hand on my arm.

'Let's say goodbye here. Don't want to give the taxi drivers an eyeful.'

'An eyeful of what?' I smile up at him.

'This.'

He guides me deftly into the recess at the entrance to the closed newsagent's and pushes me against the wall, his body taut and muscular as it presses against the softness of mine. He leans down to kiss me and I allow myself to respond, my fingers entwining themselves around his neck, up into his hair. His hands drift up inside my top and find my breasts. My nipples respond to his touch and I give an involuntary moan.

A couple of adolescent boys walk past.

'Get a room, Grandma,' one of them says and they both snigger.

I come back to earth with a bump. What the hell am I thinking, getting groped in a shop doorway like a teenager?

I reach up for Cooper's hands and halt their exploration.

'Sorry,' he grins, stepping back. 'Like I said, I can't resist you. You're not upset, are you?' He peers at me in the semi-darkness.

'No, of course not,' I laugh. He's going to think I'm a right old fuddy-duddy, first questioning his very minor drug use and now this. 'Like I said, I'm not used to it. I'd better get home and have something normal and middle-aged to calm down, like a nice cup of tea.'

'Ha ha, sounds good. I like a night in with a box set as much as the next fifty-something man. I'll see you soon, yeah?' He kisses me softly on the lips and leads me by the hand to the taxi rank.

In the taxi, I lean my head against the cold glass and gaze out at the night. Every time I think of his hands on me, his lips pressing into mine, I feel a lurch of something that falls midway between desire and panic. I haven't felt this way in years. Cooper has awoken a need in me that I didn't know was there. I hope I'm equipped to handle it.

Chapter 7

A couple of days later, I stand on the doorstep waiting for my parents to answer the door, having forgotten my key. I check my phone for the millionth time. Zach still hasn't called me back or replied to any of the texts I've sent gently enquiring after his wellbeing. While I'm there, I allow myself the pleasure of reading Cooper's text again: *I hope I didn't push too hard the other night. It's only because I like you. A lot. Buy you dinner soon?* It makes my innards somersault each time. He likes me a lot. It's been so long since I felt like this – I never dreamed I'd experience it again, not at my age anyway. It's like being a teenager.

Remember Ethan Pound? I say to Caitlin.

How could I forget, darl? He was gorgeous, although God forbid we should ever have looked directly at him or spoken to him.

We were thirteen, he was a couple of years older. Me and Caitlin would walk past his dad's fruit and veg stall on the market where he worked on a Saturday. Round and round we'd go, past the nylon clothes and the bootleg tapes until we approached the stall, heralded by the sweet smell of bananas with a back note of rotting veg that had fallen to the ground.

You'd involve me in a totally fake but very deep conversation until we were safely past, I say. *Do you remember?*

There was that wrinkled, wizened old man on the next stall . . . what did he sell?

55

Watches! Or he mended them or something.

Once we were past him, we'd dissolve into hysterical, hormone-soaked giggles and then go home and talk about it endlessly – what Ethan had been wearing, whether he'd glanced our way. I wish so badly I could talk to Caitlin about Cooper.

The door creaks open and Mum appears.

'Oh, it's you.' Why is she relieved?

'I forgot my key. Who were you expecting?'

'No one. Nothing. Come in.'

She leads me into the sitting room where Dad's on the sofa with the newspaper.

'Why are we going in here? Why aren't you in the kitchen?'

It wouldn't seem strange to an outsider to find two retirees in their lounge during the day, but these two are always in the kitchen in daylight hours. This room is strictly for evenings.

'We fancied a change, didn't we?' Mum says.

'Yes. Hello, love.' Dad ostentatiously fills in a clue on the crossword.

'What's going on? Why are you being so weird?' I wish my default wasn't annoyance rather than concern.

Dad lays the newspaper and his pen on the sofa.

'It's a bit more private in here.'

'Private? What are you on about?'

'No one can hear us,' Mum says.

'No one? What? Oh – are you talking about Cooper? Why does it matter if he can hear you? I know you didn't want to get a tenant, but he's here now, and you're benefiting from the money. It's not like he's living in your house like a lodger would be – he's totally separate.'

A significant look passes between them.

'What?'

'We think he's been in the house,' Dad says. 'When we weren't here.'

'What? Why?'

'We'd gone to Christine and Lance's for drinks last night. We were only gone a couple of hours,' Mum says.

'Yes, we left at six and we were back before eight thirty,' Dad chips in. 'I know that for a fact because I thought what a bloody stupid time to make us stay until for just a few drinks. If you want someone to stay until after eight o'clock – and they did want us to stay because I kept trying to make our excuses and Lance would start another one of his interminable stories – you have to feed them. Didn't even put out a bowl of nuts, did they, Sissy?'

'No. They had a fish pie in the oven as well – I could smell it, so they were alright, tucking into that the moment we'd gone. But by the time we got back all I could be bothered to do was scrambled eggs.'

'It was like that time when you and Martin were first married,' Dad says eagerly, as if he's never ever mentioned this before. 'You served the turkey at three thirty in the afternoon! Your mother felt quite faint!'

'I did!' she says. 'That was why—'

'Yes, I know. That was why we always came to you after that. Look, even if Cooper wanted to – which I highly doubt – he couldn't get in. He doesn't have a key for your front door, does he?'

'No, we think he came in through the internal door,' Mum says. 'I actually thought I heard someone in the house when we first got in – that there was an intruder. I never dreamed it would be Cooper. Anyway, Dad went to check and there was no one here.'

'Don't you keep that door bolted from your side?'

'We must have forgotten. We never dreamed he'd abuse our trust by coming in that way when we weren't here. We've bolted it now,' Dad says.

'But what makes you think he'd been in here?'

'For one thing, my wardrobe door was open,' Mum says solemnly. 'I never leave the door open, not since we had that moth infestation in the nineties.'

'Is that all?'

'All? Clothes moths are a nightmare, Penny! You have no idea. The money we spent on lotions and potions to try and get rid of them, and then you find yourself stalking them round the room like some kind of Victorian naturalist nabbing items for his insect collection.'

'No, I meant is that the only reason you think Cooper had been in the house? The wardrobe door? You probably left it open yourself. It's easily done. Maybe you went back to grab something to wear to Christine and Lance's and forgot.'

'I never leave it open,' she says stubbornly. 'Because of the moths.'

'Never,' Dad repeats. 'And there was mud on the stairs and on the floor in our bedroom that wasn't there before we went out – how do you explain that?'

'Are you absolutely sure it wasn't there? Neither of you have got the best eyesight, let's face it. And I don't mean to be rude, but you're not the most houseproud pair I've ever met. It's not exactly a stretch to believe there could be mud on your floor.'

Mum bristles. 'I may use glasses for reading, but there's

nothing wrong with my distance vision! And I'd hoovered those stairs the day before!'

'OK, OK. What about Dottie? Did you take her with you to Christine and Lance's?'

'No. They've got this new rescue greyhound that's completely neurotic. He's alright around humans but apparently if he sees another dog, he goes for it – ears up, teeth bared, the lot.'

'There's your explanation, then.'

'Dottie can't open my wardrobe door!'

'I meant the mud.'

'She wasn't muddy – we'd only taken her for a short walk around the block. She hadn't been off the pavement, had she, Heath?'

'No, definitely not, because we bumped into Nina and Patrick, and they were saying how clean she was compared to the last time we saw them at Smithdown Park.'

'It wasn't Smithdown Park,' Mum says irritably. 'It was by the canal.'

'No, I clearly remember it was Smithdown Park. We were by the bandstand and Dottie had got into that pond and she was filthy.'

'It wasn't, Heath! It was the canal! Nina was wearing her whole set of turquoise jewellery, not just the earrings.'

'What the hell has that got to do with anything?'

'I'm not saying I don't believe you.' I drag them back from this tangent they've veered off on. 'But I still don't know why you've jumped to the conclusion that Cooper's been in here?'

'It's not just those things,' Mum says. 'My bag is missing too.'

'Your handbag?' That's more worrying – is there something in this after all?

'Not my main one with my purse in, but the little one I take when I'm going out in the evening.'

'Did you take it to Christine and Lance's?'

'Yes.'

'Well, if this intruder broke in while you were out, they can't have taken it, can they?'

'Oh. That's true.' Mum frowns.

'Did it have any money in it?'

'No, but my bank card was in there. I know that for sure because when we came in and I thought I heard an intruder I remember thinking I must hide it because my bank card was . . . oh.'

She reddens.

'What?' I say, although I'm fairly sure what's coming.

She goes out into the hall, Dad and I following closely behind. She lifts the lid of the oak shoe box that sits by the front door and there is her evening bag, nestled among the muddy walking boots.

'I'd forgotten I put it in here when I heard the noise,' she admits. 'But that doesn't explain the other things – the mud, the wardrobe.'

'You still haven't explained why you think Cooper's to blame?'

'We told you. He's noisy,' Dad says. 'He has guests at all hours. There's something not right about that man, I know it. Remember Jason Martinez.'

That stops me in my tracks. Jason was a tall, dark brooding boyfriend I had when I was eighteen. He wore a leather jacket and played the guitar at parties. I thought he was sensitive and complicated and in need of saving.

'The very first time I met him, I saw straight through him,' Dad says. 'He was a narcissistic, controlling nightmare. You said he'd had a hard life, that he needed the pure, unconditional love he'd never had as a child. Poppycock! You've never been a very good judge of character, Pen.'

Is Dad right? He was certainly right about Jason Martinez, but I was eighteen then.

'He told me about the visitors,' I say, trying to expunge Jason from my mind. 'Where he was living before it was difficult for him to have guests.' My voice wavers. I'd thought he meant a jealous, controlling wife who wouldn't allow him to see his friends. Last night he told me he's never been married. Who was he living with and why couldn't he have visitors? I squash that thought down. 'This doesn't explain why you aren't in the kitchen.'

'We don't feel at ease in there anymore,' Mum says. 'It's too close to the basement. He might be listening to us.'

'Ha!' This is so unlikely as to be comical, verging on the paranoiac. 'Listening to you talking about what? The price of items in the supermarket? Dottie's bowel movements?'

'Is that what you imagine we talk about, Penny?' Mum says. 'If so, you've got even less imagination than I thought.'

She's right, that was unfair and untrue. They're much more likely to be talking about climate change or fiscal policy. The jibe still stings though. It's not the first time she's said something along those lines. I've always suspected she's disappointed in my choice of career. That as the daughter of an inspirational teacher and a pioneering, feminist social worker, choosing an easy, dull accountancy job that fitted in with family life was a cop-out. But, as always, I let it pass.

'This is silly,' I say briskly. 'Let's go in there together and have some lunch.'

They grumble a bit but are eventually persuaded. I lay out whatever bread, cheese and salad I can find from the sparsely populated fridge and larder. When I open the cupboard door to get the plates out, it inevitably comes off in my hand.

'I thought you were going to get Bob to fix this.'

'It's fine,' Mum says. 'You pulled too hard – there's a technique. We've had to shell out so much to get all those bits done in the basement, we can't afford to do anything in here.'

'Really? What did you actually get Bob to do down there? Has he fixed the window?' I've been expecting a call any day from Cooper to complain about something faulty. I'm surprised so far it's only been the window catch.

'Yes, he was here to do that the other day. Charged us twenty pounds!' Dad says, indignant.

'I expect that included the cost of the new catch, didn't it? Sounds like a bargain to me.'

A thought strikes me.

'I'm just going to the loo,' I tell them. Luckily they haven't had the downstairs one fixed, so I don't need an excuse to go upstairs. I go into Mum and Dad's bedroom, which looks precisely as it did when I was a child. I have that old feeling of trespassing. It wasn't that I was explicitly banned from their bedroom. It was more that it was very much their territory, with a tacit rule that I only went in there if invited, or for a specific, approved purpose. I tiptoe over to Mum's wardrobe, a double-door teak affair that could be generously described as an antique. I put a gentle finger on the door and it swings towards me, revealing hangers laden with clothes I remember from my childhood – all cheesecloth and embroidery – alongside the loose, slubby linen tunics she favours nowadays. I examine the catch. It flops loosely in its casing. Nothing in this house is level. The bedrooms particularly are all on a slight slope. If the catch is broken, which it assuredly is, it's not going to take anything for the door to open by itself. Despite my robust defence of Cooper earlier, I feel a thump of relief. I didn't really think he'd been in their house – why would he, for a start? – but it's surprisingly reassuring to have it confirmed. Removing that worry (however unacknowledged it had been) simply makes space for another. If Cooper is not causing any problems, what is going on with my parents?

Chapter 8

'You can see my problem,' Cooper says. He's not wrong. The damp patch on the bathroom ceiling that Bob was meant to have sorted before Cooper moved in is back and bigger than ever. The paint is peeling, leaving flecks on the floor below. There's not enough room for all three of us in the bathroom, so Cooper points out the affected area while Dean and I peer through the doorway.

'You mentioned on the phone that this wasn't the only issue, Mr Brownlow?' Dean's in the same shiny suit, his forehead less pockmarked than before but a violent pink. I wonder if he's been trying a new skin treatment.

'That's right. Some of the floor tiles in here are cracked and broken – I didn't notice when I moved in because there was a bathmat over them, but I cut my foot quite badly on them the other day.'

He's right again. I don't remember the tiles by the bath being smashed like that, but as he said they were covered up, and until recently I hadn't been down here for years. I've no idea what state the place was in – and judging by my parents' own house, where they actually live, I wouldn't be in the least bit surprised if things had fallen into disrepair down here.

'I see.' Dean makes furious notes on his phone.

'I paid the deposit and first month's rent, as you know. But I did put a stop to this month's direct debit while this is sorted out.'

He hasn't paid his rent? This is news to me.

'Do Mum and Dad know? That you haven't paid the rent.'

'Oh . . . er . . . I'm not sure,' Cooper says, looking at Dean.

Dean's already crimson face deepens in colour. 'I . . . er . . . I'm not sure if Julie's been in touch with them or not,' he says, avoiding my eye. 'I think she was hoping we could resolve the issues here today. However, now that I've seen the extent of it, I'll need to report back to Julie and get her take on it.'

'Right. I'll speak to her.' Jesus, what was the point of sending this youth if he's not authorised to actually do anything? 'Thanks for coming.'

Dean departs, leaving a hint of pungent, musky aftershave lingering in the air, eau de boys' changing rooms.

'I'm really sorry,' I say to Cooper. 'I'll speak to them, try and get this sorted as soon as possible.'

'Thanks, I'd appreciate that. I'm sorry about withholding the rent, but . . .'

'No, I understand. Let me go and talk to them.'

'OK, but first . . .' He takes two strides across the room and looms large above me. Tingles ripple through me as I'm assailed by the memory of his hands on my waist. He runs his forefinger down the side of my face and plants a gentle kiss on my lips, lingering long enough for a flicker of desire to rise in my body.

'Dinner tonight?' he says, mouth inches from mine.

'Yes, lovely,' I whisper.

'Pick you up from yours at eight?'

'That'd be nice.' I'm rather touched by this old-fashioned, gentlemanly offer. 'I'll text you my address.'

He steps back. 'Off you go, then.'

Without thinking I try to open the connecting door, but of course it's shut fast. They've bolted it from their side.

'I'll go round the front,' I say. As I pass, he pats me lightly on the bottom and I give him a foolish grin which remains in place as I go round the side of the house and up the front steps. The ghost of it is still on my face as I go down the hall to the kitchen, which thankfully they have returned to.

'What are you smiling about?' Dad says.

'Oh, nothing. How are you two?'

'You know. Not too bad,' Mum says, opening the oven to check on whatever's cooking in there.

'No more problems from the tenant?' It feels peculiar to call him that when his tongue has been in my mouth, but the last thing I want is for them to find out that my relationship with him is anything other than professional.

'He's been pretty quiet,' Dad admits.

'That's good. Although I'm afraid there *is* a problem. I've just been down there with some child from the lettings agency and the bathroom roof is leaking again, plus there are cracked tiles on the floor. He hasn't paid this month's rent yet. We need to get it sorted.'

'That can't be right. Bob fixed the damp. He completely replaced the roofing felt on the bathroom, and replastered the damaged bit of ceiling. There's no way it can be leaking again so soon.'

'I'm afraid it is, Dad. I've seen it with my own eyes. And the tiles.'

'That's absurd,' Mum chips in. 'He's broken those tiles himself. There was nothing wrong with them – you remember, Penny.'

67

'I don't, Mum. There was a bathmat covering them – which, by the way, suggests that you knew they were there and were hoping no one would notice.'

'Those tiles were fine. We've heard him banging around down there. He's done it on purpose.'

'Come off it, Mum, you sound paranoid. Think about what you're saying. Why on earth would he do that?'

'So he can weasel out of paying the rent!' Dad says. 'How do you know the roof's leaking again? Taken his word for it, have you?'

'No, I can see that it is – plus he's got no reason to lie.'

'I told you the reason!' Dad's face is puce. 'We need that money. He can't just not pay us!'

'Legally, maybe. But it hardly seems right if you're not holding up your side of the agreement and providing him with somewhere that's fit for habitation.'

'It was fine before he moved in!' Tears hover in the back of Mum's throat. 'Why did we ever think this was a good idea? Can't we make him leave?'

'Oh, Mum.' I swear she's aged in the last month. She's always been youthful but now she looks every one of her seventy-five years and several more. I put my arm around her but she's stiff, resistant, refusing to be consoled. 'I don't think it's as easy as all that. Worst-case scenario is he'll move out when the six months are up and we can all move on. Lesson learned.' I close my mouth tight to stop the word downsizing escaping. Now is not the time. Crazily, I'm also thinking about my potential future with Cooper. How would things work between us if he's irreparably fallen out with my parents? I have to stop this. My priority should be – *is* – my parents. It's extremely unlikely that Cooper and I have any kind of future beyond this dinner tonight.

We're interrupted by my phone ringing. Once I've wrestled it from the bottom of my bag, I swipe furiously to answer in time.

'Darling! How are you?'

'Not great.' Zach's voice is wobbly. He sounds about five years old.

'What is it? Where are you?'

'I'm at home,' he says. It's mid-week in the middle of term – why isn't he in Winchester? 'Where are you?'

'I'm at Grandma and Grandpa's. What's going on?'

'I'm not happy there, Mum. I've left. I don't ever want to go back.'

Chapter 9

'Tell me everything,' I say, placing a mug of tea and a plate piled high with toast slathered in peanut butter in front of him. I sit down opposite him at our tiny kitchen table which is only just big enough for the two of us.

'I'm just not really enjoying it,' he says with his mouth full, spraying crumbs everywhere.

'Lots of people struggle at first,' I say. 'I know I did. Why don't you spend a few days here, let me look after you, and then go back? I'm sure there's loads of parties and stuff going on – you don't want to miss out on that.'

'Not really,' he says. 'I don't think university's for me.'

'You can't say that after a few months! You've got to give it a chance. Your flatmates seemed nice when I dropped you off that first time.' I can hardly bear to think of that day – me all false jollity, Zach's face sheet-white as I kissed him goodbye, Martin piling the last of his belongings into the beige box of a room. To anyone else he would have appeared fine, but I know every inch of him and I could feel the fear and anxiety seeping out of him like gas from a leaky valve.

'They're OK,' he says in a small voice.

'What is it? Zach?'

'They haven't always been very nice to me.'

'Oh, darling. You mean, like, bullying?'

71

He stares mulishly into the murky depths of his tea, muddy brown just as he likes it and I want to kill them, these unnamed flatmates. When he was five, he was obsessed with a boy in his class called Parker. Some days Parker would play with him, but there were days when he wouldn't, days when he would stop everyone else from playing with Zach too. On the walk home from school, Zach would dissolve into sobs that broke my heart. I used to fantasise about taking our largest, shiniest kitchen knife to school and surprising Parker when he was alone, holding the knife to his throat. I wouldn't have hurt him – even in fantasy I knew that was a step too far – but I wanted to scare him so badly he would pee his pants, and never mess with my son's happiness again.

'Have you told the university? You should report it. They're so hot on bullying these days.'

'There's no point. They're not doing anything reportable. It's just, like, they've formed a little clique and they never ask me to go out with them. They do a joint weekly food shop and all cook together, but I'm not invited.'

'That's so rude!' Those hateful, vile bastards.

'And they . . . ignore me. I mean not, like, if I speak directly to one of them. Like, they'll answer. But they never start the conversation. And now I don't either, because it's got too embarrassing. There's one girl, Becky . . .'

'Oh, I remember her from the day we dropped you off. Perfect size eight with a swingy, blonde ponytail? Reminded me of Helena Purcell from my secondary school. She used to take the piss out of me because of Grandma, saying she was a hippy who hung around with druggies and women who were stupid enough to let their husbands bash them about.'

'Did you tell Grandma?' Zach says, momentarily distracted. He loves hearing tales of his grandmother's fierceness.

'Eventually. She hit the roof! Went charging into school all guns blazing. I pretended to be mortified, but I was secretly proud. I don't know what she said to them, or what they said to Helena Purcell, but she never bothered me again. But tell me about this Becky.'

'She's kind of the . . .'

'Ringleader?' I say.

'I dunno. I just think if it wasn't for her, it wouldn't be so bad.'

'What about friends on your course?'

'There's one girl, Hayley, who's asked me to go out a couple of times. She's OK, I suppose, but she's a bit boring. I don't think we've got much in common.'

'What about the others?

'I don't know them that well.' His cheeks darken in shame. 'It's hard to get to know anyone in the lectures. And the others are all better at it than me.'

'Better at filmmaking? You're so talented – those movies you and Saul used to make when you were younger!'

'That was just kids mucking about. And it's not filmmaking, it's film production. Anyway, I meant better at making friends,' he mutters.

'What about asking for some help? Counselling? There must be something available through Student Services.'

'That won't make any difference. It won't change what they're doing. It's not going to make me any friends.'

'You're right,' I say carefully. 'You can't change other people's behaviour – but you can change your reaction to it.'

'That's what Maggie used to say.' Zach had some counselling when he was eleven or twelve and Martin and I were worried that his anxiety was spiralling out of control. It was a mission to get him into school at all some days. He always claimed the talking therapy didn't help him. He reckoned the only reason things got better was because he made friends with Saul who was into the same geeky stuff as he was – gaming, and making and editing their own movies. I've always thought it helped more than he realised.

'And you're not . . .' I have to approach this with care or he'll fly off the handle. 'You haven't been smoking a bit too much? Gear, I mean.'

'Gear?' he says, making quote marks with his fingers. 'Ooh you're down with the kids, aren't you?'

I smile, despite myself. 'Alright, whatever you cool cats are calling it these days. Ganj. Smoking a doobie.'

'Argh, stop.' He puts his hands over his ears in mock dismay.

'Seriously, though.'

'Seriously, Mother, no I'm not, like I've told you a million times before. Everyone smokes a bit, it's no big deal.'

'What about these flatmates? Do they smoke?'

'No, they're all super sporty health freaks.'

'Ah. I can see why they might not be quite your cup of tea. Talking of which, every time I see Dad these days he's dressed top to toe in skin-tight activewear. I think Elaine's got him on a regime.'

He rolls his eyes and we giggle. Taking the piss out of Martin with Zach has been something of a guilty pleasure since he left me.

'Can we order pizza and watch a movie?' he says. '*Star Wars* marathon?'

Oh God. My date with Cooper. And he's picking me up here. I won't buzz him in, I'll run down when he gets here.

'I'd love to, but I'm going out for dinner.'

'Who with?'

'A friend.' I'm hopeless at lying on the spot. I should have prepared a cover story, but I didn't know I was going to need one.

'Who?'

'No one you know. A friend from work.'

'Mum, you're not . . . going on a date, are you?'

'Would you mind if I was?' This is not a conversation I ever envisaged having with my son. First I thought me and Martin would rub along together for the rest of our lives, and then, when he left, that no one would be interested in me.

'I suppose not.' His face is pale, his freckles standing out even more than usual. He looks about seven years old.

'Come on, Zach, you can't begrudge me one date when Dad moved straight from my bed into Elaine's. Am I not allowed any happiness?' My sadness and frustration at his situation has been translated into a snappy anger. I want to bite the words back as soon as they're out of my mouth. Humorously ribbing Martin is one thing, slagging him off to our son is another.

'Elaine's alright,' he says quietly.

'Of course she's alright to you, she's buttering you up, wants to get on your good side.' I can't stop the words flying out of my mouth. I'm not even making sense – I should be glad Elaine is nice to him rather than being some cartoon evil stepmother. 'That's not going to last long though, unfortunately for you. Elaine's going to have her hands full elsewhere soon.'

'What d'you mean?'

I fall silent. I shouldn't have said anything.

'What do you mean?' he repeats. 'She's not . . .' Realisation dawns. 'She's not *pregnant*, is she?' The way he says it, pregnancy might as well be a terminal illness.

I don't answer.

'Mum?'

'I shouldn't have told you. Dad'll kill me.'

'Urgh, that's gross.'

'I know, it kind of is,' I admit and suddenly we're both giggling and everything's OK again. It's like the old days before he went to university when we'd stay up late drinking beer and he'd play me new music he thought I'd like, stuff I'd never hear otherwise because they don't play it on Radio 2.

'Don't say anything to Dad. Let him tell you in his own time. I'll transfer you some money to get pizza, you hunker down tonight and we'll talk more tomorrow. I need to go and get ready.'

It's a long time since I've been on a date, and I had considerably better skin back then so getting ready takes longer than I anticipated. I'm so caught up in it that I lose track of time and when the doorbell goes, I'm in the bathroom frantically flossing my teeth. I yank the floss out, almost dislodging my tooth and leap for the bathroom door, but I'm too late, Zach's already let him in.

I decide to finish my preparations and emerge a couple of minutes later, the metallic tang of blood from my gum still lingering, to the sound of chat and laughter from the sitting room.

'Sorry to keep you waiting. I see you've met my son.'

'That's OK. It was worth the wait,' he says looking me up and down appreciatively.

I sense Zach wants to do a theatrical performance of a vomit, but he manages to hold himself back.

Cooper stands and reaches down to shake Zach's hand. 'Nice to meet you, mate.'

'Yeah, you too. Have a good time, you two. Don't do anything I wouldn't do!'

He's changed his tune. Cooper must have made a good impression.

'I won't be late, darling. See you when I get back.'

We're walking down the street to Cooper's car when I stop dead.

'Sorry, I've left my phone in the kitchen. I'll run back and get it – won't be a mo.'

I let myself back in and scamper up the stairs in the dark. Zach's on the phone.

'Yeah, I know, brilliant.'

As I pass through the sitting room, he looks up guiltily.

'Gotta go, bye.' He hangs up.

'Just back to grab my phone!' I trill. 'Who was that?'

'Saul.'

'Oh right.'

There's no reason why he shouldn't be chatting to his old mate on the phone, but there's an indefinable hint of something wrong in the air between us.

'See you later, then.'

I scoop up my phone and trip back down the stairs. There's no need to worry. I fix on a big smile and walk towards Cooper.

Chapter 10

The cocktail I had on arrival has blurred the world around the edges. A candle stuck in an old wine bottle flickers on the table between us. As Cooper pours me a glass of red wine, the rest of the room ebbs away. Tucked away in this alcove, we could be the only people in the restaurant. I'm wearing a wide-necked top and he reaches out and runs a finger across the exposed top of my shoulder. I shiver and something shifts inside me.

'You look lovely,' he says.

'Liar. I saw myself in the mirror before I came out and I look about a hundred and three.'

'You need to learn how to take a compliment.'

'I suppose I'm not used to them.'

He trails his hand back down my arm. 'Maybe it's a defence mechanism.'

'Defence against what?' I say, still feeling the imprint of his finger on my skin.

'You tell me. Did Martin ever compliment you?'

'Back in the day, I guess, when we were first together. Although now I come to think of it, I can't call a single occasion to mind.' Our wedding day – he must have said I looked beautiful then, surely. Why can't I remember?

'We've already established that he's a dickhead, so that doesn't shock me.'

'He's not so bad.' I'm surprised to find myself defending Martin.

'Really? He left you for someone else. You're very tolerant.'

'Whatever he's done, he's still my son's father. I don't want to be on bad terms with him.'

'I wouldn't be so magnanimous in your situation.'

'Have you ever been – in my situation, I mean?' Alcohol has emboldened me to get personal. 'Has anyone ever cheated on you?'

'Once,' he says. 'Let's just say I'm not big on forgiveness.'

'What happened?'

'Put it this way – I made sure she regretted it.'

'Why? What did you do?' I ask, agog, imagining him snipping up her favourite dress or stuffing prawns into her curtain hems.

'I paid the other fella a visit, made sure he wouldn't be able to do it again.'

'Oh.' I sit back in my chair, the pleasant wine-haze that has surrounded me evaporating.

He chuckles.

'I'm joking, Penny. She regretted it because the bloke turned out to be an arsehole. She came crawling back to me but I was having none of it.'

'Oh, phew!' I lean back in. 'So tell me more about you. You mentioned your family last time we went out. Do you get on with your mum now?'

'Yeah, we get on fine. I think she feels guilty, can see now that she handled it wrong back then. But it's all good now. Seems like you get on well with your parents?'

It must be the wine, but I find myself spilling more and more of my life into Cooper's willing ears. I don't feel I'm giving him much space to talk, but he's such a good listener, it's hard to stop. By the time we're digging a spoon each into one rich chocolate mousse, dimly illuminated by the last, guttering light of the candle, he's had my entire life story.

'I can't eat any more of this, it's so rich.' I lay my spoon down on the table.

'Fancy a nightcap?' he asks. 'We've missed last orders. I would say you could come back to mine, but might be a bit weird for you with your parents on the other side of the wall.'

'Yeah. I haven't told them we're . . .' I stop. I've led myself down a dead end and now I've got to finish the sentence. What are we doing?

'Having dinner?' Cooper suggests with a smile.

'Yes, exactly.'

'We could go back to yours for a drink?' he suggests. 'Zach seemed pretty relaxed about me being there.'

'OK. Just a quick drink though.'

'Scout's honour.' He holds up two fingers in a mock salute.

Back at the flat, I close the front door softly behind us. It's quiet and in darkness – it's later than I realised. Zach must have gone to bed, for which I'm thankful. I'm aware of how drunk I am as I gingerly get out glasses, bottle, corkscrew, trying not to clink any of them against anything that might wake Zach. When I go into the sitting room with the drinks, Cooper is sprawled in the middle of my two-seater sofa. There's only a small space either side of him, so I wedge myself into one of them. He gives me a lazy smile and downs half the glass in one go. I leave mine on the coffee table. I've already had too much.

'So . . . have you had . . . dinner with anyone else, since you and Martin split up?' He puts his hand casually on my knee and traces circles with his fingers which go a little higher each time. My stomach churns, a jittery mix of desire and nausea. I was – am – attracted to him, but I feel trapped, like I've lost any agency I had in the situation. That in letting him into my flat, I've relinquished the right to say no to him.

'No. Only you.'

'I think it's time you did something for yourself, don't you?' He strokes the side of my face gently. 'You do so much for everyone else.'

'I don't know what that would feel like,' I say.

'Like this.' He leans in to kiss me.

My initial impulse is to pull back, but I don't. I allow my mouth to respond. I've spent an enjoyable evening with this man. We've kissed before. I find him attractive. It's unthinkable that I should want to stop this, tell him to leave. Do I? I try to quieten these thoughts that spin around my brain as his tongue pulses in my mouth and he slips his hand around my waist. I make a faint noise of protest, but he takes it as a sign of enjoyment and burrows further up inside my top. He continues to kiss me without pausing for breath. I'd like to speak, but I don't have the chance with his probing tongue invading my mouth. I try to inhabit my body, be present, like my mindfulness app tells me. I focus on the sensations of Cooper touching me. They're pleasant feelings, I tell myself. It's been a long time since anyone touched me like this. I should be enjoying it. I am.

I allow him to lower me back on the sofa, the length of his body on top of mine, pressing down, hard and heavy. I put my arms around his neck. He reaches down between us and unbuttons my jeans, his hand snaking inside, over my knickers. I stop kissing him and push him up, away from me.

'What's the matter?' His eyes are glazed. It's as if I'm not here – not as a sentient human being anyway. I'm just a body.

'Zach's here. I feel a bit . . .'

'We can be quiet.' He buries his face in my neck, kissing and nuzzling. I fix my gaze on the pendant lamp above me. There's a crack in the ceiling, threading out from the light fixing. I should get that looked at.

I help him pull my jeans down and over my feet, taking off my socks at the same time. They're mismatched. One has a hole in the heel. I didn't think anyone would be seeing them. I'm not sure I want to go through with this, but it feels inevitable. It would cause too much of a fuss to stop, plus I don't want to wake Zach. And deep down, there's a part of me that is frightened of how he'll react if I stop him now. It's easier all round if I just get it over with.

Cooper doesn't seem to be much of a foreplay man which should be a disappointment, but I'm thankful. I want to get it over and done with. He reaches under my top to undo my bra and kneads my breasts, tweaking my nipples until I gasp in what I suppose he thinks is pleasure. He slides his hand inside my knickers, fingers burrowing, but it doesn't spark anything pleasurable. In fact I have to steel myself not to jerk away. After a couple of minutes, he pulls my knickers to one side and thrusts into me. My arms meet around his back and I hold my own hand tightly, eyes screwed shut. When he's finished, he rolls off me and I wriggle out, wrenching my knickers back into place. I retrieve my jeans from the floor and put them on. The underwire from my bra is digging into my armpit. I reach inside my top, pull it down and do it back up.

'Just going to the loo.'

Outside Zach's room, I put my ear to the door. Total silence. Thank God he didn't wake up. What was I thinking, risking him walking in on us? In the bathroom, I avoid my reflection in the mirror. I don't want to see the blankness I know will be there, to see how little I look like a woman who has recently enjoyed sex. I should be flushed, smiling, relaxed. I am none of those things.

Back in the living room, Cooper is sitting up on the sofa, buttoning up his shirt. He beams at me as if we've enjoyed a mutually satisfying experience. Surely he can't believe I actually got any gratification from that?

'I'd better go,' he says. 'Thanks for a great evening.'

'Yes, sure.'

I walk with him to the flat door and he kisses me goodbye. I force my lips into the appropriate shape. He jogs down the stairs, disappearing into the darkness. The front door to the building slams, and I'm alone.

I walk back into the sitting room and replace the sofa cushions slowly, as if I'm moving through water. I try to reassure myself that this is all part of dating, of being a single woman. I should be relishing it after all those long, safe, stultifying years of marriage, laughing it off, chalking it up to experience.

Caitlin? I say out loud, my voice wavery.

She doesn't reply. I know it's my subconscious but even that seems to have deserted me. If only I could really speak to her. She was the one person I could have phoned at this hour who wouldn't have minded. She would have pretended she was awake anyway.

I'm dying for a shower but I don't want Zach to wake and wonder why I'm washing at this hour. I undress and get into bed, first wrapping the duvet around me like a cocoon, and later

84

throwing it off, drenched with sweat. At five thirty I give up on getting any more sleep and step into the shower. I stay much longer than I normally would, in the vain hope that copious amounts of hot water will wash off my confusion and shame.

Chapter 11

'OK, OK, Mum – don't panic, I'll come round. I'll see you shortly.'

This is the last thing I need. I'm exhausted, and was hoping to avoid Cooper after last night's events, but I can't not go, Mum sounds distraught. I couldn't get much sense out of her, but it's clearly something to do with Cooper. I was a total fool to ever get involved with him. I should have known it was a terrible idea to date the man who's renting my parents' annexe. What was I thinking? I suppose I was seduced – less by Cooper himself than by the idea that someone found me attractive. I dress in baggy tracksuit bottoms and an over-sized hoodie – a ludicrous outfit for a woman of my age, but one that covers and disguises as much of my body as is humanly possible. I draw my hair back into an unflattering ponytail and don't bother with any makeup. I'm making this very easy for Cooper – one look at me in the harsh morning light and he'll be delighted I don't want a repeat performance of last night.

On the way over there, my phone rings on Bluetooth in the car. I answer without checking to see who it is, assuming it'll be Mum and Dad again.

'Why the hell did you tell Zach that Elaine's pregnant?'

Oh God. Could this day get any worse?

'I'm sorry, Martin, it kind of slipped out.'

'Slipped out? How does something like that slip out? You told him in a deliberate attempt to make him angry with me! You've always wanted to be the favourite parent!'

'Come off it, Martin.'

'Don't deny it! It's always been the two of you against me. You would never put up a united front with me, would you? You always had to take his side.'

'Take his side? Of course I'm on his side. I'm his mother. You should be on his side too.'

'I am! But that doesn't mean giving in to his every whim.'

'I don't have time for this right now. I'm on my way to Mum and Dad's to sort some crisis. I'm sorry I told Zach but the fact is, Elaine *is* pregnant. It's not as if I've made up some malicious lie about you.'

'I specifically asked you not to tell him. I wanted to do it myself, in my own way, my own time.'

'I'm sorry. But he was going to find out sooner or later, unless you were planning to tell him Elaine had a balloon up her jumper. Does it really matter?'

'Yes, it matters! He's furious with me! He asked why I didn't have the balls to tell him myself.'

I pull into Mum and Dad's driveway. My heart sinks when I see Cooper's car parked around the side.

'I've got to go, I've just arrived at Mum and Dad's. Don't worry about Zach, he'll come round.'

'That's all very well for you to—'

I cut him off mid-flow, trot up the steps and let myself in as quickly as I can. I find Mum and Dad in the kitchen, both looking exhausted and older than ever.

'What's going on?' I say before I've even taken off my coat or put my bag down.

'We've got to get him out,' Dad says quietly. 'He's dealing drugs out of our house. We can smell it! I may be old but I'm not completely naïve – I was a teenager in the sixties. I know what marijuana smells like. We could end up in prison!'

'Come off it, I think you're catastrophising a bit. Just because he smokes the odd joint doesn't mean he's a drug dealer.'

'Then who are these people that arrive at all times of the day and night?' he says. 'Don't tell me they're his friends. What sort of friends pull up in a car, music blaring, stay for two minutes and go screeching off again? They're his customers! I saw one of them at the door, handing over money, getting a little bag of something in return. He can't even be bothered to hide it!'

Is Dad imagining, exaggerating? He may be getting older but I can't deny he is as sharp as he's ever been. He's always had an uncanny ability to see through people, to see them as they are, rather than as they want to be seen. And Cooper does have drugs in the flat, that I know. Plus when I think about it, he's told me very little about himself – his job, his past, his family. All that time I've spent with him and I know barely anything about him. When I think about it, he deflects most personal questions and turns them back on me. I thought he was a good listener, but is it a deliberate strategy?

'And he still hasn't paid this month's rent,' Dad continues. 'We need it. We got a final demand from the electricity company this morning. I tried to get another credit card to pay it off but we got turned down.'

Another credit card? How many have they got?

'Have you fixed the problems? The damp, the tiles?'

'We were going to get Bob round, but how can we if he won't let us in, doesn't answer the door, or his phone?'

'He was probably out when you tried.'

'We could hear him,' Mum says in anguish. 'He was in there, but he wouldn't come to the door.'

'Maybe . . . maybe he couldn't hear you?' I'm clutching at straws here.

'Of course he could,' Dad snaps. 'He's making a fool out of us, Penny.'

Oh God, this doesn't sound good. Surely there's some benign explanation, though?

'I'll go down there now. His car's in the drive, so I presume he's in.'

'I'm not sure,' Mum says. 'I saw him go out on foot earlier and I don't think he's back yet.'

'Let me go and see.' I go straight back out into the cold and round to the side door. As I rap smartly on it, I try not to think about last night and how I can still feel the imprint of Cooper's hands on my body, the pressure as he nudged my legs apart with his knee, the soreness between my legs. There's no answer. I peer through the dusty window. There's no sign of him. I look round. Nobody can see me from here, unless Sue from next door happens to be peering out of her utility room window, the only one that has any vantage point on my parents' house. I knock again and press my ear to the door. Nothing. I reach into my bag and find my keys. I've had a key to this and all the outside doors for this house since I lived here. I unlock it and open the door a fraction.

'Cooper?' I'm ready with an excuse – we heard noises and knew you were out, thought it was an intruder – but no answer comes. I poke my head through the gap. He's nowhere to be seen. The place is silent and feels uninhabited. I swiftly cross the room and check the only other place he could be – the bathroom. He's not here, but my eyes are drawn to the cracked tiles by the bath. I kneel down to take a closer look and the strap of my bag slips off my shoulder. I allow it to fall to the floor as I run my fingers over the jagged edges of the tiles. On a couple of them, the cracks splinter out from a central point, as if something heavy has been dropped on them. I'm getting to my feet when something beneath the basin cabinet catches my attention. I crouch back down and reach for it. It's a hammer. I inspect the head more closely. Clinging to the metal are tiny flecks of what looks like paint or plaster, the exact shade of terracotta as the tiles. I drop to my knees, suddenly weak. Did Cooper damage the tiles deliberately?

Up above me, the damp patch on the ceiling is worse than ever. Feeling sick, I go outside and round to where the section of flat roof is, the one Bob repaired before Cooper moved in. I can't see the roof from the ground. I know there's a ladder in the shed, but there's no time to get it out – I'm terrified of Cooper coming back and finding me snooping. Instead I step onto the low wall that extends out from the house and use it to clamber onto the green wheelie bin. The bin is slippery – there was a frost last night and this side of the house doesn't get any sun – and I cling onto the drainpipe for support as I pull myself precariously up to standing. I transfer my grip to the edge of the flat roof, the black roofing felt gritty and rough beneath my fingers. I stare, baffled, trying to make sense of what I'm seeing but I don't have time to order my thoughts because I can hear someone walking up the drive. I freeze. There's nowhere to hide – I'm in full view. There is absolutely no reasonable explanation for why I am standing on the bin – or for why the external door to the annexe is open and my handbag is inside on the bathroom floor. For one brief, mad moment I consider opening the brown recycling bin next to me, jumping inside with the cans and bottles and closing the lid, but before I have a chance to consider whether I'm seriously going to do it, the postman appears, whistling cheerfully.

'Hello!' he says in surprise. 'Are you alright up there?'

'Yes, I'm fine, I thought I . . . er . . . heard a cat but there's nothing up here.'

'Ah right – I'll keep an eye out. Post for Brownlow through this door, right?'

'Yes please.'

He puts a handful of letters through the open door onto the mat and regards me curiously.

'Would you like me to help you down?'

'Yes. Thank you.'

I might as well take the opportunity to avoid breaking my leg. I've seen everything there is to see up here. Bob has repaired the roof as Mum and Dad said – the felt is brand new and fully sealed around the edges. But on one corner, which corresponds with where the damp patch is inside, the new felt has been cut away with what must have been an incredibly sharp knife or shears. Whoever did it – I frame it like this although it's painfully obvious who must have done – hasn't even bothered to take away or hide the removed section. It's lying there on the roof, taunting me. Underneath, the timber is bare and exposed, water pooling on the uneven surface. No wonder it's coming through into the annexe. I don't have time to stand here and dwell on it. Cooper could return at any moment.

I crouch down on the bin and reach my hand out to the postman. There's a frightening second where I wobble, grasping air, then I grab his hand and steady myself by slapping my other hand against the wall of the house. The brick grazes my skin, and blood beads on my right palm as I shakily make my way to the ground, almost falling into his arms.

I thank him and he salutes me and continues off on his rounds. I long to scurry back to the safety of Mum and Dad's, but I need to retrieve my handbag. As I step over the post on the mat, I glance down and see that one of the letters has been forwarded from a previous address. I pick it up, mindful to use my left hand, rather than my bloodied right. It's an address near Blackhawk Point, about twenty minutes' drive away. I wonder who he was living with before – one of the many things I didn't find out about him on our date. I can't waste time thinking about it here and now though. I cross the room, grab my bag from the bathroom and take out my phone. I take a photo of the address and replace the letter on the mat. As I walk back I do a sweep of the room to make sure I haven't inadvertently left any sign of my having been here. On the sideboard next to the TV there's a pile of opened post. I hesitate, listening intently, but there's no sound apart from the gentle rise and fall of voices from Radio 4 in my parents' house above. I go to the outside door and check the drive. Nothing. I close it and go back to the pile of post and flip through it. The top few are junk mail – pizzas, mattresses, estate agents. At the bottom of the pile, there's one that looks different – official. It's been opened and shoved back in the envelope. Gingerly, careful to keep my grazes away from the paper, I extract it. The letter is addressed to Cooper Brownlow and confirms an appointment with his probation officer. My knees almost give way beneath me. I feel like I've been whacked over the head with a blunt implement. Cooper has been in prison? For what? As I'm standing there, staring in bewildered consternation at the letter, I hear footsteps outside. It could be a visitor for my parents (or for Cooper more likely, if what my parents say is true) but I can't take that chance. For a terrifying few seconds I'm genuinely unable to move, each breath following too closely on the heels of the one before.

Finally, my brain kicks in. It's too late to go out the external door – if it is Cooper I'll run slap bang into him. My only hope is the internal door. I stuff the letter back in the envelope and replace it under the junk mail. As I fly across to the door, I pray with every fibre of my being that my parents haven't bolted it on their side. I slide the bolt on this side and push. It doesn't budge. Of course they've locked it, they're petrified of him. Why didn't I listen to them from the start? And then I see Cooper. He passes the window. He's going to be in here any second. The only saving grace is that he's on the phone. If he decides to finish the call outside before rooting around for his keys and letting himself in, I've got a sparse wedge of time. I pray it's enough. I need my parents to come down and unbolt the door, but if I bang on it loudly enough to attract their attention up in their kitchen, Cooper will hear it from outside. I fumble in my bag for my phone, hands slippery with sweat and call their landline – there's not a hope in hell either of their mobiles will be on while they're at home. I can hear the phone ringing in the hall above me. They take an agonisingly long time to answer it. Cooper speaks angrily into his phone, pacing around outside the window. I press myself flat against the wall, attempting to stay as still as I can so I don't catch his eye.

'Hello?' Oh no, it's Dad, the deafer of the two.

'Dad, it's me,' I say under my breath.

'Hello? Who's that?'

'Dad, it's me,' I say as loudly as I dare.

'Penny? What's going on? Was he there? What did he say about the drugs?'

'There's no time to explain, I'm in the basement and I need to get up to you right now. Come down and unbolt the door and I'll explain everything in a minute.'

'What are you talking about? Why don't you come up the other way?'

'There's no time!' On the drive, Cooper puts his phone in his pocket and moves out of my view. He's right outside the door. 'Cooper's outside! He's coming! Please, Dad, hurry!'

Finally, he recognises the urgency and puts down the phone. I can hear the thud of his walking stick on the stairs on the other side of the door and I have a horrible fear that he's going to fall, but that's soon overtaken by my terror at being discovered as I hear the jingle of Cooper's keys. There's a clunk as Dad draws the back the bolt and opens the door, his huge frame filling the doorway. I whip through, barely having time to register his confusion. As I close the door behind me and draw the bolt, the external door opens and Cooper's footsteps resound in the basement. I put my finger to my lips and motion Dad back up the stairs. Thankfully he grasps the situation and tiptoes up ahead of me without a word, placing his stick carefully and noiselessly on each step.

In the kitchen, I close the door behind us and lower myself down at the table, my whole body quivering. Mum looks from me to Dad questioningly.

'Do you want a glass of water, love?' he asks me.

I nod, momentarily unable to speak.

Mum gets a glass down from one of the many broken cupboards and fills it from the tap. She doesn't leave it to run, so it's lukewarm but I gulp it down gratefully.

'Thanks.'

'What happened down there?' Dad says.

I wipe a drop of water from my chin and place the glass on the table in front of me.

'I'm so sorry.' I take in their dear, careworn faces, this man and woman who have loved me for a lifetime, more than anyone else ever has or will. Recently I've been viewing them as an inconvenience, but now I see them properly, as people. I've been worrying about being invisible as a middle-aged woman, but I've been doing the same to them – seeing them as their age, not as who they are. A sob rises in my throat and my resolve hardens as I think about what this means for them. If it's the last thing I do, I will get them out of this situation.

'You were right about Cooper.'

Chapter 12

The bell jingles merrily as I enter the offices of Woodford Peters, but Dean doesn't look up. Their logo is gaudy – a bright-orange building with four windows and a fat triangle of a roof, squat and symmetrical like a child's drawing of a house – but inside everything is faded and tatty. I should have asked Mum and Dad earlier where they'd found the lettings agency – it turns out their friend Linda recommended it because it was cheaper than all the others. I can see why. I guess the carpet was originally a speckled beige, but it's so dirty and stained it's hard to know for sure. There are four chipped melamine desks, all empty apart from the one occupied by Dean. He continues tapping away at his keyboard for a few seconds as if finishing some vital piece of work before raising his head condescendingly.

'Can I help you?'

'I'm Penny Whitlock. Sissy and Heath Whitlock's daughter. They rent their annexe through you – on St Mary's Road. We've met before?'

'Ah. Yes.' He fiddles with his tie. It's one of those fake ones on elastic like Zach had when he started primary school. 'What can I do for you?'

'There's a problem with the tenant.'

'I thought this was all in hand, Mrs Whitlock.' He glances nervously towards the rear of the shop.

'Ms,' I say through gritted teeth.

'I'm sorry, Mzzzz Whitlock. I did check actually,' his voice becomes bolder, 'and Julie said the easiest way for you to resolve this is to effect the necessary repairs in the property.'

'What if I told you I've discovered that the tenant himself is deliberately causing the problems to give him an excuse not to pay the rent?'

'What? I don't think that's . . . I don't think so . . . is he?'

'I don't mean to be rude, but is there someone else I could speak to? Someone more . . . senior?' Someone who's more than a year out of school. Someone who doesn't have teenage acne and a TikTok account.

'I'll get Julie.'

He scuttles off gratefully into the back room, reappearing a couple of minutes later with a woman of about my age; buxom and well-preserved in a cream belted shirtdress. Her hair is high-lighted with copper tones and she sports a matching set of hammered silver jewellery – bracelet, necklace and large, dangling earrings. A waft of her perfume hits my nostrils and I recognise the musky smell of Dior's Poison. I've not smelled that since the days when I wore it myself as a teenager in the 1980s, thinking myself frightfully sophisticated. Dean resumes his seat at the computer. I'm pretty sure he's pretending to type, his ears on stalks.

'I'm Julie Woodford. Can I help you?' She couldn't sound any less like she wants to help, but I plough on regardless.

'My parents rent out their annexe through you – 62 St Mary's Road.'

'Yes, Dean's filled me in.'

The tips of Dean's ears turn red.

'It seems your parents are not keeping the property in a reasonable condition,' she goes on. 'Obviously I would never advise a tenant to withhold rent for repairs, but in this case I can understand why he is reluctant to pay.'

It occurs to me that I don't know whether we still have to pay the agency management fees if the rent isn't being paid. I suspect we do, otherwise she'd be more interested in making sure Cooper paid his rent. However, that feels like a battle for another day.

'I'm afraid there's been a . . . development since then. I have reason to believe that the tenant is deliberately damaging the property to avoid paying the rent.'

'And what reason is that?' she asks coldly. I have the unpleasant feeling she knows what I'm about to say and has the perfect counter argument ready to go.

'Somebody has cut away the roofing felt so that water is leaking into the annexe.'

'Somebody?'

'Cooper! The tenant . . . Mr Brownlow. And that's not all – when Dean came last time there were some broken tiles in the bathroom.'

'Yes, I believe Mr Brownlow cut his foot on them,' she says. She's very well-informed.

'Has he been speaking to you?'

'Who?' she asks coolly.

'Coop— Mr Brownlow.'

'We keep in touch with all our tenants, Ms Whitlock,' she says woodenly.

'In that case perhaps you can ask him to explain why there are more broken tiles than there were when he moved in, and why there was a hammer under the sink that had clearly been used to smash them.'

'May I ask how you know all this?' she asks.

'I . . . saw them. When I was visiting him in his flat.'

'Visiting?' She purses her lips and a wave of revulsion passes over her features. Surely she can't know I slept with him. 'You went into the bathroom, did you?'

'No, yes, I . . . happened to see . . . as I was passing.'

'You do know that in the contract you have with Mr Brownlow it states that you must give him written notice before entering the property, no matter what the reason?' I feel like a child who's been summoned to the headteacher's office to be accused of a crime I thought I'd got away with.

'Yes, I . . . of course I know that.'

'That's very interesting, because I had a call from Mr Brownlow earlier, claiming that you or your parents had been in the property without his permission while he was out.'

'I . . . no . . . that's . . .' I can't believe he's already been on to her.

'He said that the internal door between his property and your parents' was unbolted on his side, despite him having left it bolted. Suggesting that one of you used your key to gain access to the property from the outside, and left via the internal door.'

'He's . . . mistaken. He must have left it unbolted.' I mustn't admit to anything. He's wheedled in his way in and somehow persuaded her that we're the bad guys.

'That's a possibility,' she says evenly.

'But the roof,' I say, feeling myself on firmer ground here. 'I went up there to check on it because he said water was coming through, and the repair my parents' handyman did has been deliberately sabotaged. The repaired section has been hacked away. He didn't even bother to hide it.'

'Ah, Mr Brownlow did tell me about that. He said he decided to take a look at the roof because your parents weren't showing any interest in getting it fixed, and as you say, it seems that some-one has deliberately damaged it.'

'Yes, him!' I say, my voice betraying me with a wobble. 'Who else would it be?'

'I'm sorry to bring this up,' she says silkily, not sorry at all, 'but he did suggest that your parents are elderly, and possibly don't have all their faculties, as it were?'

'There's nothing wrong with their faculties! They may be elderly but they're both perfectly compos mentis.'

'Hmm. Mr Brownlow said he's had some rather confusing conversations with both of them, where they didn't appear to know who he was. I'd suggest that one of them may have damaged the roof themselves. He said he found your mother wandering outside on the street recently saying she didn't know where she lived. He very kindly made sure she got home safely, but it's not on. He's their tenant, not their carer. It's not fair to put him in this position.'

'This is utter bullshit!' Rage burns in me, fiery and hot.

'I don't appreciate being spoken to like that in my place of business,' she says primly. 'I think you'd better leave.'

'How dare he say that? It's completely untrue. He's made it all up! And . . .' I'm in so deep, there's no point holding back, 'he's been in prison! How did you miss that? Surely you're supposed to check these things?'

'Don't worry, I know all there is to know about Cooper,' she snaps. 'As you will have seen in the files, he had an excellent reference from his previous landlord. I think this conversation has gone on quite long enough.' Despite her bravado, there's a tremor in her voice. 'And one more thing. I advise you to keep your relationship with your tenant on a . . . professional footing.' She knows. She knows about that horrible night on my sofa. Why the hell did he tell her?

Dean taps away furiously, seemingly absorbed in his fake document. Julie stares me out defiantly, arms folded. Defeated, I turn and leave. As I walk down the street, tears pool in my eyes as I think about having to explain this encounter to my poor, darling parents. Beneath the anger and anxiety, something niggles at me, and eventually I work out what it is. Throughout our encounter, Julie had referred to Cooper as Mr Brownlow. But at the end, when I asked her about prison which was the only time she came anywhere close to losing her cool, she forgot herself and called him Cooper. I could be imagining it, but there was something disturbing about the way his name rolled off her tongue. It sounded familiar. Affectionate. As if she knows him on more than, as she might say, a professional footing.

Chapter 13

'They'd better be here soon, I've got a Zoom with Janine at 2:00.'

'Surely she can see that meeting with the police is more important,' says Mum with the confidence of the retiree.

'I doubt it. She's been a bit off with me lately. I've been late with one or two things.'

I wasted a lot of time yesterday going to see Julie Woodford and then Googling Cooper to find out more about his time in prison. In the end, it was simply a matter of typing in 'Cooper Brownlow' and 'court' and bingo – the local paper came up trumps with a helpful regular feature called 'In The Dock'. Man, 51, sentenced to a year's imprisonment for possession with intent to supply Class B drugs. I'd known it when I saw the letter from the probation officer, but to see it there in black and white was a kick in the guts. Did Julie Woodford know about this? She didn't seem surprised when I brought it up yesterday. In which case what the hell was she thinking, allowing him to rent from an elderly couple?

What with all the recent developments with Cooper, I've buried my encounter with him the other night deep in the back of my mind. I had no intention of repeating it even before I discovered the damage to the flat and the fact that he'd been in prison, but now the memory of it turns my stomach. I told Zach the dinner date hadn't gone well and asked him not to tell Mum and Dad, seeing as it wasn't going to go anywhere. I pray they don't find out any other way. The only other person who knows about it is Cooper himself, and surely he wouldn't tell them. I'm so ashamed. How desperate, how stupid must I have been to be attracted to him, to not have seen what sort of man he was?

The doorbell rings and Mum and Dad turn to me, plainly expecting that I will answer it. The weight of responsibility for this mess sits heavily on my shoulders as I walk down the hall and open the door to reveal a porcelain-skinned, ethereal female officer in her early twenties, dressed in a neat, charcoal grey suit. Her hair, smoothed back in a severe ponytail, is so blond it's almost white.

'Good morning. I'm Detective Constable Esther Blake.'

She's well-spoken and offers me a firm handshake at odds with her faerie-like appearance.

'Hi, I'm Penny Whitlock. Come through.' I point her in the direction of the kitchen and she walks in and greets my parents. As I go to close the door, Cooper materialises from round the side of the house, almost as if he'd been waiting there on purpose.

'Morning, Penny. If I'm not mistaken, you've got a visitor from the police. Everything alright?' He indicates the car on the drive. He has the gall to look amused. How dare he, when my parents are sitting in there, shells of their former selves? A year ago they went on the coach to London on a climate change march and now they're afraid to walk out of their own front door in case they bump into him.

'Yes, fine,' I say. 'A routine visit.' Where did I dredge that up from? What sort of routine would this be?

'Really?' he says. 'I heard differently. I heard you've been going around saying all sorts of things about me. And after that lovely evening we spent together, too.'

'What?' Who has he been speaking to?

'Don't think you're cleverer than me,' he says. 'People have made that mistake in the past and it never ends well.' He disappears back round the side of the house and I close the door, my heart hammering.

In the kitchen, Mum twitters around making tea for us all. Once we're settled around the kitchen table, DC Blake asks Mum and Dad to take her through the reasons they've called the police.

'Well,' I begin, trying to shake off the memory of Cooper laughing at me, 'as I said on the phone, we think he's dealing—'

'Yes, I know what you said and that's why I'm here – I'm actually doing a lot of work on drug dealing in this area – but if you don't mind, I'd like your parents' perspective on all this,' she says. 'As they're the ones most affected.'

'Right. Sure.' I take a sip of my tea. It's far too hot to drink – Mum's only put a splash of milk in it – and I splutter and spit and put it back down on the table.

'He has people coming and going at all hours,' Dad says.

'And the noise!' Mum adds. 'Banging around and playing music. And he smashed up those lovely tiles in the bathroom.'

'Yes, but that's not why we've called them, is it?' I can't help myself. Blake looks around at the decrepit kitchen units and flaking paint – in a moment she's going to dismiss this as a neighbourly dispute, or the ramblings of a confused, elderly mind, and leave. 'We discovered he's been in prison for drug dealing, which we didn't know when we rented the basement to him, obviously.'

'I can see that's not ideal from your perspective, but what is the actual problem now?' Blake says to me, giving up on them.

'As I said, I've seen marijuana in his flat, and my parents have smelled it. They've also seen multiple people coming and going from the annexe, staying a few moments each time. I don't think it's a stretch to suspect that he's dealing again.'

'OK. I can go down now and have another word with him, but—'

'Another word?' I say. 'You've already spoken to him?'

I'm impressed. I didn't think they'd speak to him until they'd had the full story from us.

'Yes. I received a call from Mr Brownlow yesterday.'

'He called *you*?'

'Yes. Perhaps you'd like to discuss this in private?' she says to me, looking pained and faintly embarrassed.

'No, it's fine,' I say impatiently. I know I've been guilty of thinking of my parents as fragile old things who must be protected, but there's no need for her to do the same.

'Alright. Well, Mr Brownlow mentioned that you and he had been . . . er . . . involved in a . . . relationship.'

'Of course she hasn't!' Dad says instantly, but Mum is looking at me with suspicion and I know my skin is betraying me, the hot stain of shame spreading up from my neck to my hairline. That absolute bastard.

DC Blake looks at me apologetically.

'He told me that he wasn't interested in pursuing the relationship further and that you were angry about that and had threatened to make up a story to get him in trouble with the police. He said you knew about his former conviction and were going to use that against him.'

'No! That's not true.' I just about manage to get the words out.

'You weren't in a relationship?' she says.

'No. Well, sort of,' I mumble, eyes glued to the table. 'Not a relationship, as such.'

'So there was something? Mr Brownlow wasn't lying about that?'

'No,' I say in a small voice. I daren't look at my parents but I can feel the shock and disappointment radiating from them. 'There was something. But it was nothing really, and it's not true that I'm doing this to get back at him.'

I'm trying desperately to hold on to the fact that I haven't done anything wrong. 'As soon as I found out he'd been in prison, that he'd been lying to us, that was it. I didn't want anything to do with him.'

'I see,' Blake says. 'Is there anything else?'

If she'd asked a moment ago, I'm fairly sure Mum and Dad would have launched into a litany of complaints, but the news that I have been 'involved' (and there's only one thing that word can mean in this context) with Cooper has taken the wind out of their sails.

'No, that's all,' I say dully. 'We appreciate your time. Thank you.'

DC Blake leaves her tea untouched and I let her out of the front door, whereupon she turns left and goes around the side of the house. I can't bear to go back into the kitchen and meet my parents' accusing faces so I leave the door ajar and stand there listening. There's a knock and a moment's silence. Another knock. She reappears.

'He's not in, but I'll come back another time.'

'Not in? You saw him when you arrived!'

'Perhaps he's gone out in the meantime,' she says patiently.

'He hasn't gone out!' Mum pops out from behind me and pushes me aside. 'I can hear him moving around down there! He's laughing at us!' Only now do I notice that she doesn't seem to have brushed her hair today and her jumper's on inside out. I'm pretty sure Blake has noticed too.

'Don't worry, Mrs Whitlock,' she says in a soothing tone. 'We'll speak to him as soon as we can.'

'That's no use to us! We could be murdered in our beds! He broke into our house, you know. The wardrobe was open and I never leave it open. And there was mud all over the floor.'

Blake struggles to keep a neutral face. I know she's thinking of the pile of unwashed dishes in the sink, the crumbs on the kitchen table, the smeared windows. My parents have never been houseproud but it does seem to have got worse in recent weeks.

'As I said, we'll have a word and be sure to keep you informed. I'll be in touch.' This last is directed at me and I nod, helpless. She gets into the car and drives off.

'How could you?' Mum says as I close the door.

'I didn't know, then,' I say, scarcely louder than a whisper. 'I thought he was nice. I was lonely.'

'Out of all the men you could have picked, you chose him?' she says. 'Did he . . . coerce you?' she adds hopefully. 'There's no shame in that, if he did.' It's a refrain I've heard often enough from her with regard to the victims of domestic violence she used to support in her work. *People ask why didn't they just leave, but it's never as simple as that,*' she used to say to me.

'No,' I say as firmly as I can, given that I'm not convinced of my answer. 'It wasn't like that.'

Dad comes out of the kitchen, his face ashen. I go to speak but he hurries up the stairs without a word. Mum follows him. As I stand alone in the hall, my phone beeps with a text. It's from Cooper: *Did you hear about my nice little chat with the police? Don't fuck with me, Penny. You'll regret it.*

Chapter 14

I haven't heard from my parents for four days. I can't remember the last time we went this long without speaking. I try to put them to the back of my mind – the whole situation has been taking up too much of my oxygen. Not only do I need to focus on Zach, my work is beginning to suffer too. The day DC Blake came, I was so distracted by Cooper's betrayal in telling the police we'd slept together that I completely forgot to log on for my two o'clock meeting. At ten past, Janine rang on my mobile and asked me coldly if everything was alright. Since then she's been much more on my case than she ever has before, wanting a daily update on what I've been doing. I wake up each day with a stone in the pit of my stomach, knowing I need to work harder than ever to catch up on what I've missed, but so lethargic and distracted that I fall even further behind.

At least today is Saturday. I've managed to cajole Zach out for a meal with Martin. We sit in the restaurant, waiting for him. Zach keeps sneaking glances at his phone.

'Waiting for a call?'

'No, just looking to see how late Dad is this time. Thirteen minutes so far.'

We've tried to continue doing occasional things as a family since the divorce. It's healthy for Zach to see us together, to see

that we're not at war, that we both still love him and are committed to co-parenting, even though he's no longer a child.

'How's the online learning going?'

'Fine.' The sullen teenage answer to everything. The truth
behind it could be anything from spectacularly amazing to wrist-
slittingly awful.

'That's good, but it's not the same, surely? It's been a week
now. You don't want to get behind.'

'I said it's fine, Mum. Loads of it's online anyway now. It's
not like it was in your day.'

'Sorry, sorry. I got a puncture on the way and had to stop and
repair it.' Martin swoops in, his face slick with sweat. He pulls
his lightweight, aerodynamic windcheater over his head, revealing another of his vibrant Lycra tops, this time combined with
sleek black leggings that leave little to the imagination. The
couple on the next table – him in smart trousers and a shirt, her
in an eye-catching tropical print shirtdress – try to disguise their
double-take.

'Bloody hell, Dad. What are you wearing? This is a nice
restaurant.'

'I'm trying to cycle instead of driving when I can. Better for
the environment and for me. Elaine's starting to get a bit annoyed
with me going on long rides on a Sunday morning and leaving
her alone, so I'm trying to use the bike for trips I'd be doing
anyway.'

'I thought the bike was Elaine's idea?' I say.

'Yes, it was, but now she's . . . you know . . .'

'Up the duff,' Zach says with a back note of disgust.

'Yeah . . . she prefers me to be at home a bit more. And, Zach,
I know it's difficult for you – and I wish I could have told you in

my own time,' this bit aimed squarely at me, 'but it's not going to change anything. The baby won't replace you.'

'Jesus, Dad, I know that. I'm not three years old. You don't need to read me a special story about becoming a big brother. It's . . . gross, that's all.'

'Come off it, that's a bit harsh.' Martin lays a crisp linen napkin over his shiny crotch. I don't think Zach and I are the only ones in the restaurant glad to see the back of it. 'Back me up here, Pen.'

'Don't bring me into it,' I say, my hackles rising at the hint of one of our old favourite arguments – that I always back Zach over Martin. 'I've got enough on my plate.'

'Like what?' Martin says.

'Cooper. Mum and Dad's tenant.'

'Oh, that guy. Are they having trouble with him? I could have told you that the day I met him.' His chest puffs up, threatening to escape its Spandex prison. God, Martin's insufferable when he's proved right. 'What's he done?'

'I don't want to go into it. The one saving grace is he's on a six-month contract so they've only got to put up with him for another few months. After that, I'm going to try my best to persuade them to downsize.'

'I thought he was alright,' Zach says, as he peruses the menu.

'When did you meet him?' Martin asks.

'Oh . . . er . . . one time when I was at Grandma and Grandpa's.'

'Yes, he came up about the window, didn't he?' I shoot him a grateful look. 'Anyway, I don't want to talk about him, I'm sick to the back teeth of it. We're here to talk about Zach.'

'Are we?' Zach says, startled. ' I thought we were here to have a *nice family lunch*.'

'Yes, we are,' I say, choosing to ignore the sarcasm, 'but also to have a sort of joint think about what you're going to do about university. How do you feel about going back tomorrow? I could drive you – or Dad could.'

'Oh ... er ... I don't think I can tomorrow,' Martin says. 'Elaine and I have got plans.'

Zach rolls his eyes theatrically.

'Whatever – let's not get side-tracked by *becoming a big brother*,' I say. 'The point is, are you going back?'

'I can keep up with my studies online,' he says.

'Well, that's good but it's not really the point, is it? We want you to enjoy the full university experience, all the socialising and the clubs and stuff. It's not going to be the same at home, is it?' I nudge Martin's leg under the table. I need some back-up here.

'Zach, we've spoken about this before,' he says. 'I'm concerned that you're shutting yourself away, smoking too much and becoming isolated. You're not giving yourself a fair chance.'

'So it's all my own fault?' Zach crosses his arms and I slump back in my chair. I know Martin's trying to help, but all this is going to do is put Zach on the defensive.

'Dad's not saying that,' I say, falling back into my familiar role as hostage negotiator. 'Let's think more practically. You said the main problem is with your flatmates. There must be a process whereby you can move accommodation.'

'I don't think there is this late in the academic year,' he says. 'Everywhere will be full by now.'

'You don't know that. It's only February – that's only a third of the way through the year. I'll call them on Monday and get the ball rolling.'

'No, Mum, let me handle it.'

'But you won't! I know you won't! You'll sit in that awful flat with those horrible kids and nothing will get any better!' I press my lips together. Getting emotional won't help. All it will do is make Zach retreat even further into his shell. Martin reaches across the table and takes my hand and for a second it all fades away – the outfit, the late-stage baby to appease the younger woman, the obvious mid-life crisis – and I see my husband, the man I fell in love with. The one other person in the world who knows Zach as well as I do, who was there for his first steps, his first words, who feels the same stab of pain I do when someone hurts him.

'What about trying to access some counselling?' he says to Zach. 'There must be support there.'

'That won't help.' He shuffles down in his seat, looking every inch the reluctant eleven-year-old he was last time he had counselling. Back then I could bribe him with a trip to the ice cream parlour, but I don't think that'll fly now. 'You don't want me at home, that's what it is. Too busy with your own life, your nights out,' he says meaningfully to me, knowing I don't want Martin to know about my date with Cooper.

'That's not true,' I say evenly. 'All I want is for you to be happy.'

'I'll go and stay with Dad and Elaine if you don't want me.'

'Oh!' Martin flushes. 'I don't know, Zach. I'd have to speak to Elaine. She gets very tired at the moment, what with the pregnancy . . .'

'I see. The baby not replacing me didn't last long, did it? Thanks a lot. You know, I'm not that hungry after all. See you.' He pushes his chair back roughly and storms out. The couple on the next table make a show of earnest conversation with each other, clearly agog at this unfolding drama.

'Well done,' I say, my momentary affection for Martin dissipating as quickly as it came.

'You're angry with me. What a surprise. You don't think there's a teeny chance that he was over-reacting?'

'No, I think you handled it badly. As usual.'

'I'm sorry if I don't jump to attention every time he wants something as if his needs are the only ones that mean anything. I can't say he can stay without checking with Elaine. It's her house.'

'It's yours as well, isn't it? Are you telling me she wouldn't allow your own son to come and stay with you?'

'Of course he could stay . . . temporarily . . . but I can't have him smoking in the house with Elaine pregnant.'

'For goodness' sake, Martin. Anyway, it doesn't matter. He can stay with me, that's not the problem, it's more that . . .' I trail off, my attention caught by Zach who is standing outside the restaurant, laughing and chatting on the phone.

'Who's he on the phone to?' says Martin.

'How should I know? One of his mates.'

'What mates? He's been telling us he doesn't have any.'

'Saul then, I guess.'

'Well, that's not good. Saul's as big a stoner as he is.'

'He's not a bad kid.'

Saul was always a bone of contention between Martin and I. Martin thought he was a bad influence and that we ought to encourage other friendships. Whilst privately I thought he had a point, I was just happy that Zach wasn't sitting alone in the playground at lunchtime.

'What are we going to do, then?' he asks.

'What can we do? I can't force him to go back and I'm certainly not going to throw him out on the street.'

'If you think for one minute that's what I'm suggesting, you know me even less than I thought you did when we were married!' He's almost bursting out of his shiny top with indignation.

'What exactly didn't I know about you? Your dormant passion for cycling?'

'Yes! Why not? We were stuck in our ways, you can't deny that. It's good to develop new interests as you get older. Keeps you young.'

I long to ask him if that's why he left me for a younger woman, to beat him over the head with the massive cliché that is his life, but I don't. I'm too tired, and too worried about Zach. It's better for him if Martin and I are on the same page, so I squash it all down and smile.

'I'm sure you're right. Tell me about the cycling – don't you worry about being hit by a car?'

'Ah no, you see that's the key – if you're deathly afraid of getting hit, it'll make you tentative and indecisive on the road, and that's actually more dangerous than anything else. The trick is to deal with cars confidently and assertively.'

As he bores on, I allow my thoughts to roam, unable to stem the flow of the worry – about Zach, work, Cooper, my parents – that eats away at me, a constant almost imperceptible thrum, like a heartbeat.

Chapter 15

From my parked car, I have a clear view of the front of the house. It's a small, unassuming terrace with a front door that opens straight onto the pavement. It's not far to the coast from here – Blackhawk Point is five minutes further down the road. Many of the houses look like they've been buffeted by the sea winds and could do with new windows or the brickwork re-pointing, but this one is well cared for; the view into the front room shielded by wooden venetian blinds.

I've been sitting here for twenty minutes trying to pluck up the courage to ring the bell at Cooper's previous address, the one I saw on the letter in his flat. No one's been in or out but thin strips of light filter between the slats of the blind so I think someone's in. I don't know who'd want to be anywhere but home on a damp and blustery February evening like this. I wish I was safe in my cosy flat, even if Zach's presence is currently casting a constant, glowering shadow across it.

This is the last place I want to be, but it's now a week since the police came (and since I last spoke to my parents) and they still haven't been back to speak to Cooper. I'll count to ten and then I'll go in, something I've done since childhood to make myself do things I didn't want to do. It works – I reach ten and open the car door, battling to stop the wind forcing it closed again. I cross the road and then hesitate outside the front door. The weather helps me – I don't want to stand out here any longer than I have to. I screw up my courage and ring the bell.

When the door opens, Cooper's hazel eyes look at me, enquiring but with a touch of suspicion, out of a younger but strikingly similar face.

'Oh . . . hello . . .' I stammer, taken aback. This guy has got to be related to Cooper.

'Can I help you?' He closes the door a fraction.

'Yes, sorry. Look, you don't know me. My name is Penny Whitlock, and I think you know my parents' tenant, Cooper Brownlow.'

'Sorry, no.' Any pleasantness drains from him and he goes to close the door. I put my hand out to prevent him from shutting it.

'Please. I'm not here for any trouble or . . . anything bad. I just want to ask you a few questions. I'll be quick. Please.'

Something in my face must make him relent and he sags back, defeated.

'Fine. You'd better come in.'

I feel suddenly vulnerable on this quiet street, light pooling under the streetlamps, faced with someone who is clearly a relative of Cooper Brownlow. I know nothing about this guy except the fact that he shares blood with a criminal who if not proven to be dangerous, shows scant regard for the impact of his actions on others.

'We can talk out here,' I say.

'I can hardly hear you over the wind,' he says irritably. 'Come in for a minute.'

My need for information is greater than my fear, so I follow him inside, down the freshly painted hallway into the small kitchen at the back of the house. It's clean and well maintained in here too apart from a splintered hole in the plaster near the fridge. I gather my coat more closely around me.

'Sit down,' he says sharply, then looks at my frightened face. 'I mean, would you like to sit down? Sorry, any mention of my brother gets me a bit angsty.'

'So you're Cooper's younger brother? I thought so – you look very alike.' I perch on the edge of a chair and he sits opposite me across the glass-topped dining table.

'Half-brother. We have different dads. I'm Scott Hamilton.'

I remember Cooper mentioning him in one of the few snippets of personal information he let slip on our date.

'And he was living here with you, until recently? I saw some of his post that was forwarded from here. I'm sorry to intrude, I didn't know who else to ask.'

'It's OK, I've been expecting something, to be honest. My advice to you – and I wish I'd taken it myself – would be to avoid him like the plague.'

'Unfortunately it's too late for that. He's renting my parents' basement annexe. He's not been paying the rent – I think he deliberately damaged the property so he can claim that's why he's not paying it. And we're fairly sure he's . . . well . . .' I don't know why I'm being so reticent. Surely Cooper's brother knows he's been in prison and what for – and if he doesn't, I have no interest in protecting him.

'Is he dealing again?' Scott looks ashamed, although I don't know why he should.

'I think so. My parents say there are people stopping by at all hours of the day and night. Obviously we didn't know he'd been in prison when we rented the annexe to him. It was all done through an agency who claim he came to them with glowing references from his previous landlord.'

'I didn't give him a fake reference, if that's what you're thinking,' Scott says, answering my unspoken question. 'Although I would have done if he'd asked. Sorry, but I was desperate to get him out.'

He scrapes the chair back and goes to stand by the window, staring out into the darkness although I can see his face dimly reflected in the glass.

'I didn't – couldn't – think about where he was going to end up. I just needed him out. Jane – my girlfriend – is pregnant. I couldn't risk him still being here when the baby was born. He was getting violent – he did that,' he indicates the hole in the wall, 'and I didn't know how much worse he was going to get.'

'Why did you let him stay in the first place?'

'Because I'm an idiot, basically. He had nowhere else to go when he came out of prison and I had our mum's voice in my head. She always gives him the benefit of the doubt – trying to assuage her guilt.'

'Why guilt, if you don't mind me asking?'

I sort of know the answer, but I'm interested to get Scott's take.

'My dad met Mum when Cooper was twelve. His own dad had left when he was little – he was a bit of an arsehole by all accounts – so it had just been Mum and Cooper for all those years. Mum says she'd tried, you know, but it was tough, they didn't have a lot of money. My dad says he did his best with Cooper but he was wild, out of control. Cooper'll claim he was left out, ignored, a stranger in his own family, and Mum's swallowed that narrative hook, line and sinker since her and my dad split up. But I know the truth. My dad went out of his way to make sure Cooper didn't feel pushed out when I was born and it was all thrown back in his face.'

'He told me he was chucked out of home at sixteen.'

'He wasn't chucked out, he left of his own accord. And I have to say things were a lot better after that, even if Mum's rewritten that particular piece of history. Even after he left home, he stole from her and lied to her but she forgave him every time. He can be quite . . . charming when he wants to be.'

'Yeah, I know,' I say with more feeling that I intended.

He raises an eyebrow. I hope I haven't given myself away. I don't want anyone else to know what happened between Cooper and I. If I could, I'd wipe that soulless encounter on the sofa from my own memory.

'He came to me when he got out,' Scott goes on, 'said he'd changed, that he was going to go straight, wanted to make amends. Mum was pressuring me to take him in – she doesn't have room at her flat. So I decided to give him one more chance. What a dickhead. He stole money out of Jane's bag, he was smoking weed in the house when we'd told him he absolutely wasn't to and he was dealing again within two weeks of getting out. When we found out Jane was pregnant, that was it. I had to get him out, I didn't care what it took. I told him he had two weeks to find somewhere else or otherwise I'd speak to his probation officer, call the police – basically make his life hell.'

'And he went? We've called the police on him too but neither he nor they seem to give a damn.'

'I think he'd had enough of living here anyway, otherwise I doubt he would have gone. He saw an opportunity to get his own place. He said he knew of an agency who'd find him a flat – Woodbridge is it?'

'Woodford Peters,' I say glumly. 'My mum's friend Linda recommended them to her because they were cheaper than the others.'

'I'm sorry. If it hadn't been for the baby I might have let him stay.'

'It's OK, I understand. I'd do anything in my power to get him out and away from my parents.'

'I don't know what to tell you,' he says. 'Maybe keep on at the police, if you're sure he's dealing.'

'I'll speak to them again, but I don't hold out much hope. Could we swap numbers? In case anything else comes up?'

He seems reluctant but unable to come up with a good reason why not, and reads his number out to me. I call him briefly and he stores mine.

'Good luck,' he says to me at the door. 'And be careful, with calling the police.'

'What do you mean?'

The clouds part for a second and his face is illuminated by the moonlight, shadows hollowing his cheekbones below Cooper's eyes.

'Just . . . watch your back, that's all. Cooper can't stand to feel that someone's got the better of him, and it's worse if he feels cornered. That's when he lashes out.'

Chapter 16

'So what's this good news? I could do with some.'

When Mum and Dad invited me and Zach over, I'd jumped at the chance, hoping this meant they'd forgiven me for my dalliance with Cooper. This last week, the silence from them has been deafening. I should be working really – I keep sneaking looks at my phone to make sure my boss Janine hasn't called – but I couldn't resist the opportunity to normalise my relationship with my parents after the grenade that's been thrown into it.

'The police were coming out of the basement this morning when we were on our way out – we actually saw Cooper speaking to them so he obviously answered the door this time.'

'That's positive.'

'It's wonderful!' she says. 'It'll all be over soon.'

'I wouldn't count on that.' I've still got Scott's words from last night ringing in my ears. Is that it, the good news?

'Don't be silly! The police will sort everything out, they'll be able to see what he's up to now.'

'That's great news.' I try to sound enthusiastic, pathetically grateful that my parents seem to have forgiven me for sleeping with Cooper, or at least decided to sweep it firmly under the carpet. 'Isn't it, Zach?'

'What?' He raises his head from his phone. 'Oh, yeah. I guess so.'

He continues scrolling. I want to tell him to stop, but it took a lot of persuasion to get him out of his room at all today, and I don't want to rock the boat.

'He's been quiet as a mouse ever since,' Mum says triumphantly. 'And there haven't been any visitors. I think it's done the trick.'

'Let's hope so.' I wish I shared her blind faith in the power of the police. It's only been a few hours, but I don't want to rain on their parade.

'And my ankle's so much better,' Dad says, hoisting up his trouser leg to show me. 'I've stopped using the walking stick and I think I'll be able to start running again soon.'

'Take it easy, yeah?'

'Fiddlesticks!' Dad says, bouncing from the room. It's hard for someone like him, who has always been so fit and strong, to accept that he needs to slow down.

'We've got some good news of our own, actually, Mum,' I say. 'Haven't we, Zach?'

'Yep.'

'Well, come on, tell her.' It's like cajoling a five-year-old to speak nicely to an adult.

'I'm going back to Winchester tomorrow.'

'Are you sure? What about those horrid flatmates?'

'Mum!' She's normally so no-nonsense, but she's always had a blind spot as far as Zach is concerned. The golden boy who can do no wrong. 'That's not hugely helpful.'

'Don't be so unsympathetic. You know you're always welcome here, Zach.'

'Thanks, Grandma. They are pretty horrid.' He grins and gives her a hug. Frustration and sadness bubble up in me.

I can't remember the last time he spontaneously embraced me.

'They can't be that bad,' I say snippily. 'One of them called you and apologised, asked you to come back.'

'Oh, yeah. True,' he says, going back to his phone.

I roll my eyes at Mum, inviting her to join me in mock despair at his uncommunicativeness, but she won't, patting him on the hand and cutting him another slice of cake.

'There's a rather foul smell in the hall,' says Dad, coming in from the garden where he's been checking on the progress of their new rose bush. 'I think Dottie must have had diarrhoea again although I can't see anything out there.'

'Oh no, has she not been well?' I say, looking down at her in her basket, where she's fast asleep.

'She's had a bit of a funny tummy,' Mum says, 'but she's been asleep the whole time you've been outside, so I don't think it can be that.'

I step out into the hall. Dad's right. The smell takes me back to primary school, where we girls would go out of our way to avoid going anywhere near the boys' toilets. I tiptoe down the steps towards the internal door to the basement, my nose wrinkled, but the smell fades as I do so. Thank God. I thought for a minute that Cooper had done something unspeakable in the annexe. It must be poor Dottie. As I walk back up the stairs, my phone rings. A sense of doom descends when I see it's Janine calling.

'Hi Janine,' I say, leaning against the wall and trying my best to sound like a busy, successful accountant who's been interrupted in her important work.

'Penny,' she says curtly. 'I thought you were going to send me the Treadwell files yesterday?'

'Oh yes, yes I was. Something came up at the last minute that's going to take a bit more time. I'll have them to you by the end of the day today.'

I haven't even looked at the account yet. I'll have to work all evening and send them so she gets them first thing tomorrow. Midnight is technically the end of the day, after all.

'Make sure you do. And, Penny, I'd like you to come in one day next week. It's been a while since we've caught up face to face.'

I lower the phone from my ear with a horrible sense of foreboding. I can't lose my job, I simply can't. I'm only just making ends meet as it is and I've got no back-up, no nest egg, and nowhere for me and Zach to go if I had to sell my flat. I must go home and tackle the Treadwell account.

But as I go back into the hall, the smell gets stronger again. A thought strikes me. It's been so long since the downstairs loo was usable I'd almost forgotten it was there, but as I get nearer to it, the smell worsens. Holding my breath, I put my hand on the door handle and push. Oh dear God. It's not dog excrement we can smell. A human has emptied their bowels in the toilet, which has been blocked and un-flushable for over six months. Whoever it was doesn't seem to have been for a while beforehand as what they have deposited is almost up to the top of the water. Brown smears streak the sides of the toilet bowl. My stomach rises in protest and I retch and slam the door shut, my hand pressed over my nose and mouth.

On shaking legs I make my way back to the kitchen. Dad is whistling as he makes us all a cup of tea and Zach is showing Mum a video on his phone of a cat sliding down the banisters. For a few wild seconds I consider if I can get away with not telling them, if I can somehow clear up that repulsive scene and never have to burst their bubble. I know it's impossible, but their sadness affects me in the same way that Zach's does – their pain is my pain, the one indistinguishable from the other.

'Has one of you . . . did you forget that the downstairs loo can't be used?' It's depressing that this is my only hope, that one of them is losing their marbles to such an extent.

'No. Why?' says Mum.

'Is that what the smell is?' says Dad. 'I should have known leaving it unused for so long would cause problems with the plumbing. I'll get Bob round.'

'Grim,' says Zach.

'And to think you blamed poor Dottie!' says Mum.

'It's not that.' I wrench the words from my mouth.

'What is it then? Let me have a look,' Dad moves towards the hall.

'No!' I shout. 'Don't go in there!'

'What's the matter?' he says, bewildered.

'Don't go in there,' I repeat. 'It's . . . someone has . . . used it.'

'What do you mean?' says Mum. 'I told you we haven't been in there.'

'No, I know you haven't.'

'Then who . . .' The colour drains from her face. 'No,' she whispers.

Puce with fury, Dad strides from the room. A few seconds later he comes back into the kitchen and in a heart-stopping moment I see there are tears in his eyes. In all my life I have never seen him cry, my big, strong mountain of a father. Mum steps towards him and takes him in her arms. She's crying too, and Zach watches them in dismay, seeing them as fallible for the first time in his life. Pure, unadulterated rage spreads through me like water soaking into a sponge. I'm about to storm down to the basement and throw Cooper out with the force of my fury – nothing and no one could resist it – when there's a strange choking noise from the corner of the room. Dottie lurches out of her basket and throws up copiously. Diarrhoea flows from the other end and she collapses, convulsing at my parents' feet before lying still in a pool of vomit and faeces. We all stare at her in horror. Mum crouches beside her, sobbing, calling her name as if that will rouse her. There are a few seconds of silence and then it begins – music thumping up from the basement; the heavy bass shattering the fragile peace that had only ever been an illusion after all.

Chapter 17

I managed to get the toilet fixed straight away yesterday (at enormous expense) by an actual plumber, not Bob the handyman. I was crippled by embarrassment at the state of it, but he laughed and said he'd seen worse. I had to put his fee on an already overloaded credit card, but that's a worry for another day.

Work is the last thing on my mind, but losing my job will make everything even worse so I get up early. I finished the Treadwell account and sent it back to Janine at ten minutes past midnight last night, but it was patently rushed and she sent it back to me at 8:15 this morning, pointing out several glaring errors. However, by mid-morning I'm beginning to get somewhere. Hopefully this will go some way towards placating Janine. I cannot afford to lose my job.

At 10:30, my phone rings. I'm engrossed in a spreadsheet and answer without checking the screen, assuming it's the client I'm expecting a call from.

'Penny Whitlock.'

'Penny, it's me,' Mum quavers down the line.

What now?

'We had a call from Tom – you know, the chair of the allotment committee?'

'Not really, but go on.'

'One of the allotments has been vandalised – plants ripped up, shed windows smashed, that kind of thing.'

'Oh no, not your plot?'

'No, it wasn't ours. It was . . . Val and Clive's – you know . . .'

'Do I? Who?'

Even though she's upset, I can't help finding her customary insistence that I must know the details of her many and varied friends – including their children's names, what they do or did for a living and what they grow in their allotments – grating.

'Val and Clive. They're jealous of me and Dad because of our cauliflower crop.'

'Ah yes, the criminals who planted the fateful trowel that Dad tripped on.'

'Don't make jokes!'

'Sorry, Mum, but I'm not going to get that upset about someone I've never met, and who it sounds as though you don't even like.'

'Tom's accusing us! He's saying Dad and I did it!'

'What?' My smile drops abruptly. 'Why would he do that?'

'Because whoever did it . . . ha! Whoever did it! We know who did it! *Cooper* used my shears.'

'How does Tom know that?'

'They're my personalised shears, the ones Dad bought me for my birthday with *Sempervirens* inscribed on the handle.' *Sempervirens.* Evergreen in Latin. 'Everyone knows about them at the allotments because they all thought it was frightfully romantic . . .' She dissolves for a second, then pulls herself together. 'And that evil man took them out of our shed, used them and left them right there on the vandalised plot all covered in bits of vegetation.'

'Do you not lock your shed?'

'We've never needed to. We're all friends up there, and anyway we don't have anything much of value in it.'

'Did you explain to Tom about Cooper? Surely he wouldn't believe that you or Dad would do such a thing?'

'Yes, of course we did. He acted sympathetic, but I can tell he still thinks it was us. Val's spitting feathers and demanding we be cast out from the allotment. I can't bear it, Penny, I just can't.'

She dissolves into wracking, piteous sobs that travel down the line and straight into my heart. I'm almost frightened by the rage that courses through me. I want to take those shears and slash at Cooper with them, to make him as frightened as he has made them, but I force myself to concentrate on a more realistic approach.

'Have Val and Clive called the police? If not, we should do it ourselves. Have you called DC Blake about . . . what Cooper did in the house?'

I can't bear to actually say it, to allow those disgusting words into my mouth.

'We didn't call them. I know what they'll think – that we're senile and one of us forgot and went in the downstairs loo and doesn't want to admit it to the other. There's no point.'

I hate to admit it, but she's right.

'This allotment thing, though – Tom should be calling the police. He shouldn't be accusing you on such a flimsy piece of evidence.'

'Will you call them?' she pleads.

I look ruefully at my open laptop. Janine will have to wait. This is more important.

Amazingly, I manage to get through to DC Blake after a lot of explaining and holding on the line.

'Hello, Ms Whitlock.'

She doesn't sound pleased to hear from me.

I outline the situation as briefly as I can, and wait. She sighs.

'Do your parents have any evidence that their tenant was involved?'

'No, but it's perfectly obvious!'

'Not to me. It sounds as though your parents have a feud with this couple.'

'It's not a feud! That'd be massively overstating it! It's nothing. There is no way on earth my parents did this. They love plants. They would never in a million years do something like this.'

'Have the couple themselves called the police?'

'I don't think so.'

'In that case, it's not currently a police matter. And if they do I have to say it's very unlikely that we'll have the resources to look into it. We might be able to send a community support officer round for a chat.'

'There's no point doing that. I'm telling you that Cooper Brownlow is the one who did this. He's trying to set my parents up – he's insidious. He knows exactly how to get to them. He's . . . he's evil. Mum and Dad said they saw police going into his flat the other day. Did you speak to him about the noise? And the visitors? He's clearly dealing from their house.'

'Yes, one of my colleagues did pay him a visit and reported that there was no sign of drugs in his flat, so that's good news.'

'It's not good news! It just means he's keeping them elsewhere!'

'My colleague also checked and he's been religiously sticking to his appointments with the probation officer. He had a word with him about the noise and Mr Brownlow was very apologetic and promised to keep it down in future. I'm afraid there's not a lot more we can do.'

'So that's it? My parents just have to deal with the fact that their tenant has broken into their home – a home he's dealing drugs from – and is generally trying to destroy their reputation and their lives? They're supposed to get on with it, is that right?'

'I'm sorry, Ms Whitlock, but at present this is not a police matter, and certainly not one we have the resources to deal with. I'm so sorry your parents are distressed by this, but—'

I slam the phone down. I can't bear another second of her faux concern. It's painfully clear that the police are not going to help us. We are alone and helpless, and utterly at Cooper Brownlow's mercy.

Chapter 18

I head over to Mum and Dad's, my conversation with DC Blake weighing heavily on my shoulders. They said they'd be here, but when I let myself in, the house is silent and empty. Perhaps they're in the garden. The thought is comforting. If they're gardening, it must mean they're feeling more comfortable in their home again. Perhaps Cooper is done now. He's punished them for the police visit. They just need to wait out the rest of his tenancy and soon he'll be a distant memory.

I go down to the back door. It's propped open – so they are in the garden. However, any brief spurt of happiness this gives me is quenched the minute I step outside. First I see my mother, very still, one hand gripping a trellis, the other pressed to her heart, and then I understand the reason why. Cooper, dressed in black jeans and a thick, expensive-looking wool jacket, is squaring up to my father. My father is both taller and broader than him, but despite his size and strength, he has never been a violent man and he is clearly intimidated. As I walk across the patio, I feel like I'm having an out-of-body experience. I can't really be here, rushing to protect my father from an attack by the tenant that I suggested they move into their home. Before I get there, before any of them have even seen me, Cooper shoves my father hard in the chest. Dad stumbles backwards and falls to the ground, his foot twisting awkwardly under him.

'Leave him alone!' My voice comes out more childlike and feeble than I hoped or intended and Cooper turns with a sneer, his face ugly with contempt. I can't believe I ever thought him attractive.

Mum releases the trellis and goes over to Dad.

'Or what?' Cooper says scornfully. 'What are you going to do, Penny? Call the police again? I wouldn't bother. As far as they're concerned, I'm quite the reformed character – a real rehabilitation success story. Whereas you lot – I think you're becoming a nuisance to them, if anything.'

Slowly, helped by Mum, Dad gets to his feet, muddy and defeated.

'I think the police will be interested to hear that you've assaulted my father.' I make an immense effort to sound adult and unemotional.

'Assaulted him?' He gives a lazy smile. 'I didn't assault him. What on earth gives you that idea?'

'I saw you.' I force the words out through the chokehold my emotions have on my throat. 'I saw you.'

'That's your word against mine,' he says pleasantly as if we're discussing something else, something normal. 'I don't have any history of violence against you – or anyone, for that matter. Yet you three have a very recent history of unsubstantiated complaints against me. In fact, it's beginning to look a bit like harassment. What do you think, Heath? Did I push you, or did you trip and fall?'

Dad's head stays down. He closes his eyes.

'You can say what you like,' Mum says, eyes burning, stepping in front of Dad as if to protect him. 'It doesn't matter who believes you. We know the truth. That's the important thing.'

Cooper takes a step closer to her. She turns her face away but stands her ground.

'I don't think that's true, Sissy,' he says quietly in her ear, as if he's imparting a delicious secret. 'It doesn't matter what you know if no one believes you.'

He leans in even closer and for a second I think he's going to kiss her on the cheek, but he laughs and steps away.

'I've got to go out now but I'll see you all very soon. Have a great afternoon.' He strides easily across the garden and around the side of the house. His car revs into life and he drives off.

'Are you OK, Dad?'

'I'm fine.'

He tries to take a step towards me but falters, wincing in pain.

'You're not OK, Heath,' says Mum tightly, two spots of colour in her cheeks.

'I've twisted my ankle, that's all,' he says stoically. 'I'll be alright.'

'What happened?' I say. 'What was he doing out here?'

'How on earth should we know what goes on his twisted little mind?' Mum says. 'We thought he was out so we came out to do a spot of tidying up in the garden. People think there's not much to do at this time of year but they're absolutely wrong. For a start—'

'Mum! Never mind about that!'

'Oh sorry, darling. We'd only been out here about ten minutes and he came out and just stood there . . . watching us. He didn't say anything, just stared. Your father muttered to me that we should go in, but why should we? This is our home. And suddenly I was furious, and it all came spilling out about breaking into the house, and the . . . the toilet thing, and Dottie and the allotment and he *smiled*, like he was enjoying himself and he said, he said . . . *You're so funny, Sissy.* And then Heath . . . well . . .'

'I couldn't have him speaking to your mother like that,' Dad says shortly. 'I told him to leave us alone or we'd call the police again, and that was when he came over and . . . well, you saw the rest.'

'You're right, Dad, we have to call the police. He physically attacked you. You're hurt.'

'What's the point?' he says heavily. 'He'll deny everything. He'll say I "had a fall".' He looks at me accusingly. 'That's what we do, isn't it? Us old people? We have falls, we get confused, we get things wrong, we have "little accidents". I've seen the way people look at me – in shops, at the doctors, everywhere. I'm old, I'm not stupid. I'm still the same person I was. I haven't had a lobotomy.'

'I know.' I squeeze his arm, knowing that he's right, that I have dismissed him and Mum like that, many times. 'I know that, Dad. That's why we should call the police. I'll make them listen this time.'

'No,' he says, limping back towards the house. 'It's futile. Don't waste your breath.'

'Mum?' I say in a small voice.

'Your father's right,' she says, all the fight gone out of her. She follows him slowly across the grass, dragging the weight of her sorrow along with her.

I watch them go, my heart breaking into a million pieces. I cannot bear it. I cannot sit by and watch while he not only breaks their spirit but puts them in actual physical danger. I'm afraid Dad is right about the police. They're not going to help us.

There is no other solution. I will have to take matters into my own hands.

Chapter 19

When I hear Cooper's car start up in the drive, I race into the front room. I sidle up to the window, staying close to the wall, out of sight and watch him drive away. I need to grab this opportunity – it's the first time he's left the house since I arrived yesterday to see Mum and a still-limping Dad off. Dad's been using the walking stick again since the altercation with Cooper two days ago. They've gone to stay in Norfolk with Marie, one of Mum's oldest friends from her school days, taking a thankfully recovered Dottie with them. The vet said she must have found and eaten something that disagreed with her. I can't bear to think that Cooper had anything to do with that, but I have to consider it a possibility. Marie lives alone and is happy for the company, so they can stay as long as they like to give me a chance to sort things out here – with the allotment and with Cooper. I've promised them that's what I will do. The problem is I have no idea how I'm going to fulfil that promise.

The first thing on my list, achieved thanks to my credit card which has taken another battering, was to get the locks changed. Although the first time he broke in he used the internal door (I can only assume Mum and Dad were right about that – the mud on the stairs, the open wardrobe door), there was no sign of a break-in when Cooper left his deposit in the downstairs loo, so he must have a key. If he tries to get in again, he'll find it no longer works.

Blake said on the phone that there was no sign of drugs in the flat. Cooper's obviously keeping them elsewhere, and I'm determined to find out where. This is my chance – he's gone out in the car so presumably I've got minimum half an hour or so – if he was popping to the shop he would have gone on foot. But I mustn't waste any time. I run down the stairs to the basement and slide the bolt open on this side – I won't make that mistake again. Hopefully I'll have time to come back out the external door, but if he comes back unexpectedly I can leave this way. The problem is Cooper will know I've been in because I'll have to leave it unlocked on his side, but maybe that's a good thing. He's very happy for us to know when he's been in here, after all. Two can play at that game.

I hurry outside and around the side of the house and let myself in. Everything seems as it was last time I was here, but I don't have time for a close inspection. I'm looking for anything that will tell me where he's keeping his supplies so I can pass that information to the police. I've got one ear out for the sound of his car coming back – if I hear it, I've got time to let myself out through the internal door. To make it even quicker, I unbolt it from his side and leave it ajar. There's some post by the TV where I found the probation letter last time, but it doesn't yield anything except junk mail. I open the doors of the sideboard that the TV sits on, but it's empty. I check under the bed where there's nothing except a grey carpet of dust. I turn my attention to the chest of drawers. The top drawer contains socks and boxer shorts (I repress a shudder at the latter at the memory of the last time I saw his underwear and, worse, its contents). The second, T-shirts and jumpers. At first I think the third and bottom drawer is more of the same, but when I feel beneath a pile of neatly folded jeans, I touch paper – an opened envelope – and when I take out the contents, I realise I've struck gold. It's a rental agreement for some garages that back onto a local council estate. I've driven past it a few times and know exactly where it is. Cooper has a lock-up. I take a photo of the agreement, replace it carefully in the envelope and put it back in the drawer. I should take the opportunity to see if I can find anything else incriminating although there's not that many other places to check. I take a quick look in the wardrobe but there's nothing in there except a few shirts. In movies and books, people hide things under their mattresses, don't they? I kneel down, heave up the mattress as far as I can and peer underneath. I can't see anything untoward, but I slip my hand in to be sure.

'If you wanted to get into my bed, you only had to ask.'

My heart plummets and I drop the mattress, trapping my hand between it and the slatted base.

'I was . . . just . . .'

'Expected to hear the car, did you?'

I extract my hand and stay kneeling by the bed, immobilised.

Cooper walks over and kneels close behind me. I want to get up, to get away, but I am rooted to the spot.

'I knew you'd be in as soon as I left, you stupid cow,' he whispers as if it's an endearment. 'Did you honestly think I'd come back in the car and give you fair warning?' His lips are right by my ear, almost close enough to touch, his hot breath moistening my skin. I hold myself rigid. He snakes his hands around my waist and pulls my body into his. I begin to shake.

'Don't you like it?' he says. 'You liked it last time, didn't you? Couldn't get enough, you dirty slag.'

A sob escapes my lips. What was I thinking, sleeping with him? How did I not see what kind of man he was? No. I have to stop thinking that way. He didn't show me, that's how I didn't see. He hid it. He lied. It wasn't my fault.

'How's the little dog? I saw you rushing off to the vet's with her. Ate something that disagreed with her, did she?'

So he did poison Dottie. There was a part of me that believed he wouldn't stoop that low, but I see now there's nothing he wouldn't do.

'How did you get in?' I need to know everything if I'm to somehow get the better of him.

'It wasn't hard.' He gives a mirthless laugh. 'Your parents have a bowl full of keys in the hall. I took a selection the first time I was in there. Thought they might come in handy.'

How am I meant to protect my parents from this? I made them a promise that I would make this go away, that I would keep them safe, but I don't know how.

'What were you doing in there that time? You'd just moved in – why were you so keen to . . . well, what were you doing?'

'Getting the lie of the land. Always good to know who you're living with.'

'What's wrong with you?' I choke the words out. 'Your tenancy is up in a few months anyway and you know we're never going to renew it. Why can't you leave us alone?'

'It's very difficult to evict a sitting tenant, Penny, if they simply refuse to leave. Can be quite a costly, lengthy process, I believe.'

144

Oh God, he's never going to leave. I had thought at the very least that there was nothing he could do to stay once the tenancy was up.

'But why? Why did you do all this in the first place?'

He releases his hold on me and stands up. I stagger to my feet, legs like water. We stand facing each other.

'Why not?' he says. 'Because I can. Why should I have to spend every penny I earn paying off someone else's mortgage and have nothing left at the end of every month? Why should other people have everything handed to them on a silver plate while I'm scraping up the crumbs off the floor? I know you've seen my brother's house. He owns that outright. How d'you think he paid for that? He's a fucking brickie and his girl-friend's a care assistant.'

'I don't—'

'His dad paid for it. After all that talk about how he'd treat us both the same. Where's my fucking house?'

'Please, Cooper. My parents are old, you're making their lives a misery.'

'They shouldn't have messed with me then, should they? If they hadn't called the police, I would have left them alone. Maybe they'll think twice next time.'

I want to rant and rave and tell him I know where he keeps the drugs and whatever else he's got in his lock-up, but I have to be smarter than that. I keep my mouth shut and walk towards the internal door, which is still open. I'm about to close it behind me when Cooper speaks.

'How's Zach?' he says.

I stand stock still, the door almost closed.

'What?'

'Just wondering how he is,' he says innocently.

'Not that it's any of your business, he's gone back to university.' Well out of this mess.

'Has he now?' he says, smiling.

I close the door and stumble up the stairs to the kitchen. What is Cooper on about? Zach is back at uni. Isn't he? I bring up his number and call him.

'Hi, Mum.' He sounds reassuringly normal.

'Hi. You OK?'

'Yeah, I'm fine. Why?'

'No reason. What are you up to?'

'I'm on my way to the uni library. There's my friend – we're going together – I'd better go.'

'Alright, darling, speak soon.'

I sit there for a moment, doubt nagging at the edges of my mind. If only there was some way to check if Zach really is where he says he is. Then it hits me – there might be a way. When he first got a phone in year seven, it was on the condition that he shared his location with me. At first, I'd log in to the app every day at 3:10 when school broke up and obsessively follow his progress. I'd know before he got home if he'd stopped to buy sweets at the shop, or taken a different route. When he started going out in the evenings I'd do the same, not able to rest until I heard his key in the door. It's been a while since I felt the need to check it. He probably switched it off long ago – but there's a small chance he's forgotten all about it. I click on the icon and wait as the familiar map loads. It shows me here at Mum and Dad's and underneath, under the heading 'people' is Zach. It makes me wait as the distance from me to him spins in a twinkling circle and then it pops up. He's two miles away, on Marchant

Street. By the looks of it, at Saul's house. Could this be old information from whenever he last shared his location? I refresh, but it remains stubbornly the same, the word 'Now' screaming at me. The truth hits home like a sandbag slugged against my head: Cooper isn't lying to me. Zach is.

Chapter 20

Before I go to Saul's, I give Charles a call. He's an ex of Caitlin's that she stayed in touch with – as she did with many of her exes. Charles is a lawyer – I'm not absolutely clear what kind, but I'm hoping he'll be able to give some kind of a steer on the situation with Cooper. There's got to be a way to get him out. The police have been worse than useless, but we must have some legal redress.

'Penny!' He sounds genuinely pleased to hear from me. 'How are you? I haven't seen you since the funeral. You did a brilliant job that day, by the way. There's no way I could have stood up in front of all those people and spoken without breaking down.'

'Thanks. Yeah, it wasn't easy, but I was determined to get through it.'

Time had seemed to stand still as I stood there quaking in my bright-red dress (no black, as per Caitlin's request), looking out over the congregation – Caitlin's many friends, her shell-shocked, bewildered parents and her sister, so painfully like her. I wasn't sure as I opened my mouth to read the eulogy I'd written whether anything was going to come out. But as I read, I gathered strength from the words I'd written about Caitlin – about her faith in me, her steadfast commitment to a life lived truthfully and to the full.

'What can I do for you?' he asks.

'I don't know if this is your thing, but I have a legal question for you.'

'Happy to help if I can.'

'My parents are having some trouble with their tenant – he rents the basement of their house. We've found out he's been in prison in the past for drug dealing – we called the police but they say there's no evidence that he's dealing now and he's seeing his probation officer and all that. Also he's not been paying the rent – we let it through an agency but they're backing him up, saying my parents need to do certain repairs. But when they've tried to access the flat with a tradesman to fix the problems, the tenant won't answer the door.'

'It's not really my area to be honest, although I can certainly recommend someone else for you to speak to. However, I will say I have a friend who had a similar situation with his tenants and I'm sorry to tell you it's no picnic. There are procedures you can follow depending what type of tenancy agreement you have, and what the terms are. But if the tenant refuses to leave, the sad truth is that it's incredibly difficult to get them out. Tenants have rights – they're protected by law. You'll be able to do it eventually, but it'll be a time-consuming, unpleasant and extremely expensive road if the tenant is determined to stay regardless.'

'Oh, God,' I say miserably.

'It's not impossible. The important thing is to get the ball rolling. Why don't you send me a copy of the tenancy agreement and I'll take a look at it and I can ask around at work – there are people there who are much more up on this than me.'

'Would you? That's very kind.'

'I will, but Penny . . . It's not going to be easy.'

I hang up more despondent than I was before. Still, I can't sit around despairing, I need to go and confront Zach.

The sweet, distinctive tang of marijuana hits my nostrils when Saul opens the front door. He doesn't recognise me at first, his expression vacant. Then it dawns on him.

'Oh, hi.'

'Hello, Saul.' I take on the schoolmarm-ish air I always do when speaking to him. I don't mean to signal my disapproval – I'd hoped originally to be one of those cool mums who was pals with her son's friends – but I can't help it. 'Is Zach here?'

'Um . . . no . . . he's at uni, isn't he?'

'Cut the crap, Saul. He's here, as you very well know. Can I come in?'

'I don't know . . .' He looks pained.

'Hi, Mum.' Zach appears in the hallway behind him and Saul ambles off, glad to be released. Zach leans against the door frame, arms folded.

'How did you know I was here?'

He doesn't seem overly bothered, but that could be because he's stoned.

'Lucky guess.' I'm not going to remind him about the app in case I want to use it again in the future – plus he'd be (rightly) furious about me spying on him. My anger rises, but I try to press it down. If Martin was here he'd be going ballistic, but that's not the best approach for Zach, he'll just dig his heels in even further. 'What's going on?'

'I told you I was unhappy at uni. I told you I didn't want to go back, but you weren't listening. It was just easier to pretend.'

'But you said your flatmate called and apologised. Are you saying you made all that up just to get me off your back?'

''Spose,' he mumbles.

'So what . . . are you going to live here with Saul? Is his mum alright with it?' I never got to know Martha, Saul's mum, beyond the occasional bit of chitchat when I picked Zach up from their house.

'She's working on a project up in Manchester for six weeks.'

'So she doesn't know you're staying?'

'It's fine! She's fine with it! Jesus! You're focusing on the wrong thing here!'

'Am I? What's the right thing? The fact that you're stoned at your mate's house in the middle of the day instead of studying at university?'

'No, the thing is that I'm really unhappy and you don't care.'

'Oh, Zach, I do, of course I do.' There's nothing in the world I care more about, nothing I want more than to take him in my arms and soothe away this hurt, make everything better like I did when he was little.

'No you don't. And anyway, you're going out with a drug dealer so don't get all funny about me smoking the odd joint.'

'I'm not going out with him – I went out for one meal with him and you know quite well I knocked it on the head when I realised what a nightmare he was being to Grandma and Grandpa.'

'He's not that bad. The annexe is falling apart – no wonder he's not paying the rent.'

'How do you know about that?' I say sharply.

He shrugs, mutinous.

'Zach, where did you get the weed from?'

'From your *boyfriend*.' He laughs, but there's no mirth in it.

'You've been buying drugs from Cooper?' Is there no area of my life this man won't invade? Is nothing safe from him?

'So? You went out with him.'

'Once! And that was enough! He's bad news, Zach. You know he did that disgusting . . . what he did at Grandma and Grandpa's house. And I'm sure he gave Dottie something to make her ill. The vet said it was touch and go – he could have killed her.'

'Come off it, Mum. Cooper didn't do any of that. Grandma or Grandpa obviously just forgot not to use the downstairs toilet, and Dottie could have eaten anything off the street. You're making it up because he didn't want to go out with you again.'

I hate it when he's like this. We're so close, and he can be so sweet at times, but right now he's like a cold stranger. There's a little voice in my head (probably Martin's) saying this is what the drugs do to him, but I ignore it.

'Is that what he told you? He's lying to you. Can't you see?'

'Is he?' he says. He eyes me mutinously, but I can see the little boy behind the bravado so I persist.

'I'm sorry if you felt I didn't listen to you about university. I'm listening now. Come home with me and we'll talk about it.' I swallow hard, trying to keep my voice level. 'I won't try and make you go back if you really don't want to.'

'No thanks. I'm fine here.' He goes to close the door.

'Please.' It's more of a sob than a word.

I see a twist of pain and the real Zach is there for a second, but then he's gone and the door is slammed in my face.

I stand there for a moment, broken. I want to bang on the door, scream and shout, make my son come back to me. Rage builds inside me – not against Zach. Against Cooper. How dare he try and turn my son against me? I run back to my car and as soon as I've closed the door behind me, I'm on my phone, Googling 'UK police anonymous tip-off line'. I don't have any hope that Cooper will think it's anyone but me, but at least I'm protecting myself to some degree. I don't care anymore anyway. My parents would probably beg me not to call the police after Cooper's retribution last time, but we need to be rid of him once and for all.

I bring up the photo I took with the details of Cooper's lock-up ready to read them out on the phone. Surely this will be enough to get him arrested and out of our lives forever.

Chapter 21

'This really isn't good enough, Penny.'

Janine regards me beadily across the desk, her features even more pinched than usual.

'Sorry,' I say, trying to discreetly rearrange my top which is clinging to my sweaty skin. Since the pandemic most of us work from home, so she's relocated the company to a cramped office in a local business park manned by a skeleton staff. She kept me waiting for fifteen minutes in the overheated, shabby reception area.

'I'm afraid that won't cut it. You're missing deadlines left, right and centre. It'd be bad enough if you were just letting me down, but it's clients. I've had Rob from Treadwell on the phone to me this week complaining. I managed to smooth it over this time, but he made it pretty clear they'll take their business else-where if it happens again.'

'I'm aware I've been a little distracted. I've been having some problems with my elderly parents.' I'm not sure Janine has any mercy, but I intend to throw myself on it regardless. She must have parents, at least. I don't want to get into the whole Cooper saga (it's been a whole week since I called the tip-off line and nothing's happened), but surely vulnerable old people have to count for something. 'They've been requiring a little more support than usual lately, and I'm their only child. It may have meant that I've taken my eye off the ball, but I'm firmly back on it now.' I mentally cross my fingers, thinking of the reams of unanswered emails clogging my inbox.

'I'm sure it's all very difficult, but everyone has a personal life, Penny. Not everyone allows it to impinge on their work.'

Does Janine have a personal life? I can't imagine her existing outside this grey office, or wearing anything other than an ill-fitting polyester trouser suit.

'I'm afraid I have no option but to give you a verbal warning.'

I feel as though I've been plunged into cold water.

'You understand what that means?'

'Yes, I think so,' I say from under the water.

'It's a first step. If things don't get better, I'll have to issue you with a written warning, and if things still fail to improve, well . . . I'll have to consider your position here altogether.'

I stumble out, thoroughly humiliated and with a hard knot of fear coiled in my stomach. If I lose my job, I could lose my home. What else is Cooper going to take from me?

Outside in the car park, my phone rings. It's Marie's landline number in Norfolk. What now?

'Darling, it's me.' My mother's voice assaults my ear. 'We really need to think about coming home.'

'I thought Marie was happy to host you as long as you want?'

'Yes, she is, but we want to get back to our lives. Has he been arrested yet?'

'No, Mum. I don't know if he's going to be.'

'But it's a week since you called that line! What are the police doing?'

'I guess it's not a priority.' I've driven past Cooper's lock-up a couple of times but it looks the same, with no sign that the police have paid it a visit.

'Not a priority! He's selling drugs, not to mention terrorising us in our own home!'

'I know, I know. But I don't want you to come back until there's been some development, or it'll all go back to the way it was before. I'll swing by the house now and check everything's alright. But don't come back until you've heard from me, will you?'

'I suppose so. But we can't stay much longer. Dad needs his own bed, he says the one here is made for Lilliputians. His feet hang over the end.'

Before I pull out of the car park I send my daily breezy text to Zach – *Just checking in!* – my pathetic attempt at keeping the lines of communication open. He never replies. I've been poring over his location on the app, but he barely leaves Saul's house.

I drive to Mum and Dad's with a heavy heart. Cooper, Zach, work . . . it feels as though my many problems are clogging my arteries, stemming the flow of blood around my body. When is it going to get easier? As I pull into the drive, the sight that greets me sends a little green shoot of hope in answer to that question. An unmarked car has evidently just arrived and I recognise the white-blond hair and slight frame of DC Esther Blake as she gets out accompanied by a thickset, dark-haired man in a black suit. A ripple of excitement rushes through me. Please let this be what I think it is. The two of them go round to the side door.

I park my car out of the way so that there's room for them to leave, and sit motionless, my palms sweaty. There's a loud knocking and Cooper answers. I open the window a crack and strain with all my might to hear what they're saying, but I can't make out the words. A few minutes pass, and then Cooper comes out, Blake and her colleague on either side of him. As they guide him into the back of the car, he catches sight of me and his face darkens. The car moves off and although I try to force myself to keep my eyes down, as it draws level I can't resist looking up. For a second, Cooper is looking straight at me, his expression murderous, and then with a spin of the wheels on the gravel, he is gone.

Chapter 22

Is this it? Dare I hope that he's actually been arrested? I start the engine and drive straight to Cooper's lock-up. As I approach, my heartbeat accelerates. I turn the corner and the garages come into view. Tears spring to my eyes and I pull over. Cooper's garage is closed, as it has been every time I've driven past. At first I think it doesn't look any different but then something catches my eye, fluttering in the breeze. It's the remnants of police tape. It must have taken them this long to get a warrant but they've obviously found something in there.

'Oh, thank God. Thank God,' I say aloud.

I've been so worried Cooper knew I'd found the details and would have removed anything incriminating, but it seems not. He really has been arrested. Even if he's granted bail, surely Woodford Peters will be on our side now as regards evicting him. This has got to be the beginning of the end of this hideous saga. I imagine telling my parents, how happy they'll be and the tears flow faster. I finally allow myself to think about what I've known all along but hadn't allowed myself to consider – that this could have been the end of them. They've aged unprecedentedly over the last few months and I honestly believe it would have driven them into an early grave. I'm tempted to call them, but I force myself to wait until I have all the information. I mustn't count our chickens, although I'm aware as I drive back to Mum and Dad's that a massive weight has been lifted from my shoulders.

I decide to give it twenty-four hours. If he's not back by then, I'll let them know. I stay overnight at the house, revelling in the silence. In the morning, I set up my laptop at the kitchen table, diligently working my way through the emails I've been ignoring. At the very point where I've decided I can't wait any longer to give Mum and Dad the good news, I hear a car pull up in the drive and the sound of feet on the gravel. The side door is unlocked and then slammed shut with unnecessary force and, a moment later, music blasts out from underneath me, louder than it's ever been before.

Hot tears bloom in my eyes. He's back. What's happened? Has he not been arrested? Or has he been released on bail? I have no idea how these things work. Thank God I didn't call Mum and Dad. After half an hour or so, the house falls silent. The side door bangs and I tense, but don't hear anything further. I creep to the front room and peer between the drawn curtains. There's no sign of him. I return to the kitchen and sit at the table, every inch of my body on high alert.

Caitlin? I say silently.

Hi, darl.

She's back. Every time I've tried to consult her since the night I spent with Cooper, nothing's come.

What am I going to do?

He's an absolute bastard. She never was one to hold back with her opinions. *You can't let him get away with this. Sissy and Heath will be devastated.*

How could I have been so stupid as to sleep with him? I didn't even want to.

You made a mistake. Everybody makes mistakes. Don't beat yourself up about it, darl.

What should I do? Should I call the police?

They haven't been much use so far, have they? I think you're going to have to deal with this one on your own.

I wish there was someone I could call. Zach and I couldn't be further apart, and it wouldn't be right to burden him with this anyway. I haven't told any of my friends what's been going on. I've been too busy trying to manage the Cooper situation – plus attempting to keep on top of work and worrying about Zach – to find any time for socialising. The only person I can think of to call is Martin, but I have to accept that he's no longer my confidant. I can talk to him about stuff to do with Zach, but nothing else. He's Elaine's person now and although I'm mostly used to that, right now I want him to hold me and tell me everything's going to be alright. I put my head down on the table and weep. After twenty minutes or so a noise rouses me from my well of self-pity. It's not a knock at the door, it's softer than that, but it comes from that general direction. Cautiously, I venture into the hall. Everything is quiet. I pad noiselessly into the front room and look out through the window. Nothing. I go back into the hall, open the front door a crack and peer out. Still nothing. I'm about to close it again when a flash of scarlet on the front steps catches my eye. It's a rose – deep crimson, almost artificial-looking although I'm pretty sure it's real. For a second I think it's from my parents' rose garden but I quickly dismiss this – it's the middle of winter, the roses aren't flowering. This one has come from a garage forecourt. I open the door wider, bewildered, and see there's another rose at the bottom of the steps. A horrible sense of foreboding settles on my shoulders. I look around.

There's no sign of Cooper but I can't be sure he's not watching. I long to close the door on whatever this is, bury my head in the sand, pretend it's not happening, but that's simply not an option. My parents want to come home. It's my responsibility that they have a safe home to come to, and I will do whatever it takes. I force my legs to carry me down the steps and around the side of the house. There's another rose, near Cooper's front door. There's no way I'm going into the basement again. Then I see that the trail, if that's what this is, isn't leading that way. There's a fourth rose past the door to the annexe, almost at the rear of the house. As if in a dream, unable to feel my legs, I move towards it and around the house into the back garden.

I stop stock still for a second and then my legs give way and I fall to my knees, weeping. The soil is torn up and scattered everywhere are leaves, roots, stems. He has wreaked havoc on the lovingly tended rose bushes, pulling them up or hacking them to pieces with a scythe that he's left casually lying on the ground. My parents have been watering and pruning and cherishing this garden for almost fifty years. It might sound unbelievable to a non-gardener, but after family these roses are the most important thing in their lives. What Cooper has done thus far has already turned them into shells of their former selves, but this is going to break them. I should never have snooped, never have told the police about the lock-up. This is his retribution and it's all my fault.

I pick up the scythe and run the blade across my thumb. It bites into my flesh, blood oozing from the wound. I stand as if in a dream and head back round the side of the house towards Cooper's front door. With the scythe heavy in my hand, I vow that I will never allow him to hurt them again.

Chapter 23

'Come quickly. The garden . . . the . . . body. We need you, Penny.'

Dad's words echo through my mind as I speed back to my parents' house, blood still seeping from the cut on my thumb. What does he mean, the body? My brain tries to come up with different scenarios that would fit his words, but they are all too disturbing to contemplate so I close my mind and concentrate on not crashing the car.

Light spills out of the annexe window at the side of the house as I park in the drive. If I'd known Mum and Dad were coming back tonight I would have been here, but once I'd established that Cooper was no longer there, I couldn't stand to be on the property a second longer. My plan was to come back in the morning and attempt to clear up the mess.

I can't worry about that now though, I'm thinking only of Mum and Dad. I don't know how they'll ever recover from the destruction of their beloved garden. The driver and passenger doors of their car are open, the internal light still on. As I close them to prevent the battery going flat, I see their suitcases on the back seat.

As I let myself in to the house, my ears are assaulted by a high-pitched keening coming from the kitchen. Dad shuffles out into the hall without his stick, one hand on the wall, grey-faced, wordless. I take him in my arms like a child, expecting him to fold and weep but he holds himself rigid in my embrace for a few seconds and then extricates himself. I follow him into the kitchen. Mum is sitting at the table, rocking back and forth, an unearthly wail pouring, unstoppable, from her. I kneel next to her.

'Mummy.' I haven't called her that since I was a child. 'Look at me.'

She continues to stare blankly into nothingness, arms wrapped tightly around herself.

'You need to come out to the garden and see,' Dad says in a low voice.

'No, I don't. I was here earlier. I know . . . what happened. I would have warned you if I'd known you were coming back from Norfolk. Why didn't you let me know?'

'It was a last-minute decision. Marie's lovely but we'd had enough of staying in someone else's house. We wanted to get back . . . home.' He chokes on this last word. 'Come out and see.'

'I don't need to, Dad. I told you, I know what's happened.' Mum's the more manifestly in shock but Dad doesn't seem to be taking in what I'm saying at all.

'You don't understand,' he says, pulling at my hand. 'You need to come outside and see.'

I don't want to see it again – it was bad enough the first time – but Dad's not going to take no for an answer, so I allow him to lead me back into the hall, where he grabs a torch from the hall table. As we go down the front steps I realise he's less leading me than holding onto me for support. When they left for Norfolk, he was relying heavily on his walking stick due to Cooper's attack. As we round the corner into the back garden, I understand why he's walking unaided. The torchlight glints off the silver fox's head where his cane lies abandoned on the churned-up earth.

'Look what he did.' Dad sweeps the torch beam across the debris of the desecrated rose garden with its splintered, smashed-up trellises and fifty years of lovingly cared for plants destroyed in a matter of moments.

'I know,' I say, laying my hand on his arm. 'I'm so desperately sorry.'

This was what I didn't want them to see. It had been hard enough for me. I'd gone to look for Cooper, fuelled by pure rage. God knows what I would have done if I'd found him, but he was either out or not answering the door. I wonder where he is now.

'It's not that,' he says dully. He moves the torch beam down to the ground a couple of metres from our feet, and I get my answer. If I felt earlier that I was moving through a dream, I'm now living in a nightmare. Cooper lies spreadeagled on his back on the ground, eyes closed. For a few seconds I'm suspended in utter terror. Dad is looking to me as if for guidance and I have no idea what I'm supposed to do next. I stagger the few steps to where he lies and kneel beside him.

'Cooper?' I put a tentative finger on his neck. There's no response and I can't feel a pulse. I lower my cheek to his mouth and nose. There's no rush of air. No rise and fall in his chest. As I lift my head, Cooper's flops to one side and in the torchlight, I catch a glimpse of the back of it, dark red, hair matted, a glint of white that might be bone. The contents of my stomach swirl and I clap a hand over my mouth. I look up, unable to hide my horror.

'What happened? Is he ill? Or did he . . . fall?'

It's horribly clear that he is not and he did not, but the alternative is too shocking to consider.

'No,' Dad whispers.

'Well then . . . what . . .?'

'We got home and we saw roses on the steps, on the drive.'

I should have removed them, but I was in such turmoil when I saw what Cooper had done to the garden that I drove home without thinking. Why didn't they tell me they were coming back?

'We followed them round and we saw . . . this . . . what he'd done. Your mother was distraught, hysterical. She was hyperventilating. I thought . . . Pen, I thought for a minute that she was going to *die*. And then . . . he came out from the basement and asked what had happened, as if he didn't know. As if he hadn't done it . . .' Tears threaten to overwhelm him but he gulps them back and continues. 'He was *laughing*. He thought it was funny. And I was so angry. So very, very angry. I couldn't bear what he'd done to us, not only tonight but since he moved in. And I knew, I just knew, that we were never going to be rid of him. Even if we managed to evict him, he'd find a way to make us pay, like he has all the other times. He's . . . he's bad, Penny, He's evil.'

'I know, Dad, but . . .'

'It wasn't meant to happen. It was like someone else had taken over. But my stick was lifting high into the air and then it was swinging down and smashing against the back of his head. And he looked so surprised, his mouth was hanging open, and he went crashing down and then everything was quiet and still.'

'Oh my God, Dad. What have you done?'

He looks me dead in the eye.

'It's over, Penny. I killed him.'

Chapter 24

I hold a cup of warm, sweet tea to Mum's lips and encourage her to drink. She's stopped making that awful noise but despite the fleece blanket I've wrapped around her, she can't stop shivering. She hasn't said a single word since I got here.

'We have to call the police,' I say.

Mum lets out a whimper.

'You're right,' Dad says, pacing around the kitchen as far as space allows. 'I have to take responsibility for what I've done.'

'It was self-defence,' I say, the words gossamer thin. 'He's a criminal. You're an upstanding citizen. You were a teacher.' Even I know how ridiculous I sound.

'But the police have got all these complaints from us on record,' Dad says. 'They know how much we wanted to get rid of him. They won't believe it was self-defence.'

'This is all my fault,' I say miserably.

'No, love.' He continues his trail back and forth past the table. 'You weren't to know, when you . . . you know.'

'No, not that,' I say. I can't believe that even in this time of extreme fear and tension I'm still blushing, still experiencing the shame of my parents knowing I slept with Cooper. 'There's something else. I found out he had a lock-up. I told the police about it and they searched it. They came and took him away this afternoon. I think they arrested him, but I'm not certain because later he was back – I guess he was released on bail. It's my fault. I'm so sorry.'

'Don't be sorry, love.' He puts one huge arm around me and pulls me into his chest. 'You were doing your best to protect us. You've been wonderful throughout all of this.'

Have I? I think of my date with Cooper, of how I lay under him and closed my eyes trying to blank it out while he pumped away at me. It makes me feel sick.

'No, they'll never believe it was self-defence – they'll say it was retribution. It'll be . . . murder – or manslaughter at the very least. I'll go to prison.' I know he's trying to be calm but his voice rises and he has to stop to regain his composure. Mum trembles ever more violently.

I can't bear it. If Dad goes to prison, he will die there, and Mum will die here alone. A memory pops into my head, fully formed. I was seven or eight and we were on holiday in France, on one of those wide, windy beaches where the Atlantic crashes relentlessly onto the sand. Dad and I would go running down the beach, salt in our hair and sun on our skin, gloriously free, shouting 'We've got to work and do SERIOUS things'. Together, we would go piling into the waves until they washed us back higgledy piggledy, panting and helpless with laughter onto the shore.

'No.' I slap my hands onto the table. They both jump. The protectiveness I've increasingly felt towards my parents as they've got older swells to unimaginable proportions. Everything they did for me as a child – every story read and reread, every sideline stood upon and goal cheered, every hurt kissed and soothed – I'm going to repay it all. 'You will not end your days in prison. I will not allow it. Not because of that evil man. Legally you might be in the wrong, but ethically there's not a person alive who would blame you for what you've done. He was making your existence a living hell.'

'But . . . what are we going to do?' Dad says.

Mum's still vacant – I'm not sure she knows or understands what's going on. I take a deep breath. Once I've said this, once we've done this, there will be no going back. It's almost unthinkable, but the alternative is even worse.

'We need to move the body while it's dark,' I say. 'Even if it's to somewhere temporary while we decide what to do.'

'Are you serious?' Dad says.

'Deadly. I will not let this happen to you.'

'My darling girl, I can't let you do this for me. If we go to the police and I confess, it'll only be me that gets punished. If you do . . . this . . . what you're suggesting . . . you're implicated too. And your mother. We could all end up in prison.'

'Not if we're clever about it. All we need to think about is where to hide the body. We haven't got time to think about the best way of . . . disposing of it. Let's get it out of the garden and hidden away for now. We'll worry about the details later.' I'm almost frightened of this cold, clinical version of myself. I didn't know she existed.

'This is madness.'

'It might be, but I won't let you go to prison. Dad, you wouldn't survive it. And how would Mum cope?'

The shaking has calmed down a bit but her expression is glazed and I still don't think she's listening or taking any of this in. Dad looks at her, and his expression reminds me of my favourite photo in their wedding album, a candid shot from the reception. Mum, beautiful in a plain ivory silk column dress, is talking and laughing with her friend, Marie. Unknown to her Dad stands beside them, his broad chest bursting from his morning suit, watching her with a mix of pride, joy and pure love.

'How are we going to do it?' he says.

I scan the room for inspiration, alighting on the second-hand wheelchair I got for Dad the first time he had a fall. It's folded up against the wall, unused and covered in a thin layer of dust.

'We'll use this to get him into the car.' I cross the room and shake it open. 'In the unlikely event that anyone sees us they'll think it's Mum.'

'Will they?' Dad sounds dubious.

'It's pitch dark out there. We need to get him into the car and I doubt we'd be able to carry him between us.'

'Then what?' he says.

My mind races, assessing the possibilities. The key thing is to put him somewhere he won't be found. If we dump him in the river, or in the woods, a dog walker will find him and by 6am we'll have police swarming all over the house. We need to buy ourselves some time.

'It has to be somewhere cold where he won't . . . decompose too quickly. Somewhere no one ever goes. Can you think of anywhere?'

'This is absurd, Pen.' Dad's tone is despairing. 'I think we should call the police.'

'No.' I will not allow him to go there. 'Come on, think.'

'I don't know . . . there's the shed at the allotment?'

'Does anyone else ever go in it?'

'Sometimes Tom comes in for a cup of tea if he forgets to bring his primus stove. And Annabel pops in for a chat if we're in there, and—'

'Oh for God's sake, that's no good.' Frustration spills out of me and he flinches. 'Sorry, Dad. Sorry. Keep thinking out loud, it might help – I won't snap again. It would at least be cold.' I try to recall the plots of every crime drama I've ever watched, every detective novel I've raced through. Where's a good place to hide a body? This is farcical. I can't believe I'm in this position.

'There's the Anderson shelter at the allotment?' he suggests timidly.

'The what?'

'You know what Anderson shelters are – air raid shelters from the war. They're made of corrugated steel and half buried in the ground.'

'I think I know what you mean. There's one at the allotment?'

'Yes. It's at the side of our patch. It's pretty much fully under-ground now, but you can still get into it. It's not used for anything and nobody ever goes in it. It'd be very cold this time of year. And no one's using the allotment the other side of it since Sheila died. But . . . I don't know if I want to go to the allotment, not after what happened to Val and Clive's plot.'

'It's the dead of night, Dad. There won't be anyone there. Don't worry about the Val and Clive thing – I'm going to sort that out. I think the Anderson shelter is as good a plan as any.' We've already made one life-changing, dramatic decision – the main thing now is to get Cooper out of the garden and leave any other decisions for a more cool-headed day. 'I'll get some stuff together – you wait here with Mum.'

I swoop around the house grabbing blankets, gloves, a hat, a headscarf – anything that could make Cooper's body in the wheelchair appear to be Mum to the casual observer.

'I'm ready,' I say, re-entering the kitchen. Dad is at Mum's side, holding her hand and murmuring soothingly in her ear. He was always the only one that could pacify her. She was mostly pretty level when I was a child but every now and then she would fly into a rage over the most trivial thing. Instead of fighting back, he would slow everything down, like a carefully constructed dam in a rampaging river, the calm to her storm. He whispers something to her that I can't hear and comes to join me.

The two of us emerge into the freezing night air. Clouds now obscure the moon and starlight so we make our way by the light of Dad's torch. A foolish part of me hopes that somehow this has all been a dream or a mistake and we're going to find the rose garden in all its glory, and Cooper alive and well in the annexe, but he's still lying there. I'm deeply grateful for Philip and Sue's leylandii so we don't have to worry about anyone seeing us. I open the wheelchair and the two of us attempt to get him into it. Cooper isn't – wasn't – tall or particularly heavy but I gain a new understanding of the phrase 'a dead weight' as we haul and heave him up. Worried that Dad isn't as strong as he used to be, and conscious of his sprained ankle, I try to carry more than my fair share of the weight, but when he slithers out of Dad's grasp for a second, I realise I've been kidding myself. Dad has been bearing the vast majority of the burden without complaint.

After a few false starts where we almost get him into position only for him to slip out and slide back to the floor, we settle him into the chair, lolling to one side. I wrap one blanket around his shoulders and tuck the other around his lap, propping him up as best I can in the process. His entire body is covered now apart from his head. I avert my eyes from the bloody mess at the back of his skull as I tug on a woolly hat. Blood immediately soaks through from the wound. I tie a headscarf over the hat, old lady style. I try to put on the gloves I brought but it's impossible – they're too small and his hands flop like dead fish. I tuck them inside the blanket instead, discarding the gloves.

'That'll have to do,' I say to Dad. 'It doesn't matter once we've got him in the car.'

He nods in agreement. He hasn't spoken since we've been out here and it's only now Cooper's bundled up that I notice how pale and shaken he is.

'Are you OK?' I ask.

He nods again and wordlessly takes hold of the wheelchair handles, pushing it over the bumpy ground. He's only gone a metre or so when the front wheel hits a rock, slamming the chair to a stop and almost tipping Cooper out. I leap forward to resettle him in the chair.

'Let me do that, Dad.' I try to remove his hands from the handles but he shakes me off.

'I'm fine,' he says impatiently, tilting the chair onto its back wheels and hefting it over the rock. We reach the side of the house without further incident. The leylandii stop here, replaced by a brick boundary wall about four feet high. If only we could get the car right down here, we'd be able to get Cooper into it unobserved, but Cooper's own car is in the way. At least the ground is smooth concrete here as he pushes the chair past Cooper's front door.

'Get the car keys out,' I hiss at Dad.

He fumbles in his pockets, hands shaking.

'Hurry up!' He scrabbles ever more frantically – at no time in the history of the world has telling someone to hurry up had the desired effect. Finally, he produces them from the depths, presses the clicker and the locks clunk open.

'He's so heavy, we're going to have to do this together,' I say. 'Open the back door. You take that side and I'll take this. We'll try and hoist him in.'

We take one of Cooper's elbows each and haul him forward. The wheelchair flies backwards, almost taking Dad with it and nearly pitching Cooper headfirst onto the ground.

'Put the brake on!' I say.

'Sorry, sorry.' Dad is grey, fear etched on every inch of his noble, craggy features. I want to hug him and calm him and tell him everything's going to be alright but there isn't time. We get the wheelchair back in position with the brake on this time. We're bracing ourselves to lift Cooper onto the back seat when Philip and Sue's Volvo pulls up in next door's drive. We both freeze. Mostly they put their car in the garage, but they don't always bother if they're going out early the next day. If they're not putting it in the garage, they're going to be getting out right next to us, separated only by a four-foot-high brick wall. For a few seconds, the engine continues to purr. Dad and I hold our breaths, praying to hear the electronic whirr of the garage door as it ascends, but the car's engine putters to a stop and the headlights blink off. Philip and Sue get out of the car and walk towards us.

Chapter 25

'Pretend it's Mum,' I whisper.

'What?' Dad says, confused.

'In the wheelchair,' I say as loudly as I dare, cursing his deafness. 'Tell them it's Mum.'

The headscarf has slipped backwards. I pull it down low over Cooper's forehead, but even in this light it's obviously not my mother. I root in my coat pockets for anything that will disguise him further. My fingers touch upon on something soft. At first I think it's a tissue, but when I feel the elastic loops I realise it's a cloth facemask, a relic of the Covid pandemic when I had one in every coat and bag I owned in case of need. I whip it out and stretch it as high and wide as it will go over Cooper's face, slipping my fingers under the headscarf to loop it over his ears. They are wet with blood when I extract them and I wipe them on my jeans, thankful it's too dark to be able to see the rusty stains that are surely clinging to the lines in my hands and under my nails.

'Hello, there!' says Philip. 'You're off out very late!'

Despite their intransigence regarding the leylandii, there have been times when I've been grateful for Philip and Sue, glad that Mum and Dad have slightly younger neighbours who are interested in them, on whom I could rely to help out in an emergency. This is not one of those times. If only they were selfish types who kept themselves to themselves.

'Mum's been taken ill,' I say, shifting to the right so that more of my body hides the wheelchair and its gruesome inhabitant from their view. 'We're taking her to hospital.'

'Oh no,' Sue says, her kind face creasing with concern. 'Is it serious?' She edges to the left, peering around me to try and get a look.

'We're not sure,' I say. 'We'd better get on though.'

'Can we do anything to help?' Sue says. 'Would you like me to come with you instead, and Philip could come round to keep Heath company? *He doesn't look too well.*' This last is said to me sotto voce, as if Dad was a child, or deaf.

'No!' I almost shout it and they recoil. 'Sorry – no, we're fine. That's very kind of you but you go on inside.'

'If you're sure,' Philip says.

'Yes. Thank you.'

They lock the car and head towards their front door, but just as they're about to let themselves in, I hear our front door opening and closing. Footsteps crunch on the gravel at the front of the house. Oh God, Mum's coming.

Sue and Philip turn, their confusion amplified by the warm, yellow glow of their porch light.

Dad's eyes widen in panic.

'That's my aunt,' I say, improvising wildly. 'Mum's sister. She's a bit confused. Dad, go and remind her we're going to hospital.'

He hurries off, grateful to be unentangled, however briefly, from this web of lies. I hear his voice, low and reassuring, and the front door closing. Sue and Philip continue to stare at me curiously as I remain steadfastly in front of the wheelchair.

'Are you sure there's nothing we can do?' Sue says.

'Yes, truly. Here comes Dad. We'll get . . . Mum into the car and be off.'

'We'll be sure to pop round tomorrow and see if you need anything.'

'Thanks, that's very kind.'

I will them with every ounce of my being to go inside, and finally they do. Dad and I look at each other over our macabre charge. I heave a shaky sigh.

'Mum says what about his phone?' Dad says.

'What?'

'His phone. If it's switched on and you take it to the allotment, they'll be able to see that he was there, if they're ever looking.'

I'm impressed, if a little alarmed, at the criminal mastermind my mother is apparently morphing into.

'See if it's in his pocket,' Dad says.

I bend down over him, unpleasantly close, and inch my hand into his jeans pocket, trying not to think of every horror film ever, where the apparently dead person reaches out and grabs the heroine. But Cooper remains still and dead – perhaps because by no measure am I a heroine here – and I manage to extricate his phone.

'Can you open it?' Dad says.

'He'll have fingerprint ID set up.'

'Can't you use his finger now?'

'Let's get him in the car first. Sue'll probably be out again in a minute with a home-cooked casserole for you to eat while Mum's in hospital.'

We take one arm each and with immense effort, haul Cooper onto the back seat. He lies across it, legs and arms splayed at awkward angles. I avert my eyes from his face which is taking on a sunken quality.

'Put the wheelchair in the back, we'll need it the other end,' I say to Dad.

We get into the front and I press the home button on the phone. The screen lights up. I kneel on the passenger seat, reach into the back and lift Cooper's limp hand, holding his forefinger to the button. The phone gives an obliging beep. It's open. I tap on the settings and change the passcode to 1234. I'm required to confirm the change with Cooper's fingerprint and I shudder as I press it to the button once more. I drop his hand, turn the phone off so it will stop giving out its location and stow it safely in my pocket.

'Right, let's go,' I say to Dad.

He obeys without question and I become aware that what happens from hereon in is completely down to me. Neither he nor Mum are going to be capable of making any decisions about this.

When we arrive at the thankfully deserted allotments, Dad and I reverse the process, bundling Cooper back into the wheelchair and bumping him over the stony ground. Once we've dragged him into the Anderson shelter, I send Dad back to sit in the car. Ostensibly he's keeping a look out (although it's very unlikely anyone would come to the allotments at this time of night) but really I'm trying to spare him any further distress.

I've managed thus far by thinking of Cooper's body as an inanimate object that needed to be moved – a problem to be solved, with no emotional component. But now I'm alone in the Anderson shelter with him, my defences crumble and my whole body shakes violently. My fingers are numb with cold as I heave him across the freezing ground.

There's a torn, muddy tarpaulin in one corner. I deploy it as a makeshift shroud, tucking it in around the edges of Cooper's body. It's not going to fully hide him, but it shields him from the view of anyone who pops their head in. Mum and Dad swear no one ever comes in here, but you never know. It's better once I can't see him anymore. I kneel beside him, head bowed in a hideous parody of prayer, deep in thought. Is there anything I've forgotten? For the first time, I consider who might miss Cooper. There's Julie from the lettings agency, plus Cooper has a brother and a mum. He must have other friends, too – and what about all the people that buy drugs from him? Are they going to be turning up at the house? Hopefully not if they're not able to get him on the phone.

In the end I decide there's nothing more I can do here tonight. We need to get back to Mum. I take a final look around. There's a chance a casual observer wouldn't notice anything amiss, Cooper's body hidden as it is by the tarp in the darkest, furthest corner of the shelter. I crawl across the dirt floor and let myself out. It's pitch black as I pick my way through the vegetable beds and back to the car.

Dad and I drive home in silence. What is there to say? Back at the house, we park in the usual spot and I unlock the door, trepidatious about what state Mum's going to be in. She's still at the kitchen table, huddled in her blanket, but she seems somewhat more present, sharper.

'Did you do it?' she asks.

'Yes,' Dad says, taking her hand and pressing it. 'We put it . . . him . . . in the shelter.'

'Well done,' she says. 'So what now?'

'I need to go home,' I say 'I'm exhausted.' It's true. I'm bone-tired, my limbs thick and sluggish, my mind shrouded in fog.

'I'll come back first thing and we can decide what to do next. Try and get some sleep.'

'This is going to sound terrible,' Mum says, 'but this might be the first night I've slept soundly since not long after that man moved in. I've been so scared about what he was going to do next I've hardly slept a wink. I know what's happened here tonight is awful, but I honestly can't feel sorry about it.'

'He's gone, love. He's gone.' Dad cups her face in his hands and rests his forehead on hers. I stand uncertainly, not sure how I feel about the fact that neither of them seem to regret what they have done.

Chapter 26

'My immediate worry is that someone will go into the Anderson shelter,' I say.

The three of us sit round their kitchen table. My eyes are sore and scratchy. I only managed a few hours of broken, fitful sleep last night, the enormity of what we'd done looming hideously large in my mind. I can feel the outline of Cooper's phone, still switched off, in my back pocket. Surely phone tracking isn't so accurate that they could tell whether the phone was in the basement or here in the house, but just in case I'll wait until I'm down there to switch it on and check if anyone's looking for him.

Although I'm besieged by a jittery, unrelenting anxiety, I can't help feeling – as Mum articulated last night – that a weight has been lifted. Ever since Cooper moved in, this house has been freighted with worry and fear. It's the first time in a while that I've been here without being tensed for disaster.

'No one ever goes in there,' Dad says.

'We should go to the allotment,' Mum chips in. 'We could keep an eye. If anyone tries to go in there, we could say there's a problem, it's dangerous and about to collapse.'

She's almost chirpy this morning, the catatonic shell of a woman from last night a distant memory. In fact, they both seem more like their old, pre-Cooper selves. It's reassuring and disturbing in equal measure.

'That's not a bad idea,' I say. 'You'd normally go today anyway, wouldn't you? It's probably wise to keep up your usual routine.'

I can hardly believe what's coming out of my mouth. However, we've started down this path now. There's no turning back – it's too late to confess because we've already done so much towards covering it up. All we can do is keep going and hope for the best.

'What about Val and Clive's plot, though?' Dad says. 'Tom still thinks we did it.'

'Why don't I call him now?' I say. 'I can't believe he thinks you had anything to do with it.'

Dad meekly hands over Tom's home number and I call it.

'Tom? This is Penny Whitlock, Heath and Sissy's daughter.'

'Ah. Penny. Yes, hello.' He sounds hesitant and shamefaced as opposed to combative, which is a good sign.

'This vandalised plot,' I say briskly. 'You can't really think my parents had anything to do with it?'

'It does seem unlikely, I must admit. But Val and Clive were putting me under a lot of pressure. It's tricky balancing the needs of all the different plot-holders, you see.'

'I understand. But in this case it was clearly someone trying to implicate my parents. They've been having some trouble with a lodger. However, that's all been sorted, so I want your assurance that my parents are welcome at the allotments.'

'Oh! Yes, yes of course,' he says. 'Please tell them I'm very sorry.'

'I will. Thank you, Tom.'

I place my phone on the table.

'Right, that's sorted. I don't think he ever truly thought it was you.'

'Darling, that's wonderful!' Mum says. 'Isn't it, Heath?'

'It really is. Well done, Penny.'

Their happiness is almost unseemly under the circumstances.

'So what are we going to do?' Dad asks.

It's scary to be the one they are looking to for answers. It reminds me of when I first brought Zach home from hospital after he was born and I was struck by the chilling realisation that Martin and I were responsible for keeping him alive.

'I need to think about what we're going to do with the . . .' I swallow. 'The body. It's cold in the shelter but that'll only give us so long. We need to come up with a more . . . permanent solution.' Bad choice of words. Solutions don't come more permanent than the one Dad came up with last night. 'And I'll go into the basement – partly to make sure there's nothing that suggests . . . what happened, and I'm going to check his phone messages, but also I'm wondering if it's worth packing up his stuff, to make it look as though he's done a runner.'

'That's a brilliant idea.' Mum says. 'You clever thing!' I swallow down my distaste at her tone, which suggests I've come up with a method of getting a red wine stain out of the carpet, not covering up the fact that her husband has killed their tenant with a fox-handled walking stick.

They bustle upstairs to get ready – even Dad's gait is sprightlier now they've been welcomed back into the allotment fold. I think I can hear him whistling. I'm thinking about going out to check their car's back seat for blood before they leave (if there are any obvious stains, I'll get the worst of them out myself and then get it valeted at the car wash place) when the doorbell rings.

'I'll get it!' I call up to them.

I open the door to see Sue from next door with a bunch of threadbare carnations.

'Hello, Penny,' she says. 'How's your mum? I brought her these.' She thrusts the flowers at me.

'She's fine,' I say, puzzled for a second before the memory of last night crashes in – Cooper disguised as my mother, the fake hospital visit. 'I mean . . . she's much better, thanks. She felt . . . er . . . dizzy. Yes, very dizzy, so we were a bit worried about her. But the hospital did lots of tests and they couldn't find anything wrong, and by that time she was feeling much better, ha ha isn't that always the way?'

'Gosh yes, isn't it just?' Sue says, peering over my shoulder, leaning into me in her eagerness to come in. I stand squarely in the doorway and take the flowers out of her hand. Unfortunately Mum chooses that moment to come tripping gaily down the stairs.

'Hello, Sue! Oh. Carnations.'

Mum, whose passion for all things floral doesn't stretch to garage forecourt bouquets, has never been one for whom the thought counts.

'You're very welcome!' says Sue, gracious in the face of my mother's obvious disdain. 'How are you feeling?'

'Wonderful!'

Worryingly, I tend to believe her, but that's not my most pressing concern.

'Wonderful compared to how you were last night, you mean,' I say. 'When we had to take you to hospital.' Mum looks confused. 'In the wheelchair,' I say desperately.

'Oh!' The penny drops. 'Yes, I felt very . . . er . . . sick last night.'

'And dizzy,' I interject.

'Oh yes, frightfully dizzy. Like I was on a ship on the ocean. Blurred vision, the lot.'

'And they couldn't find anything wrong?'

'Not a thing!'

'Surely they'll send you for some further tests or something? At your age. To be on the safe side.'

I didn't realise Sue was a bloody consultant geriatrician.

'Apparently not,' Mum says, beginning to enjoy herself. 'Sent me away with a flea in my ear!'

'That's terrible!' Sue says.

'Anyway, you were just off to the allotment, weren't you, Mum?'

'You must take it easy, Sissy,' Sue says. 'What about your sister? Is she going with you?'

Oh God, I'd forgotten about my fictional aunt.

'I don't have a—'

'No, she's not going,' I burst in, Mum having apparently forgotten too. 'She's not feeling too well herself, so I think she's going to have a quiet day. Isn't she, Mum?'

'Yes, that's right.' Thank God, she's remembered.

'I must get these lovely flowers in water,' I say, brandishing the bouquet. A few browning petals give up the fight and flutter to the ground. 'Thank you so much.'

I practically slam the door in her face and turn to lean against it.

'Golly, you're not cut out for this, are you?' Mum says. 'Give me those monstrosities. They're going straight in the bin.'

She saunters off to the kitchen, leaving me to conclude that unlike me, and rather concerningly, she was born for this.

Once I'm absolutely sure Sue is safely back inside her own front door, I send Mum and Dad off to the allotment and let myself into Cooper's apartment through the external door, first unlocking the inner door from Mum and Dad's side so I can go back that way. It's eerily quiet. There's a half-drunk mug of tea by the sink and a still-damp towel on the unmade bed. Even though I know beyond any shadow of a doubt that Cooper is not going to appear, I'm on edge. I open the top drawer of the chest of drawers. As before, there's a bag of weed in there. Presumably that's for his personal use and he keeps – kept – the stuff for selling in the lock-up.

I reach into my pocket, pull out his phone and switch it on, perching on the edge of the bed. As soon as it connects, it begins pinging with WhatsApp messages. I don't want to open any of them, so I scroll down looking at the first few words of each message. The vast majority are obviously customer orders, referencing eighths, grams and pills. There's one from Julie Woodford beginning 'Give me a call'. I'm about to close it down when I see Zach's name and sit up with a jerk. Without stopping to think about the wisdom of doing so, I click on the message, which says 'The usual pls', and then on his name, hoping against hope that it's a different Zach, but no. Zach's phone number is the only one I know off by heart and there it is in black and white. I knew Zach had bought drugs from Cooper, but I've been kidding myself that it was a one-off. I think of him holed up at Saul's smoking himself into oblivion. Is Martin right? Is Zach self-medicating with marijuana instead of facing his problems?

Someone called Smith has sent Cooper nine WhatsApp messages, but I daren't open them to see what he wants. The only one I can see says 'Where the fuck are you'. I close down WhatsApp and scroll across the other apps. His email doesn't yield anything of interest – it's mainly marketing spam. He doesn't have that many other apps apart from the standard weather, news, maps etc. My thumb hovers over photos and I tap. The most recent

photo pops up and I instinctively look away in disgust and disbe-
lief. When I force myself to look back at the screen, it's still there
– a large, angry purple penis straining towards me as if it could
pop out of the phone. Nausea roils within me. I've tried to wipe
the memory of my sexual encounter with Cooper but some
things linger in the mind, and I'm sure this appendage belongs to
him. I swipe to the next photo and the next, both of which are
different vantage points on the same thing. I keep swiping, hoping
to see something – anything – else. I get what I was hoping for
but not quite in the way I wanted. Cooper's dick pics make way
for a series of female nudes, each more gynaecological than the
last. The woman has been careful not to show her face, but there's
not much else left to the imagination, including a tattoo of a bird
in flight on the top of her right buttock. I close it down, feeling
nauseous and voyeuristic, turn off the phone, stick it in my back
pocket and get on with the job I came down to do.

Under the bed I find a large black holdall. I yank all the clothes
in the wardrobe off their hangers and into it. I cross over to the
chest of drawers, pull everything out, including the bag of weed,
and stuff it all in too. In the bathroom I gather up his toothbrush
and toothpaste, deodorant and shaving gear and wedge it all in
with the clothes. There's no more room in the holdall so I open
the inner door and sling it through into Mum and Dad's house.
I grab the two pairs of trainers from the bottom of the wardrobe
and put those through as well along with Cooper's thick winter
coat from the peg by the door. Although I've packed most of his
personal belongings, the flat still looks too inhabited. If the
police do come calling, I want them to be instantly suspicious
that he's packed up and left. In the kitchen I tear a black bin bag
from a roll I find in a drawer. Back in the main room I sweep

anything that's lying around into it – Cooper's wallet, a full ashtray, a pile of opened post, empty crisp packets, the damp towel from the bed, two phone chargers, another pair of trainers, a wireless speaker. I tie the top and put that in the pile ready to take up the stairs. I gather up all the used plates and cups and chuck them in the sink.

I'm about to step through the internal door and take it all up the stairs when there's a sharp knock at the outside door. My heart nearly jumps out of my chest. Instinctively I slam the internal door shut to hide Cooper's belongings. A second later, DC Blake's bleached visage peers through the window. I smile brightly at her and open the door.

'Good morning!' I say with madly over the top cheer. 'Can I help you?'

'DC Blake,' she says softly. 'We met the other day. And this is DS Newman.' It's the man who was with her the day Cooper was arrested. He's even bigger than he appeared then. 'We're just returning some of Mr Brownlow's property.'

She holds up a couple of carrier bags.

'I think you might be out of luck,' I say, trying to sound as breezy as I can given that all the moisture has drained from my mouth. 'Looks like he's done a runner.'

'Sorry, you are . . .?' DS Newman says.

'Penny Whitlock. This is my parents' house – they rented the basement to Cooper. You said you had some of his property?'

'Yes,' he says. 'We arrested Mr Brownlow a couple of days ago and had cause to seize some of his property, but we no longer need it.'

'He was arrested? For what? Was he dealing drugs?' I'll play this as innocent as I can.

'I'm afraid we can't share that information,' Blake says. 'And I thought you already knew he'd been arrested.'

'What? No . . . I—'

'You parked up in the driveway just as we were driving off with him,' she says mildly. 'It must have been fairly obvious what was going on.'

'Not really, I've no experience of these things,' I say, attempting to regain some kind of moral high ground – although that won't last long if they open the internal door and see all Cooper's worldly goods piled up there.

'You said you think he's done a runner?' Newman says, concerned.

'Yes, I haven't seen him for a couple of days – since that day when I saw him going off with you, in fact – and I was just passing down the side of the house on my way to do some . . . gardening,' I improvise wildly, 'when I looked through the window and saw that everything looked very empty.'

I step back to let them see in.

'Can we come in?' Newman asks.

'Of course.'

With my heart in my mouth, I watch as the two of them open the cupboards and drawers I emptied just moments ago. Every time one of them goes anywhere near the internal door I nearly throw up.

'You say you haven't seen him since he was arrested?'

'No. Although he's obviously been back to get his stuff.'

'And your parents?' Blake asks. 'Have they seen him?'

'No!' I curl my hands into fists so they can't see the sweat beading on my palms. 'They've been away for a week or so in Norfolk. They only got back last night.'

'This is rather concerning,' Newman says. 'How well do you know Mr Brownlow?'

Blake gives me a sympathetic smile. Needless to say, they all know about my night with Cooper.

'Not well at all. He was my parents' tenant.' A flashback of Cooper looming above me on my sofa fills my mind – grunting, his body pinning me down, his hands all over my body. 'I had a . . .' I search for the right word but can't find it. My shoulders sag. Does it matter how I put it? They know anyway. 'I slept with him. Once. Before I knew what kind of a man he was.'

'You didn't know he was a convicted criminal?' Newman asks.

'No, of course not.' I'm on safer ground here. 'We trusted the lettings agency – my parents never would have let the annexe to him if we'd known.'

'I think perhaps we'd better have a word with your parents whilst we're here,' he says. 'They may have heard or seen something that will indicate where he's gone. Can we go up this way?' He gestures at the internal door. The heap of Cooper's stuff pulsates behind it.

'No!' I yelp. 'I mean . . . they're not in. They've gone to their allotment.'

'Is that the ones on Albion Road?' Blake asks. 'My neighbours have got one there.'

'Yes, that's right.'

'We'll go and find them there,' Newman says. 'See if they can throw any light on Mr Brownlow's whereabouts.'

'I'll go with you, if that's OK. They're elderly, they might get a bit . . . confused.'

'No problem at all,' Blake says. 'We'll see you there. One question before we go – Mr Brownlow is currently your parents' tenant, is that right?'

'Yes. I told you that.'

'Right, right.' She smiles sweetly. 'I wanted to check because, you see, a couple of times in our conversation, you referred to him living here in the past tense.'

'That's because we'll be doing our utmost to ensure that he doesn't live here anymore, when you find him,' I say, speaking loudly as if that might disguise the hammering of my heart.

'I see. Can't say I blame you.' Esther Blake takes a final look around the apartment, her eyes lingering for a second on the internal door. Then I follow her and Newman in my car to the allotment, otherwise known as the current resting place of Cooper Brownlow's dead body.

Chapter 27

I thought we might find my parents huddled in their shed, worrying about the terrifying situation we find ourselves in, but I couldn't have been more wrong. Mum is kneeling at a raised bed, weeding away industriously, and as we wend our way through the neighbouring plot, Dad emerges from the shed, smiling broadly and carrying a steaming mug of tea in each enormous hand.

His smile drops like a stone when he spots the two police officers. I urgently need to explain what they're doing here before he gives the game away completely.

'It looks like Cooper has done a runner. These officers arrested him a couple of days ago and they're here to ask if you have any idea where he might be. That's all, that's all,' I say, my words tripping over each other in their eagerness to get out.

'Ah. Right. Can I offer either of you a cup of tea?' He recovers his composure admirably.

'No thanks,' Newman says.

'Hello.' Mum lumbers to her feet, brushing dirt from her trousers. 'Would you like to sit down? We've got camping chairs in the shed.'

'No, that won't be necessary,' Newman says. 'We wanted to ask you when you last saw your tenant.'

'We've been away for just over a week visiting a friend in Norfolk, haven't we, Sissy?'

'Have we?' Mum says vaguely.

'You know you have, Mum,' I say impatiently. 'You got back yesterday.'

'Oh yes, of course.'

'It's sometimes hard to remember things, isn't it?' Newman says sympathetically. 'I forget what I've had for dinner half the time!'

'And you returned home yesterday evening?' Blake cuts in impatiently, addressing herself to Dad.

'Yes, that's right,' Dad says.

'And did you see Mr Brownlow at all?'

'No. No. Haven't seen him since before we went away.'

'Might be a bit of a relief for you, if he has done a flit?' she suggests.

'Well, to be honest it's been a very worrying time. And now to find out he's been arrested – it's not what we're used to. We've never been in any trouble with the police.'

'You're not in trouble,' Newman says. 'We're just anxious to track this fellow down.'

'Indeed,' Blake says. 'Are you sure you didn't see him last night – either of you?' She looks intently at Mum.

'No, I don't think so,' Mum says. 'Sorry, who are we talking about again?'

I look sideways at Mum. What is she playing at?

'Your tenant, Cooper Brownlow,' Blake says. 'The one you called the police about three weeks ago.'

'Alright, Esther,' Newman says reprovingly. 'I think we're done here. It's beginning to look very much like our friend Mr Brownlow has done a runner. Do any of you have any idea where he might have gone? Did he mention friends, family?'

'No friends that I know of,' I say. 'He does have a brother.' The words are out before I have a chance to consider whether I should be owning up to knowing this. 'I think he mentioned it once,' I add. I definitely don't want them to know I was doing my own investigation into Cooper.

'Do you know his name?'

'No, sorry. Other than that, I've got no idea. Dad?'

'No, none, sorry.'

They don't bother asking Mum, who is staring off into the middle distance.

'Sissy, Heath, it's so good to see you.' Tom, chair of the allotment committee, sidles up. 'And Penny. Nice to speak to you earlier. I'm sorry again about the silly business with Val and Clive. Is everything OK?' He looks with frank curiosity at the police officers.

'Yes thanks, Tom,' I say firmly. 'The officers are just leaving, I think? Unless there's anything else?'

'No, that's fine. We'll be in touch if and when we track him down,' Newman says.

'And do let us know straight away if he comes back, or you hear from him,' Blake adds.

'Yes, of course,' I say.

They turn to go and I heave an internal sigh of relief.

'Is this an Anderson shelter?' DC Blake puts out a slender hand and runs her fingers over the curved, corrugated steel of the roof. Ice floods my veins.

'That's right,' Tom says.

'I love these things,' she says. 'They're a piece of living history. I did my dissertation on experiences of community during the Blitz.'

'Really?' says Mum, shocked out of her dementia act, if that's what it is.

'Yes, Esther joined the police on our graduate leadership programme fresh from her History degree, and just a year later she was a detective,' Newman says. I can't tell if he's sneering or admiring.

'They're fascinating old things,' Tom says. 'I've been approached by a local history society about opening it up for one of those heritage days. They've got an expert who could give a talk and everything.'

I sneak a peek at Mum and Dad. Mum's vacant look has been replaced by dread and Dad's face has drained of all colour.

'Gosh, that would be fascinating, what interesting old things they are,' I prattle, dry-mouthed, hoping no one will notice my parents (and my own) abject terror at this prospect.

'I wouldn't mind having a look inside,' Blake says.

'It's locked,' Dad yelps.

'Is it?' says Tom, wandering round to the entrance. 'I didn't think it had a lock.'

'Stuck, I mean,' Dad says. 'I tried to get in the other day. Need to bring some tools. Don't worry about it now. Let me know when the history man wants to come.' Words keep spouting unstoppably from his lips.

'It won't be for a while – Samantha and I are off on a three-week Caribbean cruise on Tuesday,' Tom says smugly.

'We don't have time for this.' Reprieve comes from an unlikely source as DS Newman taps his colleague on the arm.

'Yes, you're right,' Blake says regretfully, giving the shelter roof an affectionate pat. 'Another time.'

Newman and Blake depart and thankfully Tom isn't far behind them, having to leave for a doctor's appointment.

'We've got to get Cooper out of there tonight,' I say as soon as they're all out of earshot.

'It was a silly place to put him, really,' Mum says.

'I'm sorry,' I say, my voice dripping with sarcasm. 'Perhaps we were panicking for some strange reason. I didn't see you coming up with any better ideas. What was with you today, anyway? Were you actually faking dementia?'

'It seemed a good idea,' she says insouciantly. 'They didn't ask me any questions, did they?'

'Hmm I don't know – I think that Blake was onto you. She's not as airy fairy as she looks.'

'Onto me? What are you talking about, darling? We're not under suspicion. Anyway, they don't scare me. I've dealt with plenty of their kind before.'

'What are you talking about?' Maybe she actually is losing her marbles.

'At Greenham,' she says airily.

'Greenham?' I repeat.

'Yes, darling, Greenham Common. You know, the women's peace camp in the 1980s at the RAF base in Greenham.'

'Yes, I know what Greenham Common is.' I remember a Current Affairs lesson at school where one of the more progressive teachers told us about the time she'd spent there protesting against nuclear weapons.

'Well, I was there, wasn't I?'

'What are you talking about?'

'I went to Greenham regularly back in the eighties, when you were . . . ooh eight or nine. I was in between jobs at the time and

I'd camp there for a week or so every couple of months. I'm sure I've told you.'

'You haven't. And you definitely didn't tell me at the time.'

'Ah no,' Dad chips in. 'We didn't want you to worry if you saw the police being a bit rough with the women on the news. We'd tell you Mum was going to help Marie out with the kids or somesuch.'

'Oh.' I do remember that now. 'But who . . .?'

'Who looked after you?' Mum says tartly. 'Your other parent, perhaps?'

'We had some lovely times, darling,' Dad says. 'Our little traditions – fish and chips on a Friday night, remember?'

His words conjure up a feeling of safety, of being squashed into the sofa next to Dad, TV on, warm and cosy, the tang of salt and vinegar on my fingers. 'I do, actually. But why haven't you ever talked about it?'

'You never asked,' Mum says. 'Anyway, we don't need to worry about this lot. They're just trying to find out where Cooper's gone.'

'Yes, and we really need to hope they don't. We've got to get him out of here tonight. We can't risk Tom and his local history pal going in there.'

'What are we going to do with him?' Dad says, half-choked with fear. 'We can't let him be found.'

'We won't, we won't.' I will not let that happen.

'I've got an idea,' Mum says.

'What?' I say suspiciously.

'We don't want to put him anywhere public where a dog walker's going to find him, or chuck him into a river where he could get washed up.'

'Right.' It's unnerving how methodical she's being about this.

'So why not hide him in plain sight? We've finally got someone coming to put the new patio tiles in next week. They've already dug out the earth to be replaced with the crushed stone for the base. We could make a deep hole under that, deep enough that the patio men won't find him, and once it's done, he'll be completely covered up.'

'Well . . .' It's actually not a bad plan, apart from it being a total cliché to bury someone under the patio.

'The police aren't looking for a dead body,' Mum goes on blithely. 'They're looking for a live criminal on the run.' She's using her new-found lingo with gusto.

'What do you think, Dad?'

'I suppose we could,' he says doubtfully. 'I'm not sure I like the idea of him being on our property.'

'That's the beauty of it!' Mum insists. 'No one's going to be looking for him there. And who would suspect us? Two old fogies with barely a brain cell left between them.'

'She's got a point,' I admit. 'You could put all his stuff that I took out of the flat under there too. And what about the walking stick? Where is it anyway? Is it a good idea to bury that as well, just in case . . . I don't know? Evidence?'

'Yes, good idea,' she says. 'Right, that's decided. We'll get him tonight under cover of darkness. Penny, you can help, can't you?'

I agree that I can. I can't abandon them now – we're all in this together, like it or not. I ignore the nagging voice that wonders if my mother, far from not liking it, is enjoying it a little bit too much.

Chapter 28

I don't know how I'm ever going to sleep or concentrate on work again. The only thing that keeps me going is the desperate need to protect my parents. If I could manage the body on my own, I would do so, but I've had to let Dad help me. Unsure what state it was going to be in after twenty-four hours, I've been Googling rigor mortis. It's wildly incriminating should I ever be investigated for Cooper's death, but if I am, the fact that he's under my parents' patio will be more of a giveaway, so I don't worry too much. It seems that if Cooper's body had been at room temperature, it would have started to decay by now. However, because he's been in the Anderson shelter, which I doubt has got much above freezing since he's been in there, rigor mortis is likely to last much longer – several days at least. I find this reassuring, as I've been having horrible visions of a soft, decaying corpse dripping all sorts of revolting liquids that I don't want to think about. A cold, stiff body will be easier to deal with mentally, although I fear we'll have trouble fitting him in the car.

It's a cold, clear night at the allotments, the sky sprinkled with stars and a large, bright moon which gives everything a ghostly, shadowy air more sinister than pitch darkness. We've kept the wheelchair in the boot in case we're able to make use of it but I'm not sure we'll be able to manipulate his body enough to get him into it. The car park is thankfully as empty as you would expect at ten o'clock at night.

'Let's park up here and I'll go and see . . . what we're dealing with. You wait here.' I don't want to put Dad through any more horror than necessary. I wonder briefly if I should have brought Mum instead – she seems less bothered by the moral aspect after all – but Dad's physical strength makes him the obvious candidate.

I walk across the other plots, the ground iron-hard beneath my boots, stepping over winter cabbages, purplish, knobbly heads of sprouting broccoli and long stems laden with Brussels sprouts. Inside the shelter it's pitch dark and I fumble for my phone torch. It smells fermented and sweet, like decaying fruit. I retch.

I force myself over to where the tarpaulin covers the body, brace myself and put out a tentative hand. The body feels rigid – my research about rigor mortis and the cold must have been right. Whilst in many ways this is a relief, the wheelchair is going to be no use whatsoever – we'll never be able to bend him into the right shape to fit into it. We're going to have to carry him between us – and the easiest way will be on our shoulders in some hideous parody of coffin bearers. I let myself out and draw in great lungfuls of cold night air as I hurry back to the car.

'Right, he's very . . . stiff,' I say to Dad, getting back into the passenger seat. He winces. 'So we're going to need to get the car as near as we can to minimise the distance we have to carry him. There's no way we'll get him in the wheelchair.'

'The only plot between ours and the perimeter path is Sheila's old one,' he says. 'There's nothing in there at the moment – she'd been neglecting it while she was ill, and anything that was there has died. So if the path around is clear, which it should be, we could drive around and over her plot. Luckily it's been cold and dry, otherwise it would have been a mud bath.' Dad's clear-sightedness applies to practical situations as well as emotional ones.

'Let's go. I don't want to be here any longer than necessary.'

He fires up the engine and we drive cautiously around the path that borders the allotments. It's not made for cars and is only just wide enough. A couple of times he has to stop so I can get out and remove an obstacle – a stray watering can, a broken garden fork – but we make it round to Sheila's old plot and drive straight over it.

'Right, this is as close as we're going to get,' Dad says.

We get out and Dad follows me into the shelter. I can tell he doesn't want to look at or touch the body, but there's no time for coaxing and cajoling.

'Which end do you want to take?' I ask.

'I don't . . . what was that?'

We both stand still, ears pricked. A car has screeched to a halt somewhere nearby and doors are slamming. A group of young men rampage across the allotments. Something smashes – a flower pot, I guess – and there's laughter and whooping. They sound drunk – shouting, talking about pulling up plants, egging each other on.

'Little bastards,' Dad whispers, missing the point rather.

'Come on, lads!' one of them shouts, painfully close. The corrugated steel reverberates around us as he bangs on the shelter roof. I switch off my torch and we shrink into the shadows – a pointless exercise because if they come in we are sunk no matter what.

'What's this then, boys?' another says and there's a colossal thumping above our heads as one of them scrabbles onto the roof and starts jumping up and down. Dad and I cower in silence as the structure shudders around us. A second lad climbs up to join him and the noise becomes deafening. At the point where I'm sure one of them is going to come through the roof, slicing his flesh on shards of shattered metal, my phone begins to ring. The boys fall silent.

'Whose phone is that?' someone says.

'It's coming from inside this!' one of the boys on the roof says.

I'm holding my phone from where I was using the torch but my fingers won't work properly as I try to cut the call. It's Zach calling – Zach whose call I would never normally refuse to take – but I stab at the screen, willing it to stop. Eventually I manage it and it falls silent.

'What the hell?' says one of the boys.

They jump down and footsteps come towards the shelter entrance. This is it. This is how it ends.

Then we hear the wail of a police siren in the distance and the boys fall silent.

'Shit!' One of them says. 'We need to get out of here.'

As quickly as they arrived, they are gone in a squeal of tyres and a blast of drum and bass.

Dad and I crouch and wait in the dark.

'What are we going to say if the police come here and find us?' he says. 'We need to have some kind of story ready.'

'A story?' I say. 'What story can you think of that would explain why we're hiding in here with the corpse of your tenant? No, if they find us, that's it, Dad. It's over.'

'It might be a relief,' he says quietly.

I take his hand. 'No,' I say. 'Don't say that. I think the sirens are getting further away.'

We listen intently. I am right. The siren noise fades into the distance, having done a brilliant job of scaring those boys away.

'We can't waste any more time – we need to get it – him – out of here,' I say.

Between us, we pull Cooper's unyielding body, still loosely wrapped in the tarp, to the entrance. I check outside that there's no one around and nip over to the car and open the rear passenger door. As we attempt to lift him, I can't believe I ever considered bringing Mum instead of Dad. Almost singlehandedly, he hoists Cooper's body up, the head end resting on his broad shoulders, the feet on my much slighter ones. We stagger the few metres to the car. Dad slides the head end onto the back seat and we ram him in. The tarpaulin is slippery and he shoots in, hitting his head on the far door with a thump. The problem is his feet are sticking out a few inches on this side.

'We need to lift his head up so he's more . . . diagonal,' Dad says. 'It's like when we picked up that curtain rail that Mum bought on ebay. I've told her not to buy stuff that's collection only, but she doesn't listen. In the end we had to shove it in between the driver and passenger seats and it kept swinging round and bashing me on the head.'

'Focus, Dad!'

'Sorry, love.'

'You hold onto his feet, I'll go round the other side.'

I open the door on the other side and heave Cooper's head up. The tarp slips, revealing the matted mess that is the back of his head. A stretching, oozing movement catches my eye and I realise it's a worm. I choke, fighting the urge to throw up.

'Get his feet in,' I say to Dad. Cooper shifts in my arms as Dad shoves the other end and closes his door. I let go with one arm and in one swift movement remove the other and slam the door shut on his head, which falls back heavily against the window.

We get back into the car. Dad is breathing heavily. Hands shaking, he starts the ignition. The whole thing has only taken about fifteen minutes, but it feels like a lifetime since we arrived. I've aged about twenty years. We make the drive in silence. As we turn into their road, my phone rings. It's Zach again and this time I answer.

'Mum?' he says before I've even said hello. In that one word I can tell that something is wrong.

'What's the matter?'

'Can you come and get me from Saul's?'

I look at the corpse of my parents' tenant in the back of the car. I think of my mother waiting for us, gardening gloves on and spade poised, ready to bury him under the patio. I think of my son, and the many times I have rescued him from a situation he couldn't handle, or counselled him through yet another crisis. When people talk about the sandwich generation, I'm not sure this is exactly what they mean.

'Of course, darling,' I say. 'I'll be there as soon as I can.'

Chapter 29

I leave Mum and Dad to dig Cooper's makeshift grave, promising to come back and help them once I've sorted Zach out.

'There's no need,' Mum says. 'We can manage – gardening is our forte!' She waves her spade at me, remarkably cheerful about the whole thing.

'Yes, I know that but you need to dig a pretty deep hole, and . . . you're not as young as you were, are you?'

'For goodness' sake, Penny, look at your father! He's strong as an ox and still runs marathons – and my Pilates teacher said I had the physique of a fifty-year-old! And if you're worrying about whether I can cope with it mentally, don't. Us Greenham Common women are stronger than you can ever imagine.'

I still can't believe I didn't know she was at Greenham, although since she told me, memories of Dad and I doing things without her have been floating back to me.

'I'll ring you when I know how long I'm going to be.'

Dad follows me out to the hall and gathers me into an enormous bear hug.

'Don't worry, I'll look after her,' he says into my hair.

'Apparently she doesn't need looking after,' I say. 'You heard her.'

'Yes, but I also know her,' he says, drawing back. 'She's like one of those floating shelves – it appears as though they're just

x

x

x

stuck to the wall but actually they're supported securely by hidden internal brackets.'

'The brackets being you?' I say, smiling.

'Yep,' he says, kissing my cheek. 'Now, off you go – you've got your own floating shelf to support.'

I spend the short drive thinking about where or who my internal brackets are, and conclude as I park outside Saul's house that I don't have any. I'm a broken shelf, sagging in the middle under the weight of all the crap piled on it. Zach is sitting on the low brick wall that borders the front garden. He picks up his bag and slumps down on the passenger seat next to me.

'How are you?' I ask cautiously as we drive away. Experience has taught me not to go straight in asking lots of questions. A subtler approach usually yields better results.

'Fine,' he says.

'Good,' I remain neutral.

We sit in silence for a few minutes and then he shifts and sighs.

'Can I borrow some money?'

'What for?'

'I owe Cooper some,' he says. My stomach lurches. Zach stares mulishly out of the window.

'What for?' I ask, knowing the answer.

'You know.'

'Is he . . . chasing you for it?' I choke the words out, feeling as if my throat is closing up. I know the answer has to be no, but it's the obvious question I'd ask if I didn't know that Cooper's chasing days were well and truly over.

'He was, but he's gone quiet the last couple of days. I've been calling him today but his phone's switched off. Now there's this other guy called Smith. Huge bloke – built like a brick shithouse.'

'What?' I nearly miss my turn and slam on the brakes, swinging round at the last second. 'Sorry, lost concentration for a sec. Another guy, you said?' Who the hell is this?

'Cooper did say if we didn't pay he'd be sending someone round. This bloke came round this afternoon, says he's Cooper's 'associate'. He said Cooper's temporarily out of action and that we should deal with him for now.'

Perhaps this is a good thing for us – if Cooper's clients are going to be diverted to this Smith character, they're less likely to be turning up at the house at all hours.

'Why the hell didn't you pay Cooper?'

'He wasn't too bothered at first – he was happy for us to have a sort of account with him.'

'I bet he was. That's how they reel you in. You stupid boy.' I can't help it, my frustration spills out into the already frosty air between us.

'Thanks, Mum, that's really helpful.'

'Sorry.' I should be raging, but I can hear the anxious little boy hiding behind his sarcasm. 'How much do you owe him?'

'Two hundred and fifty quid.'

'What? How have you racked up that much?'

'Well, that's over a few weeks, and then there was this new stuff he said we should try – he gave us a bit for free, actually, and we liked it so . . .'

'Is that between you and Saul?'

'Yeah.'

'Right.' I'm by no means rolling in money but I can scrape together two hundred and fifty pounds. 'I'll pay this Smith character off, but Saul owes me his half. He can pay me in instalments if he likes. And no more staying at Saul's. Either you go back to university or you move back in with me.'

'Fine. It was getting boring there anyway.'

'And no more drugs.'

'But it helps me, Mum – there's loads of studies that show cannabis can help treat depression.'

'There's also plenty of evidence of the link between cannabis use and depression. I mean it, Zach. I agree you need help with your mental health, but I think a visit to the doctor to discuss medication and therapy is what you need, not sitting around all day smoking weed.'

'Where is Cooper anyway? Have you seen him at Grandma and Grandpa's?'

An image of the worm feasting on the mangled flesh of Cooper's head flashes into my mind and I swallow.

'He was arrested for dealing two days ago. He was granted bail but we think he's done a runner. He hasn't paid the rent and no one's seen him, and, as you said, his phone's been switched off.'

'Seriously? Oh, man.'

'I'm terribly sorry that your supply of illegal drugs has been cut off, but in case you hadn't noticed, Grandma and Grandpa have been going through hell because of him. Good riddance, I say.' Cooper is a criminal, a drug dealer, a bad and horrible man. It scares me to think it, but perhaps the world is better off without him. Is anyone really going to miss him? I'm pretty sure his brother will be as glad to be rid of him as my parents are, on my limited acquaintance with him.

'Have you got this Smith character's number? How will I get the money to him?'

'No, I haven't got it. He said he'd be in touch.'

'I bet he did.'

Zach sighs again and resumes his intent perusal of the passing landscape. We continue the rest of the journey in silence and when we get home, he goes straight to bed. I can hear the tinny blare of his phone – he's watching YouTube videos. I daren't go back to Mum and Dad's until he's asleep – where would I say I was going? I'd like to call Martin to talk about Zach, but for one thing it's too late, and for another he'd only berate me for wading in to rescue Zach once again. I'm too tired to counter his tiresome insistence that me constantly bailing Zach out is doing him no favours.

I sit down on the sofa, my body aching with the effort of holding myself together all evening. I close my eyes for a second, knowing there's no danger of me dropping off with everything that's going on. Six hours later, I jolt awake, my hands and feet like ice. I jump to my feet, shaking. I can't believe I fell asleep. It's still dark outside and I look at my phone – 5:30. The flat is dark and silent. I listen outside Zach's door to make sure but all is quiet, so I grab my keys and drive as fast as I dare back to Mum and Dad's.

I walk cautiously down the side of the house past the entrance to the basement. The entire house is in darkness. As I round the corner, I switch on my phone torch and focus the beam on the patio area. The earth there is loose as if there's been recent digging, but then I'm not sure what it looked like before. Have they really managed to do it alone? I sweep the torch around the rest of the garden. The ground everywhere is churned up, particularly around the rose garden where Cooper wreaked his havoc. I go back round to the front and let myself in, closing the door as quietly as I can behind me. Dottie comes pattering out of the kitchen, barking excitedly.

'Sshh,' I say uselessly, as if she'd be able to understand.

Floorboards creak above me and Mum comes into view at the top of the stairs in her dressing gown.

'I'm so so sorry I've been so long – I sat down, I only meant it to be for a minute, and I fell asleep on the sofa. And now I've woken you,' I say.

'It's fine, I wasn't asleep,' she says as she laboriously edges down the stairs one at a time, gripping the banister.

'Are you alright?'

'Yes fine, just a bit stiff.' Cooper's unbending, lifeless body flashes before me. I force the image away.

'You didn't . . . have you done it?'

'Oh yes, it's all done,' she says jauntily as if we're discussing planting their latest rose bush.

'And all the stuff I took out of the flat, and the walking stick too?'

'Yes, yes, all done, don't worry.'

'How long did it take?'

'We've only just finished. That's why I'm still awake, although your father was asleep the minute his head hit the pillow.'

'It's nearly six in the morning.'

'As you said, we had to dig down pretty deep.'

'And did you manage to . . . you know . . . get him . . . out of the car and . . .'

'Yes, we balanced him across the wheelbarrow.'

'Bloody hell, Mum.'

'What?' she says with some spirit. 'Did you think we were a pair of useless old dears who couldn't be trusted with anything?

I told you gardening was our strong suit. And we've always kept ourselves fit.'

'I know. It's not that. It's just you seem . . . remarkably OK about everything.'

'I'm sorry if I'm not falling apart and boohooing and going for therapy.' She reaches the bottom of the stairs and looks at me defiantly. 'When you've lived as long as I have, you've been through things. You lose people. You fall out or lose touch. People get ill. They die. At the end of the day, you have to get on with it. You're not dead. You're still alive. What else is there to do other than keep going?'

'Yes, I know that. I've lost people too.' I'd give my right arm to be able to call Caitlin and spill this whole sorry tale to her.

And implicate me in the crime? Thanks very much! Caitlin says.

'I know you have.' She softens momentarily. 'I adored Caitlin too, you know I did.'

It's true, Mum really did love her. Caitlin spent more time here than she did at her own house when we were teenagers.

'So you know very well that you have to pick yourself up and carry on,' Mum says, armour back on. 'I've never told you this but we lost two babies before you came along. Both times I thought I'd die of heartbreak, but guess what? I didn't.'

'Oh, Mum, I'm so sorry. You never said.' I put out my hand and touch her arm, but she shrugs it off.

'I'm not looking for sympathy, darling. I'm saying life's not easy and although this . . . episode . . . is difficult, we've been through worse. Let's have some tea.'

She breezes past me into the kitchen and switches on the light. As she fills the kettle, I hear a car pull up in the drive. My heart sinks. It's six in the morning, who the hell can it be? I go into the front room and peer through the gap in the curtains. A ridiculously large black four-wheel-drive vehicle has parked right in the middle of the drive, blocking any other cars from coming in or out. The security light clicks on and I can see the number plate. It's a personalised one, reading 5M1TH. The engine is killed and the headlamps go dark. I narrow my eyes to see through the gloom as the driver steps out of the car and heads down the side of the house. I can't make out much about them apart from being pretty sure it's a man. A very large man. As Zach might say, a man built like a brick shithouse.

Chapter 30

The banging reverberates through the house like thunder. Mum clutches me, her fingers, claw-like, digging into the soft flesh of my arm.

'Who is it?' she says, terrified. 'What do they want?'

'I think I know,' I say, gently disengaging myself. 'Let me sort it.'

I steel myself to go outside and round the side of the house where a giant of a man with close-cropped, greying hair is thumping on the door to the basement.

'Can I help you?' I say, sounding reedy and absurdly posh.

'Where's Cooper?' he says without any preamble. He moves towards me. In two enormous strides he's covered the not inconsiderable distance between us. He's even bigger close up. My eyes are level with the middle of his chest. His T-shirt strains across his belly, the cotton stretched tight and paper thin. I try not to wrinkle my nose at the musty scent which seeps from his pores – weed and old sweat and damp towels. This has to be Smith, the guy Zach told me about.

'I wish I knew,' I say, trying to sound breezily confident.

'Who are you?' he says suspiciously. 'I thought the house belonged to some old couple.'

Anger burns in my chest like acid reflux at the idea of Cooper describing my dear parents to this oaf in such a casual, dismissive fashion.

'Yes, it does,' I say faux-pleasantly. 'They're my parents.'

'Where is he, then? He's not answering his phone. He was meant to meet me yesterday with some money he owes me and he never showed.'

'Unfortunately I have no idea whatsoever. He's disappeared owing my parents a lot of money. We're rather afraid he's done a runner. Now, as it's six o'clock in the morning, I'd thank you to do us the courtesy of leaving us alone. I don't want my parents woken up.'

'Too late,' he says. I follow his gaze to see my mother in her dressing gown, feet bare, tiptoeing across the gravel, shivering in the freezing air.

'Hello, dear. Can we help you?' She holds tight to the side of the house as if the wind could blow her away. There's a fragility to her that wasn't there a moment ago when she was stridently advocating a stiff upper lip in the face of adversity.

'Go back inside, Mum.'

'Yeah, love. You'll catch your death.' The words themselves are kind, but the manner of their delivery gives them an unmistakeable air of menace.

She regards him blankly, eyes glazed.

'Mum, go back in. You've got nothing on your feet.'

'Haven't I?' She looks down, surprised.

'Your tenant owes me money,' Smith says to her. 'Do you know where he is?'

'He's looking for Cooper, Mum. I've told him we don't know where he is. He owes us money too,' I say to Smith. 'I'd love to know where he is.'

'Why don't we take a squiz at his flat?' he says. 'Maybe there'll be a clue in there.'

'Oh . . . well . . . I don't know about that. We're not supposed to be in there without his permission.'

'But you said yourself he owes you money, might have done a runner. I'd call that extenuating circumstances, wouldn't you?'

'I don't think—'

'You're not getting it, are you?' He lowers his face to mine, his breath sour, any pretence of geniality long gone. 'I'm not asking you. Either you let me in or I smash the window. Your choice.'

'Fine,' I say in a strangled squawk. 'I'll go and get the key. Mum, come on.'

She follows me back inside.

'What was all that about?' I say as I scrabble through random charging leads and screwed up takeaway leaflets on the hall table, trying to find the basement key.

'All what?' She slides her feet back into her slippers. 'Ooh, that's better.'

'Why did you take them off? Just to make yourself seem even more gaga?'

'I didn't want them to get wet,' she says, injured.

'You know what I'm talking about. The doolally old lady act out there.'

'I don't think it's a bad thing if we're seen to be not quite all there. Just in case. Call it another insurance policy.'

'What do you mean, another one? Oh, I haven't got time for this.' I finally locate the key and go back outside.

I let Smith in and stand in the doorway as he pokes around the flat, opening cupboards and drawers exactly as the police did the day before.

'Very convenient for you, isn't it?' he says eventually.

'I beg your pardon?' I force myself to sound level, unconcerned.

'I don't suppose he was a model tenant, was he?'

'He was alright,' I say stiffly.

'Now come on, darlin'.' He walks slowly over to me. I take a half step back. 'You've just told me he's upped and left owing you money. Must have been very stressful for the old dears. You must be angry at him.'

'Not particularly.' My mind races. What would I say if Cooper really had disappeared and I didn't know he was buried under the patio? 'As you can see, most of his stuff has gone. If he has done a runner, I can't say I'm going to miss him. But like I said, I don't know where he is.'

'This is quite the mystery, isn't it?' He smiles unpleasantly. I'm desperate to change the subject before I give myself away.

'While I've got you, I think my son owes you some money?' This could be just the thing.

'Does he now? Who's your son?'

'His name's Zach. Him and his friend Saul have been using your . . . services. He said you went round to Saul's house – on Marchant Street?'

'Oh yeah, those two. What about it?'

'I said I'd pay the debt for them – £250 I think he said?'

'Plus interest.' Silver fillings gleam from the back of his mouth, spread wide in a Cheshire cat grin.

'How much?'

'Another £250,' he says, straight-faced.

'What?'

'They're late paying. That's the arrangement.'

'Fine. If I pay you, will you . . . leave them alone?'

'Of course,' he spreads his arms wide. 'Why wouldn't I?'

'I'll need to go to the cash point. Will you follow me there, and we can get this done?'

'Sure.'

'I'll just go and tell my mum.'

As I let myself back in I catch Mum in the hallway, taking off the gardening clogs they keep by the door.

'Where have you been?'

'Nowhere,' she says, not meeting my eye.

'I need to get back to Zach. Will you be OK?'

'Yes. But I don't like this – people coming looking for him. It's never going to be over, is it?'

'It will,' I say unconvincingly. 'We just need to get through this bit.'

'No, we need to find a way to end it.'

'Mum, it's too late to confess now. We need to keep going.'

'I'm not talking about confessing.' She looks at me sharply. 'Quite the opposite.'

What's the opposite of confessing? Smith sounds his horn, long and loud.

'I've got to go. I'll come back later. Try and get some sleep.'

I drive to the cash point, frantically calculating where I can switch money from in order to pay Smith off and still be able to cover my bills this month. Every time I look in the rear-view mirror, Smith's SUV looms large, never more than a few metres behind me, trailing me like a shadow.

Chapter 31

Two weeks later I'm beginning to hope that paying Smith off has meant we'll never hear from him again. Zach is moody and withdrawn, but staying away from Saul and spending most of his time in his room. I don't think he's been smoking but my fear is that it's only because a) his supply has been cut off and b) he's skint. I've stopped asking him about university. I haven't had the headspace for anything except the crushing weight of what we have done to Cooper and whether we're going to be found out. Smith was certainly suspicious, but surely he must think it more likely that Cooper is up to something dodgy than that my elderly parents are.

Today is the day that Cooper's final resting place is covered up. We'll all feel better when there's a hundredweight of slate on top of him, but first I've got to practise my presentation ready for a meeting this afternoon with Tim Glennon, one of our biggest clients. I'm closeted in my room going over and over it, when Janine calls.

'Hello?' I say cheerily, with no sense of foreboding. She'll be calling to go over things for the meeting later – she's going to be there too, so it's an opportunity to get back in her good books.

'Good morning,' she says thinly, coolness seeping down the line.

'Er . . . is everything OK?'

'Not really, Penny. I've just had a call from Tim Glennon asking for the information he requested prior to today's meeting.'

'What?' A chill shivers through me. 'He didn't request anything in advance.'

'I'm afraid he did. I emailed you five days ago outlining the exact nature of what he required.'

Oh no, no, no. I quickly scroll back through my emails and open the one in question. I skim through the requirements for the presentation, which is all as I remember, and exactly what I've prepared. Then at the bottom, I see the crucial sentence I missed.

'Oh God, Janine, I missed that. But listen, I think you're going to be really pleased with the presentation—'

'I'm afraid the presentation is neither here nor there. I told you last time that if there were any more instances of unprofessional behaviour, I would have to issue a written warning, and that's what I'm going to do.'

'Oh please no, Janine, I simply missed one line of your email. I'll sort it now.'

'It's too late. I've sent him the necessary information, of course, but his trust in us has been destroyed.'

Jesus, we're doing his accounts, not performing life-saving surgery on his only child. I bite my tongue.

'I'm so sorry. Could you not reconsider, please?'

'I'm afraid not.' She's not afraid. I have a horrible feeling she's taking pleasure in it. 'I'll see you at the meeting this afternoon. I do hope you're adequately prepared.'

I gather up my things with a heavy heart. It's the last thing I feel like doing, but I promised to drop in on Mum and Dad on the way to work to check on the progress of the patio guys.

There's been no sign of Zach so I've left him alone this morning, assuming he was sleeping. Before I leave, I knock on his bedroom door but there's no answer. I poke my head in cautiously. He's not here. His bed is a tangle of stained sheets, dirty socks and damp towels. Every surface is littered with Rizla papers, flakes of tobacco (or weed, I suppose), half-drunk cups of tea and plates coated in grease. He must have slipped out while I was working.

When I arrive at my parents I'm expecting to see a hive of activity – vans, a cement mixer, patio tiles being hauled around on a trolley – but it's empty and silent.

'What's going on? Where are the patio guys?' I say as soon as I'm inside.

'They cancelled,' Dad says glumly. 'I think it's a sign.'

'Nonsense,' Mum says briskly. 'They got a bigger job. They said they'll be back to do ours when it's done, but they can think again. So annoying. Dad's been to the bank and got cash out for them specially. I've been asking around all our friends for recommendations and Linda has suggested someone she's used – she said they were brilliant. I'm going to get onto them.'

'No, Mum. Look what happened last time she recommended someone – you ended up with that cowboy outfit of a lettings agency and . . . *him*. Ask around, see if you can get any other recommendations – get some different quotes too.'

'She's right,' Dad says to Mum. 'I'm not taking any more advice from that woman.'

'Are you alright?' I sit down next to him at the table.

He looks pale and exhausted, and his hands shake as he lifts the mug to his lips.

'Not really.'

'He's not sleeping well,' Mum says. By contrast she's exceptionally perky, her grey curls tied up in a jaunty spotted headscarf.

'I can't stop seeing it . . . him . . .' Dad says. 'Can't stop thinking about what we've done. Whether we've made a huge mistake. I should have gone to the police – we could have said it was self-defence. He was a criminal, after all.'

'We've been over this,' Mum says. 'What's done is done. We can't change it. And we have to keep in mind that the world is essentially a better place without him. Think of all those protest marches we've been on – that was what we wanted, wasn't it? A better place for the generations that come after us.'

'Not like this, though,' Dad says.

'It's not ideal, but it's done now. And who's come looking for him, after all? The police, and that giant oaf, Smith. Nobody else. I'm sure his clients are disappointed they can't get hold of him, but it's been over a week and no one has missed him on a personal level.'

Into the silence that follows this pronouncement, my phone rings. Dad jumps and tea spatters from his mug onto his hand and the table.

'Hello?'

'Hello, is that . . . Mrs Patterson?' says a timid female voice.

I haven't been called that since Zach was at primary school and one of his teachers couldn't fathom that although Martin and I were married, I hadn't taken his name.

'Yes,' I say, too tired to argue the toss.

'I'm sorry to bother you, but my name's Hayley. I'm a . . . sort of a . . . friend of your son, Zach. From university.'

'Oh.'

I trace a pattern in the crumbs on the table with my forefinger.

'How did you get my number?'

'One of my friends has been working in the admissions office, doing data entry,' she admits, embarrassed. 'I asked her to look it up for me. You won't . . . tell anyone, will you?'

'No, don't worry. Are you one of his flatmates?'

'No, we do the same course.'

A faint bell rings in my head. Hayley. Zach mentioned her. Said they didn't have much in common.

'I wanted to check if he was OK. I went round to his flat and the others told me he'd gone home. They weren't sure if he was ever coming back. I've called him a couple of times, and texted, but he hasn't got back to me. I was a bit worried, the way he disappeared off the face of the earth.'

'That's so kind of you.' I'm moved by her concern for him. 'He's just taking a bit of time out. I hope he's going to come back. He'd had some . . . trouble with his flatmates.' I shouldn't talk about Zach behind his back, but the chance to find out a bit more about his university life is irresistible. Mum and Dad watch me intently.

'Yeah, they mentioned that,' she says cautiously. We're dancing around each other, neither of us wanting to put our foot in it. I decide to be a bit more direct.

'He said he felt isolated from them, that they were leaving him out, ignoring him.'

'Mm.'

'What? Please tell me. I'd rather know if there's something else going on.'

'He definitely had become isolated from the others in the flat but I'm not sure it was totally their fault.'

'What do you mean?' Of course I know exactly what she means. It's what Martin's been saying all along. Zach isolated himself. Getting high is more important to him than anything else.

'They said they tried to include him at first, but he never wanted to go out or do anything except . . . well . . .'

'It's alright, I know about his . . . habit.' I force the word out, foreign on my tongue. As much as I try to tell myself that Zach's primary problem is anxiety exacerbated by mean, bullying flat-mates, there's a little voice in my head that won't stop asking if in fact he's an addict.

'He spent all his time smoking in his room, so in the end they stopped bothering. It was the same with me. I tried to get him to come out with some of the others from our course, but he'd make excuses and in the end I kind of gave up. I'm sorry.'

'Don't apologise! I'm grateful to you for trying. And for phoning. I really appreciate it. I'll tell him you called.'

I put my phone down on the table and try to take calming breaths. My instinct is to shout and scream that Zach's been lying to me about what's gone on at university, but my rational brain knows that's not really the case. The weed has clouded his judgement. I'm certain Hayley's version is much closer to the actual truth.

Oh, Caitlin, I wish you were here.

She was great with Zach – the cool aunt figure every teenager needs. With no children of her own, her natural instinct was to treat him as an adult and he responded brilliantly.

What should I do?

That's easy. Talk to him, she says.

'What's wrong?' Mum says. 'Who was that?'

'A friend of Zach's from university, Hayley. She's worried about him. She suggested he may have a problem with . . . marijuana.'

'Rubbish,' she says robustly. 'He's just a normal student. Goodness, if this Hayley had been around in our day, she'd have seen some sights to make her hair curl.'

'That's what I've always thought, but now . . . I'm not so sure. Martin certainly thinks he smokes too much, that it's isolating him.'

'He's being over-dramatic, as usual. Don't you think so, Heath?'

'I don't know. If Penny and Martin are worried, maybe there is cause for concern.'

'He was fine earlier,' she says. 'I really think you're all worrying over nothing.'

'You've seen him today?' I say. 'When?'

'Around ten. He popped in for a cup of tea.'

'What, out of the blue?'

Zach adores his grandparents but I've never known him to pay them an impromptu visit without me.

'We were a bit surprised,' Dad admits, 'but it was lovely to see him.'

The wheels of my mind click slowly round. I think of what Mum said earlier about getting cash from the bank. Surely he wouldn't have stooped that low. Please no.

'Where's the cash you got for the patio?' I have to force the words out.

'I left it on the hall table,' Dad says. 'You're not thinking . . .?'

'What?' Mum says, bewildered, looking from me to Dad and back again.

Dad gets up and leaves the room, his face set. He returns, leafing through a pile of twenty-pound notes. When he gets to the end, he starts again, this time counting out loud as he places each one on the table in front of him.

'There's £100 missing,' he says woodenly.

'He wouldn't have . . .' I begin, but there's a tell-tale note of doubt.

'You can't think Zach took it?' Mum says, appalled.

'Where's it gone then?' Dad says.

'Maybe you mis-counted earlier,' Mum's hopefulness reflects the longing of my heart, the pleading for it not to be true.

'No,' he says. 'I checked it twice. I've got the receipt from the cash point.' He extracts a small slip of paper from his pocket and hands it to Mum. She looks at it for a long moment and places it on the table in front of her with a trembling hand, sorrow etched into her features. Her earlier insouciance has vanished and I think she might cry.

An unfamiliar emotion boils within me. It takes me a moment to recognise it because I'm so unaccustomed to feeling it in relation to Zach. I'm used to experiencing sympathy, concern, love, but now I feel anger – hot and sour, curdling inside me. How dare he do this to my parents – his own grandparents – who have been through so much recently? I've excused him so many times over the years, but I have reached my limit. I stab at my phone, calling him, but it goes straight to voicemail. I don't leave a message. I've been too indulgent with Zach. I've enabled him and this is the result. It has to stop.

Chapter 32

I prowl around my living room like a caged tiger. Zach's phone is still going to voicemail. Reluctantly, I call Saul.

'Hello?' he croaks.

'It's Penny, Zach's Mum. Is he with you?'

'No, he's not here.'

Do you know where he is?'

'Er . . . no. Sorry.'

No one who has parented a teenager would have any trouble spotting this as an obvious lie.

'Saul, you don't have to protect him. I don't care what he's doing. I don't care if he's gone to buy drugs.' Now who's lying? Of course I care. 'I just need to know where he is.'

'He texted me to say he was going to get some gear.'

'Where? Not from Smith? I thought you didn't have his number?'

'We don't.' He sounds disappointed.

'Who is he getting it from then?'

'He's gone over to Blackhawk Leys.'

I give a sharp intake of breath. Blackhawk Leys is a notorious sink estate between here and Blackhawk Point on the south coast. It's probably hideously snobby and middle class of me but even in my current state of rage, the idea of Zach roaming around there horrifies me.

'Does he know someone over there?'

'No, but everyone knows there's dealers there, and since Cooper disappeared and we can't get hold of Smith, he thought it was worth a try.'

'Jesus Christ, Saul, you two are so bloody naïve! Why didn't you go with him? How's he getting there? It's five miles away.'

'There's a bus,' Saul says. 'Every half an hour from the bus station in town.'

'Have you heard from him? He's been gone for hours.'

'No, I can't get through. I was a bit worried about that actually,' he admits.

'Not worried enough to call me, though? Anything could have happened to him. I need to go. Call me if you hear from him.'

I resume my pacing. What should I do? The protective mother in me wants to jump in the car and drive the streets looking for him, but should I simply let him take his chances?

Caitlin, help me, I mutter.

It's obvious, she says. *Call Martin.*

She's right. Martin is the only other person in the world who will understand how I feel. Unfortunately he's not answering his mobile. Perhaps he's out on one of his interminable, Elaine-avoiding bike rides. I leave a mildly hysterical message and hang up. Then I remember that I have Elaine and Martin's landline number stored in my phone. Martin solemnly gave it to me along with her address on the day he moved out of our marital home. I never thought I'd want or need to use it, but these are exceptional circumstances. I call it, praying Martin answers.

'Hello?' Elaine sounds suspicious, as most people do when their landline rings.

'Hi Elaine, it's Penny . . . Whitlock,' I add in clarification in case she's got a friend called Penny.

'Oh!' Surprise is added to her suspicion.

'I'm sorry to bother you, but is Martin there? I can't get him on his mobile.'

'No, sorry, he's out on a bike ride.'

Of course he bloody is.

'Are you OK? Can I help at all?'

Tears prick at the backs of my eyes. I'm not sure I can cope with her being nice to me in my current state. I've not had much to do with her for obvious reasons, but I'm self-aware enough to know she's bound to be more of a monster in my imagination than she could ever be in reality.

'It's Zach. He's gone off . . . somewhere . . .' I don't want to mention drugs as I'm not sure how much Martin has told her. 'I'm a bit worried about him.'

'I'm sure he's fine – hang on, Martin's back, he's coming up the drive.'

She goes off and I hear distant voices and then Martin's on the line, panting with exertion.

'What's up, Pen?'

'It's Zach. He . . . he took some money from Mum and Dad's house.'

'Took? What, you mean stole?'

'Yes.'

'Oh, Pen.'

'You don't have to say it, Martin. It's my fault. I've over-indulged him, I've minimised everything. I couldn't see that he had a real problem, but I can now.'

'I wasn't going to say that,' he says softly. 'Where is he now?'

'That's the thing. His phone's off so I called Saul who says Zach's gone to Blackhawk Leys to try and buy drugs.'

'Blackhawk Leys? Bloody hell, Pen.'

'What?' says Elaine in the background. 'What about Blackhawk Leys?'

'Zach's gone there to try and buy . . . you know,' he says to her. 'How long has he been gone?' he asks me.

'I'm not sure, I don't know what time he went out. Martin, what if something's happened to him?'

'Right,' he says decisively. 'I'll come straight round to you and we'll drive over there and see if we can find him.'

'Martin, no!' Elaine hisses. 'You can't go to Blackhawk Leys. What about the baby?'

'The baby will be perfectly safe here, inside you,' he says with a touch of irritation that I find shamefully pleasing. 'I'll see you in fifteen, Pen.'

Ten minutes later, my doorbell rings and I buzz him up. I was expecting him to be still in one of his hideous cycling outfits but he's in well-fitting jeans, dark-brown boots and a chunky roll-neck jumper I haven't seen before.

'I thought you'd been on a bike ride,' I say, waving a hand at his outfit.

'I had. I was sweaty so I got changed quickly. Are you OK?'

'Yes,' I say. 'Not really. No.' I crumple, and he steps forward and takes me in his arms.

'Hey, Pen, don't worry. It's going to be alright.'

I bury my face in the thick cable knit of his sweater and find my arms slipping round his waist out of pure habit. I breathe in the familiar scent of him and am hit by a tidal wave of longing – not sexual, but merely the desire for the comfort of facing the world from the familiarity of a long-term relationship. My marriage was far from perfect and certainly not exciting, but Martin is not a bad man and it is so tiring always being alone. There's a part of me that never wants to let go. I pull back a little, our faces still close. For a blurry second it feels as if we're going to kiss but then we hear a key in the door and spring apart as if we've been electrified.

Zach appears in the doorway, stopping stock still when he sees both of us. His T-shirt is ripped at the neck and a yellow bruise blossoms on his cheek.

'What happened?' Martin says, crossing the room towards him.

I stand rooted to the spot, trembling with a relief dulled by the knowledge of what Zach has done.

'I'm fine,' he says.

'No you're not.' I find my voice. 'You are very far from fine. We know what you've done.'

'What do you mean?' he says, guarded.

'You stole a hundred pounds from Grandma and Grandpa!' The words burst from me in a torrent. 'What did you get for it? Was it worth it?'

'No I . . . it wasn't like that . . .'

'Wasn't like what? Stealing from two vulnerable old people who love you more than anything in the world? They were so happy that you'd popped in to see them. What did you get? Anything good?'

I blaze over and start rooting in the pockets of his parka.

'Hey, Penny . . .' Martin says.

Zach pushes me away.

'I didn't get anything, OK? I got mugged. They took the money and my phone.'

Old habits die hard and for a millisecond my instinct is to comfort him but I can't, I won't.

'Good,' I say harshly.

His eyes widen in shock.

'I mean it. I'm glad this has happened. It's what you deserve.'

'Mum . . .' His voice cracks and I want to melt, I want to go to him, but I harden myself.

'No. You've gone too far. I want you out of here.'

'What?' His face pales beneath the bruising.

'I mean it,' I say, steeling myself. 'You've got a perfectly good room at university, which your dad and I are paying for. You can go back there. I cannot look at you right now. How could you do that to Grandma and Grandpa after all the stress they've been under lately?'

'I can't go back to uni tonight, it's too late,' he says plaintively.

'You can stay with me tonight,' Martin says. 'We'll all sit down and talk, when everyone's less stressed.'

'By everyone you mean me, I suppose? I'm not stressed, I'm furious.' It's as if every negative emotion that I've ever felt towards Zach and suppressed is rolling out of me, an unstoppable force.

'What about Elaine?' Zach says to Martin.

'She'll be fine. Come on, let's go.'

I follow them to the front door. As they step into the vestibule outside the flat, Zach looks back at me, silently pleading with me to forgive him. I slam the door.

In my pocket, my phone begins to ring. I take it out and see Janine's name flashing. Oh no. The meeting. The one that started – I check the time – half an hour ago. I'm so tempted not to answer it, but that'd only make things worse.

'Janine. I'm so sorry. I got held up but I'm on my way.'

'Don't bother,' she says icily. 'I suppose you don't have an actual reason for not turning up?'

'My son. He went missing.'

'Your son? Isn't he an adult?' she says acidly.

'Well, yes . . .'

'And have you found him now?'

'As a matter of fact, we have but—'

'I see. In that case I'm sure you'll agree that given you were already on a written warning I have no option but to terminate your employment. HR will be in touch.'

Everything is falling apart. I sink to the floor, my back to the front door and wish with all my might that I had never laid eyes on Cooper Brownlow.

Chapter 33

Zach's been at Martin's for a few days now. Martin reports that he's staying in his room, not joining them for mealtimes. He's refusing to go back to university but at least he's not smoking.

The one bright spot about me losing my job is I can keep a better eye on Mum and Dad. Dad, having always had a tendency towards the strong and silent, becomes more withdrawn and morose by the day. Mum, on the other hand, has gone the other way. A kind way of viewing it would be to say that the trauma has rendered her manic, that her almost hyperactive behaviour is a type of PTSD, but I fear that in reality she's got her spark back. That what we've done to Cooper has energised her. Neither of them has mentioned Zach since the discovery of the missing money.

I jump every time my phone rings or the doorbell goes. Woodford Peters, the lettings agency, have called a few times but I've ignored them. I assume they've been trying and failing to contact Cooper too, and I don't feel up to a conversation with the hapless Dean.

I sit on my laptop in Mum and Dad's kitchen, half-heartedly looking for jobs online, although I'm not sure who will want to hire me seeing as I was fired for poor performance. I need to find something, somehow. I've got enough to cover next month's mortgage and bills, and that's it. The well will have run dry. What am I going to do?

I can't stop worrying too about whether anyone's going to come looking for Cooper. Scott seemed a nice bloke, but how long will that last if he starts to suspect we've done something to his brother? Or there might be someone else in Cooper's life who's noticed he's gone missing. I dig Cooper's phone out from the depths of my bag where I've been keeping it. It's been switched off since that day in the basement. The idea of turning it on makes me shrivel inside. It's not just the grimness of the dick pics and the nudes. Looking at his contacts, his daily inter- actions makes him more real, and the only way I can cope with what we've done is by seeing him as a monster. However, I need to know who, if anyone, is looking for him. I switch it on and as soon as it connects to the Wi-Fi it starts pinging with messages and missed calls. I'm about to go through them when the door- bell rings. I jump up with a start, shove the phone into my back pocket and dash into the hall, Dottie yapping at my heels.

When I open the door, I'm struck by the folly of not answer- ing my phone to Woodford Peters. Instead of the spotty visage of Dean, I am greeted by the sight of Julie Woodford herself in a cloud of Dior's Poison, resplendent in tight leather trousers, a waist-length cream fur coat and full makeup.

'Oh! Good morning. Be quiet, Dottie.' I bend and take hold of her collar. She's normally extremely docile, but she strains at my hand and growls at Julie, who wrinkles her nose as if Dottie has relieved herself on her shoes.

'Where is he?' she demands.

I give Dottie a final remonstrative pat and stand up straight. No point asking who she means.

'I've no idea.' I need to keep on with this lie, 'I'm keen to find him myself. He hasn't paid the rent and we haven't seen him for almost three weeks. I was going to call you in fact, to see if you'd heard from him.'

'Really?' She raises one immaculately plucked and groomed eyebrow. 'You don't seem that keen. I've called you many times. I would have thought you'd have been eager to speak to me to see if I'd heard from him.'

'I was hoping to sort things out without involving you,' I say coldly. 'Last time we had a problem with Coop— Mr Brownlow, you weren't exactly falling over yourself to help me. And whilst we're on the subject, did you know he was recently arrested for drug dealing?'

'Only because you reported him,' she says. 'And I think we both know why you did that.'

'I did it because he'd been dealing drugs from my parents' house! As you obviously know very well. How could you have let him move in here?'

'You're just trying to get your own back on him because he doesn't want you.'

'I promise you I've got absolutely no interest in him in that regard,' I say grimly. Is there anyone Cooper didn't tell about our night together? 'Even less so since I discovered that he was in prison for drug dealing before he moved in here.'

'Yes, I know,' she says, looking me straight in the eye.

'Right. And you were happy to let him move in here, to my elderly, vulnerable parents' home?'

'He's done his time, paid his dues. He's a changed man. Everyone deserves a second chance,' she says, daring me to challenge her.

'Is that what he told you? What is it with you and him? You're like one of those insane women who marries someone on Death Row!'

'How dare you?' she says, taking a step closer, the scent of her perfume almost overwhelming me. 'I'm concerned for his well-being. I'd like you to let me in to the apartment so that I can check for myself that there's nothing amiss.'

'I'm afraid that won't be possible,' I say.

'In that case, I'll let myself in,' she says. 'I've brought my own set of keys that you provided when you engaged our services.'

'You can't do that,' I say weakly.

'Watch me.' She totters down the front steps in her spike-heeled ankle boots. In desperation, I follow her, Dottie scurrying along at my side, emitting a series of sharp barks. She extracts the key from her handbag and opens the door. I stand helplessly in the doorway as, following in the footsteps of both the police and Smith, she searches the flat for any sign of him.

'He hasn't done a runner,' she says finally, obstinately. 'He wouldn't, I know he wouldn't. Why is his car still on the drive? Where is he? What have you done with him?'

'I have no idea what you mean,' I say, the frost in my words hiding a roiling panic. 'I'm telling you that a tenant you placed in my elderly parents' house not only refused to pay the rent but is a convicted criminal, and you're suggesting I've done . . . I don't know . . . what exactly are you suggesting?'

'He's not answering his phone,' she says stubbornly. 'He hasn't got his car. Where is he?'

She gets her phone out and there's a second where I don't foresee what's about to happen but then she starts tapping at her screen with her long, curved, magenta talons. She's calling Cooper and I feel his phone, still switched on, like a burning brand in my pocket. It rings. Her mouth falls open in shock and she brandishes her phone at me like a weapon.

'Why have you got his phone? What have you done to him?'

'I haven't done anything! I . . .' My mind works furiously. 'I found his phone in here when I was looking for clues as to where he'd gone. I took it so that I could give it to the police.'

'You're lying.' Her eyebrows furrow, foundation flaking in her crows' feet. 'Where is he?'

She crouches down to look under the bed as if I might have him secreted there. As she does so, something about her being down on Dottie's level sends the little dog into overdrive. She barks furiously and scurries over to Julie.

'Get off!' Julie shoves her roughly away.

'Hey! Don't do that!' I say, moving to gather Dottie up and take her back upstairs, but she escapes and lunges at Julie's backside.

'Ow!' Julie stands up. 'That stupid thing bit me! Get away!' She kicks out at Dottie who cringes away and whines at my feet.

Julie twists round and pulls down the waistband of her trousers, revealing two small puncture marks each oozing a drop of blood.

'Look what she's done!' she gasps.

I pick Dottie up and cradle her, unable to find the words to apologise. Partly because, although she's weirdly vulnerable, I can't find it in myself to feel sorry for this woman, but mainly because I'm distracted by what I can see underneath the bite mark: at the very top of Julie's right buttock, there's a tattoo. A tattoo of a bird in flight identical to the one I saw in the nude photos on Cooper's phone.

Chapter 34

A couple of days later, I'm hanging out at Mum and Dad's again. They come breezing in from the garden, roses in their cheeks and dirt under their fingernails. Spring is in the air and it almost feels like old times, before the world spun on its axis. Before Cooper. I told them about Julie's visit, but they've taken the news that she doesn't believe Cooper has done a runner with equanimity – especially Mum.

Cooper's phone sits in my bedside drawer like an unexploded landmine. I need to make the lie I told Julie into a truth by handing it in to the police, but I'm scared it'll make them suspicious of me.

'We've done a marvellous job of tidying up the rose garden,' she says brightly. 'Luckily, thanks to the ghastly leylandii, no one can see into the garden anyway. But I think the way it looks now, if anyone does come into the garden, we could get away with saying the roses have been affected by some sort of blight and we've had to cut them right back.'

It's faintly chilling how matter of fact she sounds.

'And look at this!' Mum lays a spray of small, yellow, purple and orange-red flowers on the table. 'Tropaeolum tricolor. It's having a bumper year.'

'Lovely,' I say, brushing off the fine sprinkling of earth she's deposited on the keyboard of my laptop.

'We're down to the last few Brussels at the allotment,' Dad says with a wink. He seems brighter than he has of late, which I suppose is a good thing. 'We're going up there after lunch – I'll bring you some back.' My hatred for sprouts has always been a running joke between us, but I find it hard to raise a smile about anything at the moment. This is the longest I've ever been without speaking to Zach. Martin's sorted him out a new phone but he hasn't texted or called me. Even though I know he's safe, our estrangement is a dull ache that refuses to ease.

'Have you had any luck with the patio?' I think I'll feel better – safer – when the slabs have been laid. Until they are, it feels as if Cooper's body could be discovered at any moment.

'Not yet,' Mum says. 'I'm asking around.'

'We need to get it done as soon as possible.' I can't stop thinking about the tattoo on Julie's buttock. It was bad enough when I thought she was concerned about him as a client of her agency, but now I know that they were involved . . . I hesitate to say romantically as there was nothing very romantic about those photos, but . . . intimately. She's genuinely concerned about his wellbeing. What if she starts asking questions elsewhere – goes to the police? At the moment, they think he's skipped bail and is on the run from them, which suits our purposes very well. But if she can convince them he's come to harm, they're going to start their investigations here, his last-known address.

The doorbell rings and Dad and I start.

'Are you expecting anyone?' I ask.

'No,' Dad says. 'What is it now?'

'It's probably the post. I'll go.' Mum sweeps out, leaving Dad and I eyeballing each other over the table. She opens the door and we hear voices, then Mum comes back in, her face a blank mask, followed by the two police officers who came last time.

'You remember um . . .' She waves a hand in their general direction. 'Oh dear, I'm terribly sorry, your names have gone clean out of my head.'

I regard her suspiciously. She was fine a moment ago, fit as a fiddle and exulting over her Tropalum whatsit. Suddenly she's an OAP – a harmless old dear who can't distinguish one day from another.

'I'm DS Newman,' he says, 'and this is my colleague DC Blake.'

I stand up, dry-mouthed. Have they somehow found out about Cooper's phone?

'Is everything OK?' My tongue feels too big for my mouth and my body doesn't seem to belong to me.

'Why don't we sit down?' Blake's hair is woven into a long French plait that hangs halfway down her back. I'm assailed by a previously forgotten memory of Dad coaxing my hair into a similar style for primary school. It must have been when Mum was off at Greenham Common. I close the lid of my laptop and we take our seats around the table, awaiting our fate. I keep my eyes on the two police officers, fearful of giving something away if I look at Mum or Dad, although it may well be too late to worry about that. This may be the moment I've been fearing and imagining since I saw Cooper's dead body splayed on the ground.

'We've come to inform you of some news regarding your tenant, Mr Cooper Brownlow,' DS Newman says. 'Obviously you had registered some complaints against him, and you know that he was subsequently arrested for drug dealing and has since disappeared, breaking his bail conditions.'

'Yes.' I have to tell them about the phone before this goes any further. I can't be seen to have been withholding information.

'I've been meaning to call you, actually,' I say quickly, not giving myself a chance to back out. 'I found something in Cooper's flat. I was down there . . . checking things, you know, because we're worried that he's gone missing, and I found . . . I found a phone. . . . I was going to come and hand it in, but you've saved me the trouble, ha ha!'

'When did you find it?' Blake says.

'Oh . . . recently . . . the other day – yesterday, I think it was.'

'And you're only thinking to tell us now?'

'Well, he may have had more than one, I mean he was a drug dealer, so I thought it more than likely didn't mean anything.'

'We'll be the judge of that,' she says reprovingly.

'We'll certainly be very interested in the contents of that phone,' Newman breaks in, 'particularly in light of the news that we're about to share with you.'

I clasp my hands together under the table, every muscle in my body tensed.

'We have reason to believe that Mr Brownlow has been murdered,' he says.

'Oh God,' Dad chokes.

Mum sits in silence, her expression shrewd until DC Blake turns to look at her when her eyes film over in a parody of vacancy.

'Have you . . .' I was going to ask if they've found the body (although obviously they can't have done) but I worry it sounds too knowing. 'What happened to him?'

'That's not entirely clear at this point,' Newman says.

'So how do you know . . .? You said you have reason to believe he's been . . .' I can't bring myself to say the word.

'Yes,' he says. 'I'm afraid what we're about to tell you is rather disturbing, but we need to give you the full facts. We wouldn't normally divulge this amount of information but we have our reasons in this case.'

There's a sense that we as a family are holding our collective breaths, our fate hanging on their next words.

'Mr Brownlow had an ... associate called Neville Smith,' Newman says. 'A gentleman known to us by virtue of various drug-related offences over the years.'

'Yes, I'm aware of him,' I say, trying to keep my voice level. 'He came here looking for Cooper a week or so ago.' It seems important to tell the truth as far as is feasible. In the unlikely event that Smith has been to the police to report Cooper missing, I want my story to tally with his.

'We received an anonymous tip-off from a member of the public that Smith and Brownlow had had a falling out about some money owed by Brownlow to Smith,' Newman says.

'I see.' That wasn't what I was expecting. Can I dare to hope the finger of suspicion has fallen elsewhere than on us?

'The caller said they had reason to suspect that Smith had harmed Brownlow.' Newman continues. 'They also provided enough detail for us to gain a search warrant for Mr Smith's home and car.'

The two officers exchange a glance. Newman gives a nod and Blake speaks.

'Unfortunately, when we arrived at his home, Mr Smith absconded out the back. We gave chase, but he evaded capture. We are confident we will find him soon but in the meantime we do need you to be vigilant, which is why we are sharing this information with you. If you see him or hear from him, we would urge you to call 999 immediately. In the subsequent search of his car, we found something that, when we do catch up with Mr Smith, gives us sufficient evidence to arrest him on suspicion of the murder of Cooper Brownlow.'

I hope they can't sense the confusion emanating from the three of us. At any rate Dad looks thoroughly confused, as am I, but when I sneak a quick peek at Mum, she's half-smiling. I don't know if this is part of her 'forgetful old lady' act for the police, or something more worrying.

'What did you find?' I ask.

Esther Blake leans forward, elbows resting on the table, her light-blue eyes unreadable.

'We found Cooper Brownlow's severed finger.'

Chapter 35

We manage to hold it together until the police have left, but as soon as the door has closed behind them, Dad leans against it for support, sagging at the knees.

'How the hell did his finger get into Smith's car?'

I start to answer that I have no idea, when I realise he's addressing himself to Mum. She shrugs innocently.

'Don't pull that confused old lady shit with me!' he says.

'Dad!' I'm shocked. Dad rarely swears, and I'm not sure I've ever seen him really angry with anyone, let alone Mum.

'Well, do you know how it happened?' he asks me.

'No, of course not.'

'Neither do I,' he says grimly. 'That only leaves one person. Sissy?'

'It was an insurance policy,' Mum says as casually as if she's talking about third party, fire and theft.

'Jesus, Mum! What did you do?'

'We took turns with the digging that night. One of us would go in for a rest and the other would crack on with it and vice versa. When Dad was inside, I sawed off one of Cooper's fingers – don't worry, I was wearing gloves throughout. I thought it might come in handy – and I was right, wasn't I?'

'But . . .' Questions crowd my mind. 'What did you do with it? When did you put it in Smith's car?

'That night I just popped it in a sandwich bag and put it in the freezer drawer with the soft fruits from the allotment. Then when Smith was here the other day, I thought he was the obvious choice.'

'To frame for murder, you mean?' I say.

'Yes, exactly!' She says, pleased I've understood.

'Sissy, this is . . . too much.' Dad's face is grey. 'Doing what . . . we did is one thing, but sending someone else to prison for it?'

'I'm sure that man is no stranger to prison – any more than his "associate" Cooper was,' Mum says. 'He's a drug dealer and a thug. Think of the young people whose lives he's ruined. You can't argue that the streets aren't a safer place without him.'

I think of Zach, sitting alone in the spare room at Martin and Elaine's, jittery and miserable, instead of being off at university having the time of his life. He's not living, he's merely existing. Can I blame drugs for that? I'd like to, because if the fault doesn't lie with marijuana there's a chance that, as his mother, it lies with me.

'Even if that's true, Mum, the fact is he isn't off the streets, is he? He evaded capture, as they put it. He's very much on the streets – he could be on our street, coming after us, if he's worked out who put that finger in his car.'

'He'll never suspect us,' she says blithely. 'We're not the sort of people who go round chopping other people's fingers off.'

'Apparently we are,' Dad says pointedly.

'For goodness' sake, you two,' she says, exasperated. 'We made a mistake. Your father didn't mean to kill Cooper. Do you believe he should spend the rest of his life in prison? We went through all this on the night in question. It was an accident. And if this Smith character goes to prison for it – well, it's no more than he deserves. I'm certain there's a whole raft of crimes that he's committed and got away with. Consider this karma.'

'Karma is generally meted out by the universe,' I say. 'It's not for you to decide.'

'When did you get so holier than thou?' she snaps. 'The moment we decided not to call the police that night, we lost any moral authority. The "right" thing to do would have been to own up, take responsibility for what happened and face the consequences. We didn't do that. It's like at Greenham Common – the police were against us; as far as they were concerned we were in the wrong, but we weren't, were we? We had the moral right on our side. And we're operating by our own moral code now. That's all we can do. Isn't it, Heath?'

'I . . . I don't . . .' He's still propping himself up against the front door. I'm pretty sure if he tried to take a step, he'd collapse on the hall floor.

'Dad, come and sit down.' I take his arm and lead him through to the kitchen where I lower him into a dining chair. Mum follows and sits opposite him.

'I'm sorry I didn't tell you about the finger before. I wasn't sure they'd ever find it, so I thought there might not be any need for you to know.'

'I don't think it's the not telling him that's the problem,' I say. 'More the hacking off of body parts and planting them as evidence to frame someone for a crime they didn't commit.'

'Ugh.' She claps her hands together, dirt from the garden under her nails. 'We're going round in circles here. Someone's got to go to prison for the crime. Who would you rather it be – your father, or a career criminal?'

'And I presume it was you that called the police anonymously suggesting Smith was involved?' I say. 'So you must have known – hoped – there was a good chance they'd find the finger.'

'You said yourself that the woman from the lettings agency – Julie – was suspicious. She was bound to go to the police sooner or later,' Mum says. 'I thought it prudent to get in there before she did. And it worked, didn't it?' she says, challenging me to disagree. 'They think he did it. If Julie goes to the police now, it'll look like she's in cahoots with him, trying to get him out of it.'

'So . . . what do you suggest we do?' I say.

'Nothing,' she says calmly. 'Sit tight and let the police do their job. They'll find Smith soon enough, he can't have gone far. Then it'll all be over.'

She stands up, brushes some lingering dirt from her hands and fills the kettle at the sink, business satisfactorily concluded. Dad watches her wonderingly, as if he hardly knows his wife of more than fifty years at all.

Chapter 36

As I let myself into my cold, silent flat, my head still filled with disturbing images of my mother hacking off Cooper's finger, my phone begins to ring. I scrabble in my bag for it. It's Martin. What now?

'Have you seen Zach?'

Oh God.

'No. Why?'

'He's taken money out of Elaine's bag and gone,' he says, dull and flat.

'Why did she leave it lying around?'

'Don't blame Elaine!' he says. 'This is on Zach and no one else.'

'I know, I know. You're right. It was good of her to let him stay at all under the circumstances.'

'I thought . . .' he says miserably, 'I thought I could get through to him, if I just gave him time, patience. Elaine said someone picked him up. She heard the door bang closed, looked out of the window and saw Zach getting into a car.'

'What kind? It wasn't a black SUV, was it?'

Zach wouldn't be so monumentally stupid as to go off with Smith, would he? Although thinking about it, Smith's car must be in police custody anyway.

'No, she said it was a small car, a Fiat she thinks.'

'Have you asked Saul if he knows anything?'

'I haven't got his number.'

'I'll call him now. I'll let you know.'

I hang up and ring Saul. He answers after a couple of rings.

'Saul! Thank God. Have you seen Zach?'

'No, I haven't seen him, but . . .' He sounds awkward.

'What? Spit it out, Saul, I don't have time for this. Has he gone to buy gear?'

'Yes, that's what he said.'

'Where? Has he gone to Blackhawk Leys again?'

'No, he . . . I was thinking I should ring you actually. I told him not to go, but he wouldn't listen.'

'Go where? Who's he getting it from?'

'That Smith bloke.'

'What?' Icy fingers trickle down my spine. 'Are you sure? Has he spoken to him? I thought you didn't have his number.'

'We don't, but some woman called him earlier and said Smith had taken over Cooper's . . . clients, and she could pick Zach up and take him to him. He asked me if I wanted him to get me anything. I said no, said he shouldn't go, but he wouldn't take any notice.'

'What woman?'

'I dunno.'

'Do you know where she was taking him?'

'No, he didn't say. I don't think he knew.'

I blow out a long breath, like a silent whistle, trying to calm my whirling thoughts. 'Smith is dangerous, Saul. He's . . . the police think he may have murdered Cooper. They tried to arrest him but he escaped.'

'What?' he says, sounding suddenly like the eleven-year-old boy who used to come over to play with Zach on the Xbox.

'I haven't got time to explain, I need to think. If you hear from him, call me.'

I hang up without giving him a chance to say anything more. My fingers clumsy, almost numb, I swipe my way to the app.

'Please please please,' I mutter as it tries to locate Zach. The fact that his phone went to voicemail means it's unlikely to find him anyway, and even if he does have signal, I bet he hasn't enabled location sharing on his new phone. I watch the spinning icon, my sense of doom worsening the longer it goes on. Eventually it stops and the words 'No location found' pop up. Images of Zach as a baby, a toddler, a teenager, fill my mind and then all the previous Zachs get blotted out by a vision of him as he is now – hurt, confused, scared. The police. I need to call the police. Smith is a wanted man – a dangerous murderer as far as they're concerned. They'll find him. I go to call 999 but before I have a chance, a text pings up on my phone from a number I don't recognise. There's no message, just a video. I press play. It takes a few seconds to load, then opens on a close-up of two terrified eyes. Nobody else would recognise them, a dull blue flecked with grey and a darker-blue ring around the iris. Nobody but me because they used to be part of me. I grew them inside my body. I feel like I've been hit by a train. The camera pans out to show my darling, my little boy, tied to a chair, tape across his mouth. He's not struggling – in fact he sits perfectly still, almost frozen in place with terror. Smith strolls into shot and with a violent wave of nausea I see he is holding a small handgun.

'Hello, Penny,' he says genially into the camera. 'As you can see, I've got Zach here with me. It's not a nice feeling is it, to see someone you love hurting? So you understand how Julie here feels.' Julie? Julie Woodford is the woman who picked Zach up? Smith waves the hand holding the gun in the direction of the camera. Zach flinches and Smith gives a little smile. 'Julie was very fond of Cooper. She didn't like it when your parents took against him, started spreading lies about him. She told me all about it – oh yeah, we know each other. As you've probably gathered, Julie and Cooper were . . . friendly. Very friendly. Anyone that's close to Cooper is going to know me and all, because we work together – or worked, should I say – very closely. And one day Cooper wasn't there any more – but his car was. His phone was. And there you were, snooping around his flat. And then the day I came to visit, somebody put Cooper's finger in my car. Now I know I didn't kill Cooper, and I know for a fact that the finger wasn't there before I paid you a visit. So it's not too big a leap, is it, to suspect that you and your parents know a bit more about what happened to him than you're letting on.'

Casually, he raises the gun to Zach's left temple. Zach strains his head away from it and lets out a strangled whimper from behind his gag, but the gun follows. My head is swimming and I can't take in enough air.

'So here's what you're going to do,' Smith goes on. 'Your parents are going to go to the police and tell them the truth – whatever that is. Either they confess to murdering Cooper or you do – whichever way you want to play it – and you take the police to wherever his body is and you show them and you take a video of you showing them and you send it to me. I'll give you four hours – 'til 7pm tonight. If I haven't heard from you by then . . . pow!' He mimes pulling the trigger and Zach's head jerks back, his eyes wild and pleading.

'And don't think for a second that this gun's not real – that I'm not the kind of man who knows how to get a hold of a gun. I'm well connected, don't you worry about that.'

Smith nods towards the camera to indicate that he's finished. Instead of tapping to stop the video Julie Woodford must have accidentally switched the camera back to selfie mode, because for a second I see her face before the screen goes blank. Although this whole thing is a horrific mess, it gives me a microscopic shred of hope because Julie looks as shocked and frightened as I am.

I feel as though I'm walking through water as I go back to the car and set off, calling Dad's mobile as I drive.

'Hello, love,' he says, his kind normality like a knife to my chest.

'Are you still at home?'

'No, we're up at the allotment. There's an awful lot to do you know, even at this time of year.'

'I need to talk to you. I'll be there in ten minutes.'

'What is it? Are you OK?'

'I can't do this on the phone. I'll see you shortly.'

I cut him off without another word and try to concentrate on keeping the car on the road, rather than on the fact that effectively what Smith has asked me to do is to choose between my parents and my only son.

Chapter 37

I park next to Mum and Dad's car, jump out and hotfoot it across the allotments.

'Hey, watch it!' A bearded, grey-haired man rears up beside me from where he's kneeling, tending to a frilly-leaved dark green vegetable. 'You're treading all over my kale!'

'Sorry,' I say, veering onto the path that leads between the plots, leaving him chuntering away in my wake.

'Hello, darling!' Mum says as I come racing over. 'Are you alright? This is Beryl, who's taken over Sheila's old allotment. And good news – she's recommended a brilliant patio company.'

'Hello.' Beryl, a woman of about my mother's age, holds out a wrinkled hand and smiles, revealing snaggled, yellowing teeth. I ignore her.

'I need to speak to you both in private. Where's Dad?'

'He's in the shed. Sorry, Beryl,' Mum says, 'My daughter seems to have lost her manners.'

I take Mum by the arm and hustle her inside the shed, where we find Dad boiling water on the primus stove.

'Tea, love?'

'No, there's no time. I got this video.'

'What video?' Mum says.

'I'll show you.' My words are almost swallowed by the terror that swirls inside me. I tap Play on the video and they watch it in silence, Dad raising his hand to his mouth as it unfolds.

'We need to get down the police station right now,' he says when it's finished. 'It's over. This has gone too far.'

'Really?' I say to him thickly, through unshed tears.

'Yes,' he says. 'Come on, Sissy.' He takes a couple of strides but halts in the shed doorway when he realises she's not following him.

'Unless . . .' she says.

'Unless what?' He turns round slowly. 'You would let our grandson die to save yourself . . . me . . . from . . . to stop people finding out what we've done?'

'No, of course not,' she says crossly as if he was accusing her of forgetting to buy milk. 'But what if there's a way to do both? Save Zach and not hand ourselves in?'

I gaze at her, speechless, unable to believe my own ears.

'Like what?' Dad is fit to explode. 'You saw that . . . oaf. He's got a gun!'

'Who's the woman at the end?' Mum says. 'Holding the camera?'

'That's Julie Woodford from the estate agents. You know – I told you she came looking for Cooper that time. She was in some sort of relationship with him.'

'Let's watch it again,' Mum says. 'There might be a clue as to where they've got him.' She holds up her hand to forestall what Dad's about to say. 'That'll help the police, whatever we decide to do.'

'Fine.' I hand it to her for them to watch, not able to bear putting myself through it for a third time.

'What's that noise?' Mum says, bending to get her ear closer to the phone.

'You could lift the phone instead of—' I break off. What does it matter now?

'What noise?' Dad says.

'You won't be able to hear it with your cloth ears,' she says.

'I'm wearing my hearing aids, I'll have you know. I can hear perfectly well.'

'Listen to this, then – in the background.'

She rewinds the video and holds it to his ear.

'Sounds like a train,' he says.

'Yes! I agree. But it's not passing by – it's starting up. I think it's pulling out of the station.'

'It does sound like that,' he admits. 'But who's to say which station?'

'They won't have had time to go far, will they? And they won't have wanted to risk taking him any further than they had to. It's got to be the station in town. Let me watch it again.'

This time she rummages in her bag for her glasses first and clicks Play for the third time. She stares at the screen intently, a tightening around her lips when Smith puts the gun to Zach's head the only sign she's finding it a distressing watch.

'Right there,' she pauses the video and shows me. 'Look, outside the window.'

'What? I can't see anything.'

'Tropaeolum tricolor!'

'What?' Is she finally losing her marbles?

'The yellow and red flowers I showed you this morning – from the garden – you remember.'

'Oh, yeah. Vaguely.' It feels like a million years ago – a happier time when our biggest problem was that my parents had murdered their tenant and buried him under the patio.

'I know where he is,' she says, her eyes shining triumphantly. 'There's this block of flats round the back of the station, quite run down, and I've always thought it strange that there's tropaeolum tricolor growing up the back of it – it's really rather rare. You know the one, Heath.'

'I think so.'

'OK, Mum, but how does this help us? In case you hadn't noticed, he's got a gun.'

'Exactly. We're wasting time,' Dad says. 'Seriously, Sissy. We need to go to the police.'

'But what if they don't believe us? You've seen how they treat us – like children. As if instead of gaining knowledge and wisdom we've regressed as we got older. If they won't believe us and we can't make them come to see the . . . the body . . . Then what? He's only given us four hours – what if we can't convince them in that time? Then we'll have to tell the police the truth about where Zach is and they'll go blazing in and Smith'll be like a cornered animal and God knows what he'll do. No, we need to get Smith out of there and then we can get in and free Zach. That Julie woman won't be a problem – you saw her at the end of the video. She's as terrified as Zach is. She's got herself in way too deep – there's no way she wants any blood on her hands.'

'Your mother might be right,' Dad says with a peculiar expression that I can't fathom. 'The most important thing is to get Zach out safely.'

'But . . . how?' An inferno of rage and fear builds inside me, threatening to boil over.

'Leave that to me,' she says calmly. 'Pen, can you send me that number? That the video came from.'

'But—'

'There's a can of petrol in the back of the car, isn't there?' she asks Dad.

'Yes, there should be.'

'I don't think you're meant to keep petrol in your car.' Why am I bothering? That's the least of my worries right now.

'Right, I'll take these.' She picks up a box of matches from beside the primus stove, and, after a moment's thought, her freshly sharpened, personalised garden shears, *Sempervirens* inscribed on the handle. She tucks them into the deep inside pocket of her gardening coat.

'What are you going to do?'

'It's easier if you don't know, but I've got a plan. I hope it works. Give me an hour or so. If it doesn't, we'll think again about going to the police. You two go out there and work on the allotment – make sure you're seen – in case you need an alibi. I'll be alright – no one will suspect a dotty old bird like me.'

What the hell is she going to do?

'Mum, this is madness. I won't let you go.'

She strokes my hair and cups my chin in her hand. 'That's awfully sweet of you, darling, but I'm afraid it's not up to you.'

'Dad? You can't be happy with this?'

'I've got as much chance of changing your mother's mind as I have of flying to the moon. Let her go.'

'See? Dad knows me.' They exchange a deep, knowing look.

'Fine. Take care, I suppose.' A completely useless imperative.

'Oh, I'm tough as old boots. I was at Greenham Common, don't forget. I'm not easily scared.'

'But that was a peaceful protest, wasn't it?' I say.

'Most of the time,' she says with a half-smile. 'I may not always have told your father everything that was going on. Right, I'm going. If I haven't contacted you in an hour . . .'

She doesn't finish the sentence, picking up the car keys and tramping out of the shed in her wellies. I try not to be overwhelmed by the fear that I'll never see my mother or my son again.

Chapter 38

'We'll wait until she's definitely gone,' Dad says, watching her go.

'And then what?' I say to him, perplexed.

'We're going after her. You don't think I'd let her go after that maniac alone with a can of petrol and a box of matches, do you?'

'But . . . you just did, didn't you?'

'I let her think I did,' he says. 'She was going anyway – there was no stopping her any more than there was when you were a child.'

A long-lost memory stirs within me of overhearing an argument between Mum and Dad. Mum was off somewhere – I didn't know where at the time, but it's obvious to me now that it must have been Greenham – and I heard Dad say she ought to be grateful that he was letting her do this. I was in the next room so couldn't see her, but I imagine her eyes were nearly popping out of her head. *Letting me? You're letting me? You don't get to 'let' me do anything.* If her voice had got any higher it would have been a shriek.

'Come on,' he says. 'She's gone. Got your car keys?'

'Everything alright?' Beryl calls over from the neighbouring plot as we race past. She's sitting in a camping chair, hands wrapped around a tin mug. Her plot is barren and empty, but

I suppose she has only recently taken it over. 'Sissy left in a hurry.'

'Yes, fine, fine,' Dad says. 'She remembered she had an appointment that she'd forgotten – well, originally she'd remembered it, then forgot and then remembered again at the last moment.'

'Oh dear, that sounds about right for us oldies!'

'Ha ha, yes,' Dad says mirthlessly. 'She . . . er . . . forgot something, so we've got to go after her. See you soon.'

Beryl gives a little wave.

'If we're quick we'll catch up with her,' Dad says as he does up his seatbelt.

'And do what, though?' I start the engine. 'What's she going to do?'

'I've got a vague idea,' Dad says.

'Can you direct me to these flats?'

'Head for the station and I'll tell you where to go when we get there.'

I swerve out of the car park and head in the direction of the railway station.

'Come on, come on,' Dad urges.

'I can't go any faster – there's pedestrians. I don't want another death on my conscience.'

'Bloody hell, what's happening here?' he says as we join the back of an unmoving line of traffic.

'It'll be cars turning right at the junction up ahead. It's always a nightmare at this time. It won't take long.'

'Turn around,' Dad says, twisting in his seat. 'You could cut down Walnut Avenue and join the main road further down.'

'I doubt that'd be any quicker. There's always a bit of a queue here but it moves faster than you think. See, here we go.'

The car in front starts to move. We inch forward and then grind to a halt again.

'Turn around, Pen!' he says, taking off his glasses to wipe sweat from his forehead. 'There must be some issue up ahead.'

'Fine, I'll try.'

I put my indicator on and attempt a three-point turn. I'm so agitated that I don't notice a car coming from the opposite direction until the driver blares his horn, gesturing and shouting from behind his windscreen. I hold a hand up in apology and try to swing back into the space I vacated, but the car behind me has moved up slightly meaning I can't fit back in. I try to indicate this to the driver on the other side of the road through a series of pointing and shrugging motions. He sits there, arms folded, belligerent. *Stupid cow* he mouths. At least, I think it's cow. My cheeks burn. Before I know it, Dad is unbuckling his seat belt and climbing out of the car.

'Dad, what are you doing?'

He strides over to the driver's side, towering above the car, and mimes a winding motion. Somewhat taken aback, the man rolls down his window.

'My wife is in danger,' Dad spits. 'My daughter and I are trying to get to her and neither of us is in the mood for your pathetic games. So reverse out of our way and piss off and find some other way of making yourself feel like a man.'

'Old fucking twat,' says the man, but his heart's not in it and he reverses sharply and waits. Dad strolls back and gets in beside me.

'Right, that absolute dingbat behind you hasn't left much room, but you've still just about got space to do a three-point turn if you go up on the opposite pavement.'

He talks me through it patiently, much as he did when he was teaching me to drive thirty-three years ago, and after bumping up on the kerb and thumping back down, we're on our way. He's right about cutting down Walnut Avenue, as dads usually are about these things. The rest of the journey runs smoothly and within five minutes we're pulling up opposite a bedraggled-looking, off-white block of flats, all peeling paint and ground-in grime.

'This is the one, I'm sure,' Dad says. 'Yes – there's our car. But where's your mother?'

'There she is,' I say, clocking her. She's put on a headscarf that reminds me of the one I used to disguise Cooper in the wheelchair that night. Surely it's not the same one? I narrow my eyes trying to spot any bloodstains.

The car that Mum planted the bloody finger in is obviously still in police custody, but Smith seemingly has an endless supply, as there's a black SUV with another helpfully personalised number plate – 5M1TH2 – parked about twenty metres down the road from the front of the flats. Mum takes a loose brick from the low wall that runs between the pavement and the scrubby grass that an estate agent would describe as a delightful shared garden, and smashes it through the passenger side window. The alarm wails, but she ignores it and shakes the petrol can vigorously through the jagged glass into the car. Two young women avert their eyes as they pass. I'm struck by how easy it is to get away with doing what you want. Nobody wants to get involved.

'What should we do? What's she going to do?' I say, in an agony of indecision.

'Wait,' Dad says, laying a hand on my arm. 'We're here if she needs us.'

I watch in sick fascination as she strikes a match and throws it through the broken window. Flames leap inside the car as she walks back towards the flats casually swinging the petrol can in one hand, the other holding the phone to her ear. She rounds the corner of the block, out of sight, and waits.

'Shall we go now?' I say. 'What's she doing?'

'She's phoning him,' Dad breathes, horrified but admiring. 'Wait and see.'

Twenty seconds later, Smith comes charging out and lets out a howl of fury when he sees the fire raging inside his car. There's a dingy newsagent's between the flats and his car and he runs in there. Instantly, Mum darts out from her hiding place and into the flats through the door that Smith has helpfully left open.

'What shall we do?' I plead with Dad again. 'We can't let her go in there all alone.'

Smith re-emerges from the newsagent's brandishing a fire extinguisher which he sprays frantically onto his car although the blaze shows little sign of dying down.

'We can't go in there now, he'll see us,' Dad says. 'We need to trust her.'

'Trust her? Trust her? This is madness!'

'Don't underestimate her. I know better than anyone that you do that at your peril. Drive over and park right outside, so we're there when they come out. We can leave our car here.'

'They? Do you really think . . .?'

'You know your mother.'

I'm beginning to understand that I don't know her half as well as he does, or she him.

'She won't be expecting us to be here, though.'

'Oh, she will,' he says. 'Go on, drive over there. Now, Penelope!'

Not wanting a repeat of the earlier fracas, I check both ways and swing across the road so I'm right outside the entrance. I leave the engine running, my gaze on Smith who doesn't seem to be getting the better of the fire. A middle-aged, suited man passing by pulls out his phone, requesting a fire engine and the police.

'Look, Dad, look!'

My heart gives an enormous leap as my mother charges out of the building, petrol can in one hand and garden shears in the other like Boudica the warrior queen with her shield and spear, closely followed by a stumbling but indubitably living Zach. He looks terrified, a bruise blooming purple around his eye to match the fading one on his cheek, the skin around his mouth raw, but he's alive, he's alive. Tears roll down my face.

'I told you,' Dad says, choked with pride. 'I told you.'

Mum bundles Zach into the back of the car and clambers in after him.

'I knew you'd be here,' she says, grinning breathlessly at Dad. 'Come on, Pen, let's get going.'

I don't need telling twice. It's tempting to drive past Smith so that he sees us but I resist, swinging the car around and heading off in the other direction, towards the police station.

'She helped me to free Zach, you know,' Mum says. 'That Julie. I knew the minute I saw her in that video that she didn't want to be there.'

As we reach the end of the road, I hear the distant sound of sirens.

Chapter 39

'I'm afraid DS Newman's been called out to a car fire,' DC Blake says, sitting down opposite the four of us. Sunlight slants through the open venetian blinds, casting shadow lines across the interview table between us. The brightness makes her appear paler than ever, her skin almost translucent. 'So you'll have to make do with me. Are you alright?' she says to Zach, clocking his bruises and cuts.

'He's fine,' Mum says. 'Not seriously hurt.'

'Worth getting a doctor to have a look at you all the same,' Blake says mildly. 'Now, what can I do for you?'

'This car fire, would it be near the flats behind the railway station?' Mum asks.

'Er . . . yes, I believe so.'

'So that was me.'

'I beg your pardon? You mean, that was your car?'

'No, it was Neville Smith's. I set fire to it.'

She looks up and blinks.

'I see.'

'Neville Smith has become obsessed with implicating us in Cooper Brownlow's disappearance,' Mum says. 'Earlier today, he sent a woman called Julie Woodford to abduct my grandson Zach, and sent this video to Penny. Show her, Pen.'

I pass my phone over and she watches it in silence.

'These are very serious accusations,' she says. 'He's not only suggesting you're involved in Cooper Brownlow's disappearance – he's saying you murdered him. Do you have any idea why he would do that?'

'I would have thought it was obvious,' Mum says as if talking to a child. 'He's doing it in order to get himself off the hook.'

'Hmm,' says Blake. 'Why didn't you call us straight away when you got this?'

'We . . . Well . . .' I'm floundering, not wanting to slip up by implying there was any truth in Smith's accusation, that we'd considered confessing to the police.

'Frankly, we didn't trust you not to botch it up,' Mum says, her head held high.

'Excuse me?' Blake's words slice through the air. She may be slight, but she has a core of steel.

'There was a real risk that if the police showed up, Smith would have done something terrible, something that couldn't be undone. I would not allow that to happen to my grandson.'

'So what did you do, exactly?'

'I set fire to his car and called him so he'd come out. While he was dealing with that, I went into the flat and rescued Zach.'

'You . . . by yourself?' Blake says incredulously.

'Yes, why not? It did the trick, didn't it? It takes more than a coward with a gun to scare me. And that Julie woman was more petrified than any of us. Felt a bit sorry for her, actually. I used to work with abused women and I wouldn't be surprised at all if she was coerced into helping that awful man.'

'You were marvellous.' Dad pats her knee. 'Crazy, but marvellous.'

'She was,' Zach says, awestruck. 'Grandma was *insane.*'

'Alright . . .' Blake doesn't know what to do with any of this. 'We'll need to take statements from all of you individually, so . . .'

Her phone beeps with a message and she checks it.

'DS Newman is back,' she says with some relief. 'Please wait here, I'll be back in a minute.'

'Do you think she—' Dad begins.

'Heath!' Mum interrupts, flicking her eyes for a second at the cameras on the wall which are no doubt recording us. We sit there in strained silence for five minutes or so until the door opens and Blake comes back in followed by DS Newman.

'Good afternoon, all. Are you OK?' he asks Zach, who nods.

'Right. Well.' He opens his arms in an expansive gesture. 'I'm pleased to tell you we've arrested Neville Smith on suspicion of the murder of Cooper Brownlow. DC Blake's filled me in about what's happened this afternoon and I'm confident we'll also be charging him with Zach's kidnapping and assault. Julie Woodford was still at the scene when we arrived, and she's come in voluntarily to help us with our enquiries. We'll need to take statements from you all, and get Zach checked over by a medic. Then you can go. You've had quite a day of it – we'll debrief more thoroughly tomorrow.'

'Will we need to come back in for that?' I ask.

'Yes, that . . .' Blake begins.

'No, no, that won't be necessary,' Newman interrupts. 'We'll come to you.'

'But what about—' Blake begins.

'I think they've been through enough,' Newman says. 'Let's just be grateful we've got our man. You're quite something, Mrs Whitlock.'

Blake looks at him as though he's something horrid she's trodden in.

'Anyone would have done the same,' Mum says modestly.

'I don't think so, do you, Esther?' he says jovially.

'No, certainly not,' she says without a trace of a smile.

'If you'd all like to come with me,' Newman says, 'we'll get you a hot drink and start taking your statements.'

As we make our way down the corridor, Julie Woodford is coming the other way accompanied by a uniformed officer. She stops when she sees us, looking straight at me, white and scared. I stop too and am aware of the other three gathering behind me, a team of Whitlocks.

'I'm sorry,' she says. 'I didn't know what Smith was going to do. I just wanted to find Cooper. Smith said Zach knew where he was. I had no idea he had a gun. He kept saying you'd done away with Cooper, and I was . . . so confused . . . I didn't know what to believe.'

She's got a nerve. I'm about to tell her where she can shove her confusion when Mum steps forward, oozing compassion.

'It's alright. Sometimes it's hard to see clearly when you're in the middle of something. You mustn't blame yourself.'

'Shall we move along?' Blake says sharply from behind us. 'It's the first door on the left.'

We all troop into another room, this one complete with stained sofas and a low coffee table. Mum, Dad, Zach and I sit down. DC Blake remains standing, watching us, her expression impenetrable. Outside, the sun passes behind a cloud and the room feels suddenly grey and chilly.

Chapter 40

We're not expecting the police until mid-day the following day, but at eleven o'clock there's a knock at the door. I open it, expecting the now-familiar visages of Newman and Blake, but am greeted instead by a woman of about my age. She's dressed in baggy leggings and a shapeless jumper, her hair scrabbled into a scraggy ponytail and her face makeup free. It takes me a few seconds to recognise her as Julie Woodford.

'Can I come in?' she says.

'I don't think so. You're not exactly popular around here.'

'Fair enough,' she says, uncharacteristically meekly. 'Could we talk though? Please?'

I look behind me. The low voices of my parents emanate from the kitchen.

'Fine, just for a minute.'

I grab a random raincoat from the row of pegs by the door and step outside, stuffing my arms into it. It must belong to my dad as it engulfs my entire body, the sleeves hanging well past my hands.

'Morning, Penny!' Naturally Sue from next door would choose this moment to leave her house, her beak sticking so far over the wall she's practically knocking us over with it.

'Morning, Sue.'

'How's your Mum?'

'Er . . . she's . . .' Surely news of Mum's escapade yesterday hasn't spread to 64 St Mary's Road?

'Because I was wondering – has she had her thyroid checked? That can cause those symptoms – dizziness, blurred vision.'

'I'm not sure, Sue, I'll ask.'

I take Julie's elbow, preparing to hustle her around the side of the house into the garden.

'And how's your auntie?' Sue says.

Does this woman never let anything go? I briefly consider telling her my phantom aunt has shuffled off her mortal coil, but I fear that would only lead to further, more intense questioning.

'She's fine. Come on, Julie.'

I leave Sue twittering about how we must all get together for coffee, and lead Julie past the churned-up mess of the patio area. We sit on an old bench where we're shielded from prying eyes by the leylandii. Julie surveys the remains of the rose garden. Mum and Dad have made a decent inroad into tidying it up but even to the untrained eye it still looks a bit of a mess.

'What happened there?'

'There was a . . . problem, with the roses. I'm not sure . . .'

'Did *he* do it?' she asks, aghast. 'He did, didn't he? It's exactly his style.'

'You've changed your tune,' I say. 'Last time you came here you were defending him to the hilt.'

'I know. I'm sorry. And about yesterday – your boy . . . Smith didn't tell me what he was planning. He said he wanted to talk to Zach about Cooper, that Zach knew where Cooper was, that he could help us find him. He asked me to help because he didn't know if Zach would go with him, plus the police were looking for him so he didn't want to go out and about any more than he had to. I think I'd got so used to doing what Cooper told me to that it made me compliant. Sometimes it's easier to go along with it. Then when I got to the flat with Zach and Smith had a gun . . . I was scared.'

She twists her hands around and around each other in her lap.

'What was the story, with you and Cooper?' I say, more gently.

'We met about six months ago, not long after he got out of prison. I was at a very low ebb. My husband had left me for someone else.'

'I know the feeling.'

'I thought he loved me, but I'm pretty sure he just thought I could be useful to him, finding flats for his dodgy mates who didn't have references. I wouldn't do it for any of them though. It would have been professional suicide. But . . .'

'You faked the reference for him.' I say.

She nods, shamefaced. 'I was under his spell. I knew there were other women, but I convinced myself that I was different, I was the special one that he would always come back to.'

'I never would have . . . if I'd known he wasn't single,' I mutter.

'I don't blame you, although I was jealous as hell at the time. Ironically, it was him that accused me of cheating although I never so much as looked at another man. He got it into his head that I was having an affair with one of my clients who owned a lot of properties and rented them all out through me. Cooper scared the guy off so badly he stopped using me and went with a different estate agent. Cost me a bloody fortune. He was bad news but I couldn't see it. He would treat me so badly, then switch and be lovely, and I would gather up these crumbs of decency that he'd deigned to throw me and make a banquet out of them. You know what it's like. Although you were cleverer than me – you saw through him quickly and he hated it. He was used to treating me like crap and me accepting it and loving him anyway.'

We look at each other, two women fooled by the same flattery, the same stupid, human desire to be seen, to be wanted.

'When Smith . . . involved me in the situation with Zach, it woke me up. I couldn't believe I had allowed myself to get to that point but suddenly I could see everything clearly – who Smith is, who Cooper was. I'm glad he's dead,' she says. 'I'm grateful. And I'm glad that the right person is going to be punished for it.'

'Wh-what do you mean?'

'Exactly that,' she says. 'The police aren't going to press any charges against me for my part in Zach's kidnap. They've agreed that I was coerced by Smith, and they're grateful for my . . . cooperation in the investigation against him.' She stands up. 'You don't need to worry about that anymore.'

I want to ask her more, but I daren't articulate what I think she's suggesting in case that's not what she means at all.

'Don't let that man ruin any more of your life than he already has,' she says. 'I'm not going to. And if you ever fancy a drink, give me a call.'

'I'd love to, but I won't be able to afford a drink any time soon.'

'Why not?'

'I got fired from my job. I took my eye off the ball, what with everything else that's been going on.'

'Sorry to hear that.' She hesitates. 'You don't want to work in an estate agent's, do you?'

'You mean . . .?'

'Dean's just announced he's leaving. Got a job as a car sales-man, a job he's frighteningly suited to. The pay's not great, but there's the opportunity to earn a bit of commission. And it'll all be on the level from now on, I promise.'

'I'd love to. Honestly, that would be a lifesaver.'

'Why don't you pop in to the office tomorrow and we can discuss it properly?'

With that, she's gone, leaving me feeling lighter than I have in a long time. Not just because I'll be able to pay my mortgage after all, but because I'm not the only woman who deceived herself over Cooper Brownlow, not the only one who was stupid enough to get involved with him. And, for the first time, I can see that perhaps, just perhaps, neither Julie nor I were stupid at all.

Chapter 41

An hour later, DS Newman and DC Blake arrive for the debrief. Blake's not sporting her plait today – instead her hair is coiled into a tight, silvery bun at the nape of her neck.

Once the five of us are settled around the kitchen table with cups of tea and my mother's homemade coffee and walnut cake, DS Newman leans forward, his hands clasped in front of him.

'I'm happy to tell you that this morning, we charged Neville Smith with the murder of Cooper Brownlow. Conviction's not going to be easy in the absence of a body, but we had enough circumstantial evidence to charge him.'

Mum and Dad keep their eyes firmly on Newman, not a hint of emotion passing either of their faces although I sense a delicate shift in atmosphere.

'We've also charged him with Zach's kidnap. There won't be any charges against Julie Woodford. In our view, she was controlled and coerced by Neville Smith, who is a violent man. She's also been extremely helpful to us in the murder enquiry,' he says. 'This cake is delicious, Mrs Whitlock.'

'Thank you,' Mum says, preening. 'The secret, would you believe, is to use instant coffee, not the fancy real stuff.'

'Well, it's certainly worked.' He shovels in another large forkful.

'As DS Newman says, Julie Woodford has been most helpful.' Blake, who refused the offer of cake, seems faintly repulsed by her colleague's enjoyment of it. 'Neville Smith obviously had some sort of hold over her, but she's come to the realisation that he was lying to her – grooming her, in a way. He had her convinced that the three of you had killed Cooper Brownlow. She's being very cooperative and has provided us with some new information that will help with the prosecution.'

'Can I ask what that is?' I say.

Blake looks at Newman questioningly and he nods.

'She has shared with us that Neville Smith told her that he had killed Mr Brownlow and that he was deliberately trying to incriminate you, Mr and Mrs Whitlock.'

Dad, who had just taken a sip of his tea, coughs and tea splatters on the table.

'Sorry.' He stands and grabs a piece of kitchen towel from the roll by the sink, making a right performance of mopping up the mess.

'Neville Smith and Cooper Brownlow, as of course you know, were involved together in drug-related criminal activity,' Newman goes on. 'It seems they'd had some kind of falling out which I'm sure we'll get to the bottom of. Mr Smith has previous convictions for both drug-related offences and violent crimes. Julie Woodford and Mr Smith became known to each other when Ms Woodford was in a relationship with Cooper Brownlow, so she went to Smith when she became concerned about Brownlow's whereabouts. As I said, he managed to convince her that the three of you were responsible for his disappearance.'

'And the fire?' I ask.

'With regards to the fire that was set in Mr Smith's car, while we want to stress that taking the law into your own hands is never advised or condoned, under the circumstances there won't be any charges,' Newman says.

'That's good news, thank you,' I say, squeezing Mum's hand. 'Isn't it, Mum?'

'What's that, dear?' she says with the habitual vagueness that overcomes her only in the presence of the police.

'I'm not sure she remembers it that well,' Dad says apologetically.

Newman looks sympathetic.

'It was an impressively calculated move for someone whose memory is not working as well as it did,' DC Blake says.

Oh God, Mum's overdone it. If Blake believes she's putting on an act, she's going to smell a rat.

'Mum's fine in the moment,' I say quickly. 'She's not stupid, she knows what she's doing. It's just her short-term memory can be a bit hazy.'

'I understand,' says Newman. 'My dad's the same. He can remember the score of the Charlton Athletic v Sunderland play-off finals in 1998, but has no idea what he had for breakfast.'

'Exactly.' I shoot him a grateful smile.

'I haven't lost my marbles yet,' Mum says. 'Just a bit forgetful.'

'Not to worry at all, Mrs Whitlock,' Newman says. 'I think that's all we need to do today. How's Zach doing?'

'Not too bad, considering,' I say. 'He's staying with my ex-husband Martin and his partner, Elaine. He doesn't want to be left alone at the moment, understandably.'

Elaine has surprised me by stepping up to the mark and supporting Martin in looking after Zach, even after he stole from her. I'm beginning to think I misjudged her.

'You've got all the details for Victim Support, haven't you?' Newman says. 'Please do encourage him to contact them – the right support can make all the difference.'

'Thanks, I will.'

I'll be doing everything I can to urge Zach to get support. Martin has started researching addiction therapy services and has offered to pay for it privately. I can't believe how blind I've been to the fact that Zach's smoking is more than just a teenage rebellion – that he is an addict. I was stupid to let it go unaddressed for so long. I'm thankful at least that Zach isn't involved in this mess with Cooper – that, as far as he's concerned, the version we've presented to the police is the truth.

I see them to the door, where Newman shakes my hand warmly.

'Take care of yourself,' he says. 'And those two. We'll be in touch, but in the meantime if you need anything, give us a call. Esther?'

Blake gives me a card with her mobile number on it, her face impassive, and they leave.

Julie Woodford has done us a massive favour, but I wish with all my heart that the story we've concocted between us was the truth. I don't know if I'm ever going to be able to slough off this horrible sick feeling – a mixture of fear and guilt and shame that threatens to overwhelm me.

I'm about to close the door when a battered black transit van pulls into the drive. It comes to a halt and two men get out, one youngish, sallow and unhealthy-looking with a wispy moustache, the other older, squat and grizzled, wearing a flat cap and a khaki bomber jacket.

'Can I help you?' I say, praying they've called to the wrong house, that this isn't something else, some more trouble.

'Mrs Whitlock? We've come to have a look at your patio,' the older one says. 'Got some samples in the back for you.'

'It's my parents you want. They're inside, hold on. Mum, Dad!' I call back to them.

They come bustling out.

'Who recommended these guys?' I say in a low voice. 'Not Linda, please.'

'No, it was Beryl, from the allotment. She said they're great,' Mum says.

As I watch the younger man open up the back doors of the van and start lifting slabs out and displaying them on the gravel drive, I'm not sure whether to feel relief or yet more anxiety. It'll be good to get the patio done, to know that Cooper is well and truly buried, but the thought of anyone poking around in that area sends sparks flying through my body. Mum and Dad make their way out and start exclaiming over patterned porcelain and brushed sandstone. This is a good thing, it's moving on. It's the beginning of the end.

Chapter 42

'Where's Mum?'

Dad scrapes the remains of his cheese and pickle sandwich into the bin and puts the plate in the sink.

'She's walked into town – gone for lunch with Beryl.'

'That's nice. It's what she needs after last week – a bit of normality.'

'Yes.'

He puts the kettle on and sits down heavily at the kitchen table.

'Are you OK, Dad? You look tired.'

'Oh yes, I'm fine, love.'

That's the exact answer he's given me every time I've asked him that question for my entire adult life.

'Really?' I sit down opposite him. 'Because it's understandable if you're not. I'm not OK. After ... everything ... you know. It's perfectly normal that you'd be ... traumatised.'

He tuts. It's not a word he'd ever use, particularly in relation to himself.

'Don't be daft. I'll be alright.'

'And Mum?'

'She's right as rain,' he says with a hint of bitterness. '*Living her best life*, as Zach would say.'

'What do you mean?'

'I don't know, don't listen to me.' He passes his hand down his face as if trying to wipe something away.

'No, I want to listen to you. Please.' It's so rare for him to voice a hint of criticism about my mother.

'I don't know . . . she seems more than alright. Better than ever. Better than she was . . . before.'

'Yeah, I know what you mean.' It's bothered me too, how easily she's shrugged off what we've done. 'Maybe we should talk to her. What time are you expecting her back?'

'I would have thought she'd be back by now,' he says, looking at his watch. 'It's been hours.'

'They'll be gassing away about old times,' I say. 'Was Beryl at Greenham Common too?'

'I've no idea,' he says.

'So you didn't know her back in those days?'

'No, of course not.'

'How do you know her, then?'

'From the allotment,' he says, as if talking to a complete idiot. 'You know that. She took over Sheila's plot.'

'I know. I just thought you knew her from before, because . . .' Why did I think that? I assumed, from the way they spoke about her, that she was a longstanding friend.

'So you didn't know her at all before? When did she take over Sheila's plot?'

'I don't know . . . a few weeks ago?'

A tendril of fear, like a strand of bindweed, slowly twists its way around my intestines.

'When exactly?'

'How would I remember that?' he says testily.

'Was it before or after . . . the thing . . . Cooper?'

'Oh after, definitely,' he says, glad to be able to answer at least one of my questions confidently. 'I was surprised actually, because Tom – you know, the chair of the allotments – is away on a cruise and normally nothing happens up there without his say so.'

'She never asked you anything about Cooper, did she?'

'No, why would she? We didn't tell her anything about it. We're not totally stupid.'

'No, I know.' Something's nagging at me though. 'She's the one that suggested the guys to do the patio, right?'

'Yes. What's wrong with that?'

'How did she know you needed it doing?'

'We must have told her, I suppose. We didn't tell her *why*, obviously.'

'No, but . . . did she seem . . . interested in the patio?'

'Yes, a bit. I think she asked us if we'd done anything recently in the garden. She asked us a lot of questions. But that's because she had some guys who'd done hers that she recommended very highly, so she wanted to be able to tell them exactly what we wanted. We told her it didn't need digging over or preparing, that we'd already done all that, that we only needed the tiles laying. Don't worry, we were very clear about that.'

'Oh, God.' The bindweed entwines itself ever more insidiously around my insides, threatening to choke the life out of them.

'What?' Dad says, exasperated.

'What if . . . Beryl isn't who she seems? I mean, what if she's connected to Cooper?'

'What on earth could she have to do with that lowlife?'

'She could be . . .' I think of Scott, Cooper's brother, telling me about their mother, who always took Cooper's side, always forgave him no matter what. 'She could be his mother. She's the right age.'

'What makes you think that? You could say that about any of our friends.'

'Except they're not new friends who've sought you out recently, since Cooper died, are they? They haven't set themselves up in the allotment next to you, and engaged you in conversation about what you've been up to in your garden, and sent men to sniff around the patio? What's Beryl's surname?'

'I don't know,' he says. 'You're making quite a leap, aren't you?'

I bring up Scott's number and dial. It goes to voicemail.

'Hi, this is Penny Whitlock. Could you give me a call back on this number as soon as you can, please? It's urgent. Thanks.'

'Give Mum a ring,' he says. 'I'm sure you're putting two and two together and coming up with five.' There's a waver in his voice that wasn't there before that belies his words.

I call her mobile, but predictably that too goes straight to voicemail.

'Why won't either of you ever turn your bloody phones on?' I throw my phone down on the table and run my hands through my hair.

'Sorry,' he says, meekly.

'It's not your fault. Have you got Beryl's number?'

'No, I don't think so. Mum's got it. And Beryl's got my number – she took them both at the same time.'

'Why didn't you take hers?'

'She said she'd text me or ring me and then I'd have it, but she never did. It didn't seem that important at the time. Mum was in contact with her anyway.'

'Where's your phone?' I don't bother asking him if it's switched on. He's in the house, why would it be?

'It's in the dresser, I think,' he says, crossing the kitchen and pulling it from the drawer. 'Here we are.'

'Switch it on.'

'Alright.' He pokes at it and it buzzes into life.

'Check that you didn't save her number – you might've forgotten.'

'I doubt it,' he says, offended, but taps away. As he does so, the phone beeps.

'What's that? Is it Mum?'

He pushes his glasses up to the top of his head and holds the phone away from him. 'No, it's a text. From a number, no name.'

'What does it say?' The bindweed coils a little tighter.

'It's from Beryl. That's good. She says Mum's phone's dead so she's letting me know they've decided to head up to the allotment. She's asking if I can pick Mum up there in a bit, because Beryl's got to head off in the other direction afterwards so can't drop her back.'

'Oh.'

'So you were worrying about nothing. You had me going for a minute there.'

'Right. Good.' A handful of raindrops sprinkle against the kitchen window as if someone's throwing stones to capture our attention. 'It's not a very nice day for it, is it? Shall we head up there now? Check everything's alright?'

'I guess so. What about the patio guys? They're meant to be coming this afternoon.'

'They don't need to come inside, do they? If there's a problem they can give you a call – if you keep your mobile on.'

It's meant to be a joke, the one I always make about them never having their phones on, but it falls flat today. This brings home the fact that although we're not discussing it, and although we're both very calm and measured as I drive Dad towards the allotment, neither of us are completely reassured by Beryl's text.

Chapter 43

'Which one is Beryl's car?' I say as we arrive in the almost empty allotment car park.

'I don't know.'

'Do you actually know anything about her?'

'She's a friend!' He tries to release the seatbelt catch but it sticks. He plucks uselessly at the belt. 'We met her at the allotment. We share an interest in gardening. She and your mother get on well. What was I supposed to think? Why would I be suspicious?'

'Here.' I force the catch down and the seatbelt springs out. 'You have to be suspicious of everybody. That's how it is now. Because of what we've done. That's where we are.'

We get out of the car and walk towards their plot. It's no longer raining but the sky is a forbidding iron-grey and an icy wind slices into us like a knife. There's no one about.

'Maybe they're in the shed,' Dad says, but when we get there, the padlock is clasped tightly around the bolt, the windows dark.

'What about Beryl's shed?' I say.

'I don't think she uses it – it's falling down,' Dad says. 'The whole plot was neglected when Sheila was ill.'

'Let's have a look anyway.'

We make our way across their plot and Beryl's, but it's immediately obvious that there's no one here.

'Where are they?' Dad says, pulling his coat tighter around him, worry etched into his lined face. 'What's going on?'

'Try ringing Beryl,' I say.

'Good idea.' He calls up her number and holds the phone to his ear for thirty seconds or so. 'It's ringing out,' he says to me. 'Hang on, voicemail.'

'Leave a message. Try and sound normal,' I say hurriedly.

'Right, yes . . . Oh hello, Beryl, this is Heath Whitlock. I was wondering where you and Sissy have got to! Hope all's well. Can you give me a ring back when you get this? Thanks.'

He hangs up.

'Was that OK?'

'Yes, fine.'

As he's putting the phone back in his pocket, it beeps.

'It's another text from Beryl,' he says. 'It says sorry the signal is poor where they are, but they've gone to the garden centre at Knoxheath.'

'What? Why have they gone there?'

'I know,' Dad says. 'The one at Wreatham's nearer and it's got a much better selection.'

'No, I mean why have they gone to the garden centre at all? This feels off. I don't like it.'

'What shall we do?' he says, wanting me to make the decision as if I am the parent and he the child. It's been overcast all day and the light is dimming. 'Should we call the police?'

'And say what, though? Mum's gone out with a friend and she's texted to say they've gone to the garden centre, please send reinforcements?'

'Let's go there,' he says. 'And if they're not there, we'll . . . think again.'

We sit in silence on the way to Knoxheath. It's begun to rain again and the windscreen wipers sweep hypnotically back and forth. I fight against my instinct to speed along residential roads and jump red lights. The situation will not be helped by me being stopped for speeding – or worse, hitting a pedestrian or another car. I grip the steering wheel tightly. Dad leans forward, drumming his fingers on the dashboard.

I park near the entrance and we barrel in, ignoring the green-aproned staff member who welcomes us at the door. There are a few customers browsing the seeds and decorative pots but there's no sign of Mum or Beryl. We sweep the inside, searching down every aisle, in every corner including the small café, and then make our way out of the back doors into the outside section which is lined with plants and small trees for sale. It's not a large area and it's instantly obvious that there's no one out here.

'They're not here,' Dad says in a small, scared voice.

My phone begins to ring. It's Scott Hamilton.

'Scott, hi.'

'Hello. Are you – is everything OK?'

'I don't know, to be perfectly honest.'

'Oh. Right. How can I . . .?'

'This is going to sound weird, but I don't have time to explain. Can you tell me your mother's name?'

'Yes, it's Barbara. Barbara Hamilton.'

Thank God. Beryl isn't Cooper's mother. Unsurprisingly when you consider what I've been through in the last few weeks, I've allowed my imagination to run riot. Just to be on the safe side, I add a follow up question.

'She hasn't recently taken on an allotment, has she?'

'Yes, at Albion Road. She's been really enjoying it. How on earth did you know that?'

The pots of sage, thyme and parsley swim before me.

'Can you . . . do you have a picture of her you could text me?'

'What? Why?'

'Please, Scott. My mother's in danger.'

'What's this got to do with my mum? What's going on?'

'She is the danger! Did you know about this? Are you in on it together?'

'I have no idea what you're on about.' He sounds genuinely bemused. Whatever Beryl – Barbara – is up to, I don't think he knows anything about it.

'Fine. Just send me the photo.'

I cut him off. 'That was Cooper's brother, Scott. I think . . . Beryl is Cooper's mother.'

'Oh God,' Dad says faintly.

Scott's message pings in and I open it to reveal a close-up of the woman my parents know as Beryl grinning toothily into the camera, squinting in the sunlight.

As Dad and I gaze at it, Dad's phone begins to ring.

'Put it on speaker.'

He looks at me bemused and I grab the phone from him and answer on speaker.

'Are you getting it yet?' Her voice echoes down the line, tinny with an edge of derangement. 'Do you understand? We're off to Blackhawk Point. I hear the cliffs are particularly treacherous there right now. Coastal erosion, they call it. I know what you did to my boy, you and Sissy. I'm going to make you both pay.'

She cuts the call. I lower the phone, blood rushing in my ears.

'We need to call the police. This is serious.'

'You drive, I'll call them on the way,' he says. 'I can't believe I couldn't see it. If she hurts your mother, or . . .'

His jaw tightens. Neither of us want to say it, but I know we're both imagining Mum's body tumbling down the chalk cliff, dislodging stones and debris before being dashed to pieces on the jagged rocks below and taken by the savage waves.

Back in the car, I race off, all thoughts of keeping to the speed limit forgotten.

'Shall I call 999?' Dad says.

I think of trying to explain this situation to the call handler, of how difficult it would be to convey the real sense of emergency. Then I remember the card that DC Blake pressed into my hand.

'No, call Blake – the one who found the finger. I've got her mobile number – it's on a card in my purse.' He looks helplessly around him. 'In my bag, by your feet.'

He digs it out and dials.

'Ah hello, this is Heath Whitlock – you know, we . . . er my grandson . . . yes, that's right. We need police assistance.'

I cringe as Dad explains what's happened in a painfully laboured fashion. However, he gets the message across, and hangs up.

'She's going to come herself, with the other one. She said we shouldn't do anything 'til they get there.'

'Are you kidding? I'm not going to sit and watch that bastard's mother bundling Mum over the cliff, or whatever she's planning to do.' I bite back angry tears.

'Nor am I, although frankly, I think she'd struggle,' Dad says. 'I wonder if that's not what she's planning at all. Mum's pretty fit for her age – fitter than Beryl.'

'She could have drugged her, or have someone helping her.' I can't believe we're having this conversation, that this is my real, actual life.

'Here's the turning for the car park,' Dad says.

I nearly overshoot it, but brake just in time and we swing in and park near the path that leads through to the clifftop. We unclip our seatbelts and leap out of the car. We half-jog past the pub with views out over the sea, its windows yellow squares of warm and inviting light, and out towards the point. It's almost dusk and the wind is fiercer up here than it was inland. I can't tell whether the cries filtering through the air are sea birds or something worse.

As we stumble over the uneven ground, the clouds scud across the sky, revealing a full moon rising over the sea. For a moment the landscape is illuminated and we can see two figures ahead, one holding tight to the other, heading straight for the cliff edge.

Chapter 44

'Mum!' I scream once I'm in with a chance of being heard above the wind and crashing waves.

'Sissy!' Dad shouts, his voice weaker than mine, carried away into the air.

The figures continue their inexorable march towards the edge. I force myself to run, ankles twisting perilously as my feet meet rabbit holes, legs threatening to give way, chest burning. I pull away from Dad, gaining on the two figures.

'Stop!' I shout at the top of my lungs.

Miraculously, they do. I keep running towards them, but as they turn towards me and their white faces loom out of the darkness, my feet slow. It's not Mum and Beryl. It's two black-clad teenagers, a boy with a bleached buzzcut and a girl with multiple facial piercings that glint in the moonlight.

I reach them, panting with exertion.

'Have you seen anyone else out here?' I manage through wheezing breaths. 'Two older women?'

'No, sorry,' the girl says. She takes a step closer. 'Are you alright?'

'Yes. No. We're looking for my mum.'

'We haven't seen anyone,' the boy says.

Dad catches me up, wheezing.

'It's not her,' I say redundantly. 'They haven't seen them.'

'Sorry,' says the girl again.

Her companion plucks at her sleeve and they continue trudging towards the edge.

'Are you two OK?' Dad says, and I'm reminded that Blackhawk Point is a notorious suicide spot.

'We're fine,' the girl says. 'We're not going to top ourselves or anything, if that's what you think. It's just really cool up here when it's dark and windy.'

'Alright . . . be careful, won't you?' Dad says. I'm touched that even in the midst of what we're going through, he has the heart to worry about these two.

They leave us standing alone, scrubland stretching out either side of us along the coast, behind us to the pub and car park and in front of us to the ocean. There's no one else in sight.

'Where are they?' Dad says, a sob catching in his throat. 'Where is she?'

His phone rings.

'It's her,' he says, holding out the phone.

I answer on speaker. We have to lean in close to hear.

'What are you two doing out there on the cliff?' She laughs unpleasantly.

'Where are you? What have you done with Sissy?' Dad demands.

'Done with her? I haven't done anything with her. We had a nice lunch in town and now we're having a quiet drink in the pub at Blackhawk Point. Like I told you.'

'What? Where are you now?' I say, my eyes meeting Dad's.

'In the pub. On the left as you come in the door. Aren't you listening?'

'Mum, are you there?' I say urgently.

'Yes, darling. What on earth is going on?'

Thank God. Whatever else happens – even if Cooper's mother knows everything and can prove it, even if I have to confess to the murder myself – Mum is alive and well.

I end the call, and Dad and I walk as fast as we can after our exertions back to the pub. He opens the door and we walk into the warm snugness of it, thick with the smell of spilled beer and chip fat, musak playing softly over the speakers. On the left, as promised, sit Mum and the woman I can only think of as Beryl, each with a glass of white wine in front of them. Dad sits down next to Mum and wraps his arms around her. I remain standing, watching over the table as if Beryl's going to abscond, taking Mum with her.

'Are you alright?' he says to her.

'I'm fine.' She fights her way out of his embrace. 'What are you two doing here?'

'We thought . . .' Dad dissolves into tears. 'Oh, my darling.'

'Heath? What's wrong?' She looks around, exasperated. 'Is somebody going to tell me what is going on?'

'I'm afraid I haven't been entirely honest with you.' Beryl takes a prim sip of her wine.

'This is Cooper Brownlow's mother.' I can't hold it in, can't bear to see Mum sitting there thinking she's having an innocent drink with a friend. 'Her name's not Beryl, it's Barbara Hamilton.'

'What?' She draws back, horrified.

'She deliberately befriended you by taking the allotment next to yours.'

'However did you manage that?' Mum asks, momentarily distracted from the more pressing issue. 'There's a waiting list for those allotments as long as your arm. I thought it had only been empty so long because Sheila's kids were arguing that they should inherit it.'

'I didn't exactly go through the official channels,' she says. 'I could see no one was using it so I just . . . turned up.'

'That's completely unethical,' Mum says crossly.

'Mum, you're missing the point here. She's been texting us, calling us . . . today . . . implying that she was going to hurt you,' I say.

'I was never going to hurt her,' Beryl says dismissively. 'I'm not like that. Unlike you.'

'What do you mean?' Mum says warily.

'You know perfectly well what I mean. Neville Smith didn't hurt my boy. He came to me after Cooper disappeared, asking if I knew where he was. He wanted to find him. They hadn't fallen out – they were business partners. They depended on each other, if anything. He came to see me the day they tried to arrest him, begged me to help him. He swore blind he had nothing to do with what they found in his car – the . . . finger . . .' Her face twists with pain as she presses her lips together, trying to get her emotions under control. I feel an unwelcome twinge of empathy. She and I are both mothers. Cooper Brownlow was a living nightmare and I can't bring myself to be sorry he's gone, but he was her son. I know that no matter what Zach does, however horrendous, I will always love him. I wouldn't be able to help it any more than I can help breathing. I grew him inside my body, flesh of my flesh, as Beryl did Cooper.

'Guess where Smith'd been the week before it was found hidden in his car?' She's recovered herself. 'Your house. He knew you'd done something to him. You were desperate to get rid of him. You'd been calling the police on him non-stop, and for what? A bit of noise? Having a few friends round?'

Mum's eyebrows go up and I can see she's about to argue that it was a bit more than that – that Cooper hadn't paid his rent, that he had deliberately damaged their property and broken in to their home on more than one occasion and that he was dealing drugs from their house. Dad nudges her.

'And you can say it was more than that,' Beryl goes on, 'and maybe it was but does that justify what you did to him? You killed him – now I don't know if that was an accident or if you did it on purpose, and I don't know which of you did it, but what I do know is that you're all in on it and you were glad about it. That you lied about it and covered it up. That you chopped off his finger and planted it in an innocent man's car and allowed him to go to jail for what you'd done.'

Dad and I are speechless. My mouth is so dry I couldn't speak if I wanted to and Dad looks similarly afflicted. Mum, however, has no such trouble.

'This is all a very interesting little story,' she says calmly, 'but unfortunately it's a total fabrication. If we killed Cooper, where's his body?'

'Oh, that's an easy one,' She's like the cat who got the cream. A whisper of fear tickles the back of my neck. 'That's what you're all doing here. You didn't really think I was going to push Sissy off the cliff, did you? I'd never do anything so ridiculously melodramatic. Anyway, that would be too good for her. I just wanted to make sure you were all out of the way.'

'Out of the way for what?' Dad says.

'Well, you did keep going on about your patio. Kept on asking and asking about the company I'd used to do mine. Sissy was

OK but, Heath, you'd get ever such a funny look every time we discussed it. The same look you've got now, in fact.'

Dad is whey-faced, his knee jiggling uncontrollably.

'Those patio guys I recommended? They're there this afternoon, aren't they? They must have been there a couple of hours – I should think that'd be long enough, don't you? He can't be that far down.'

'They don't need to dig down.' It's my voice but it feels like someone else's, someone far away. 'They're laying the tiles.'

'They're not patio guys, Penny,' she says pityingly. 'They're . . . associates of Neville Smith who've kindly offered to help me out. I wonder what they'll find down there?'

Her eyes move to the door as it opens, letting in a blast of cold air. She smiles beatifically.

'Ah, here's the police. I did think you might call them – I would have done it myself but it was kind of you to save me the trouble.'

DS Newman, shadowed by DC Blake, paler and more unearthly than ever, strides over to the table.

'Mrs Whitlock, I'm delighted to see you're safe. Now, what seems to be the problem?'

Chapter 45

'What happened tonight?' Esther Blake asks, snatching a side-ways glance at me from the passenger seat. The rain has set in, hammering on the windscreen, shimmering in the beam of the headlights. With her alabaster, luminous skin, she glows like a nightlight every time we pass under a street lamp. DS Newman has taken my parents in his car. I wish I knew what they're saying to him.

Cooper's mother was happy to let us talk ourselves into a corner in the pub. She knew we didn't have a leg to stand on. As we blathered and apologised to the police about how we'd been mistaken, how we were sorry to have dragged them out on a wild goose chase, she knew that her 'patio guys' were uncovering her son's body. I shudder to think about what state it will be in by now. When DS Newman suggested he come back with us to the house to talk it all through, she piped up, saying she thought that was a brilliant idea, and that she'd follow on behind to lend her support. What could we say?

It's pointless trying to come up with an explanation for what we're about to be faced with in the garden – it can only be a matter of time before we're arrested – but an instinct for self-preservation has kicked in and I can't allow myself to give in. There's a minuscule chance that even if the patio guys have discovered the body, there might somehow not be enough forensic evidence to link us to the murder. Maybe it'll still be feasible that it was Smith, particularly in the light of his 'confession' to Julie Woodford. We could suggest that he buried Cooper in my parents' garden to try and implicate them.

'Did you . . . did you speak to Beryl . . . Cooper's mother . . . for your investigation?' I ask, eyes firmly on the road.

'Yes,' she says neutrally.

'I see. Right.'

'We talked to everyone – family, friends, associates. I must admit I was a little surprised when you said that your mother had voluntarily met up with her.'

'We didn't know who she was – she never told us. When you interviewed her, did she . . . she seems to support this idea that we . . . or my parents . . .'

'That you killed Mr Brownlow? Yes, she did mention that, and of course Neville Smith had said the same thing. We had to consider every possibility. However, the fact that your parents are elderly, respectable citizens with no prior convictions and Mr Smith was a known violent offender with Mr Brownlow's finger in his car, who absconded when we tried to arrest him, plus Julie Woodford's statement, meant that DS Newman didn't take her accusations too seriously.'

It hangs between us like one of those pine-scented air fresheners, unpleasant and impossible to ignore. DS Newman didn't take it seriously, but did Esther Blake?

'Right. Good.' I plough on regardless. 'That's what happened today. Apparently she deliberately befriended my parents by taking on the allotment next to theirs and today she— well, my father and I got the idea that she had abducted my mother and that she meant to harm her. However, it seems she was trying to get us all out of the way, because she's got this idea into her head . . .' I lick my lips, trying to get some moisture into the Gobi desert of my mouth. 'She thinks my parents have buried him under the patio.'

'I see.' Her hands stay neatly folded in her lap.

Her unruffled calm unsettles me. I hoped she would laugh but her refusal to do so suggests she thinks it's a possibility.

'It's ridiculous.' I pause to give her a chance to agree. She says nothing. 'But the thing is she's evidently sent some goons round – associates of Neville Smith – to dig it up. She says they're there now.'

'Not to worry,' she says mildly. 'We'll be able to sort them out.'

'Yes, thank you. I suppose . . .' A wave of panic engulfs me, but I force myself to keep on talking. 'What if . . . is it possible that Neville Smith buried him in my parents' garden? And he's asked Cooper's mother to uncover his body so that my parents get the blame?'

'I'd say that's highly unlikely.'

I can feel her eyes on me. I ostentatiously check my wing and rear-view mirrors, hands in the ten to two position. I know it's only a manifestation of my guilt, but it feels like she can see into my soul, like she knows what we've done.

'So,' I say, wildly casting around for another topic of conversation, 'from a History degree to joining the police – must have been a bit of a change?'

'In a way,' she says. 'There are lots of similarities between history and policing though.'

'How so?' I try to keep my tone level as if we've been introduced at a party and are engaging in some light small talk.

'When you first start studying history at school, it appears to be all about learning facts. Such and such an event happened on this date, and this was how it unfolded. But it's not really about that at all. It's about reviewing the available evidence and trying to understand what happened and why. Often you find, once you poke about a bit, that there's absolutely no good reason to believe the accepted version of events. It's the same with policing. It's important to keep an open mind.'

'Mm hmm.'

I don't trust myself to say any more and we spend the rest of the journey in silence. DS Newman is pulling into the drive when we arrive. Beryl squeezes her car in behind the patio guys' black van, leaving Blake and I to park on the road.

We all get out of our cars. You could cut the atmosphere with a knife. Beryl doesn't speak but she's burning with a hectic, fevered energy. Even the usually phlegmatic DS Newman is on edge. I'm on the alert, trying to interpret any eye contact between him and Blake. I can't take a full breath. My head swims. The only ones who seem relaxed, strangely, are my parents. Maybe they're relieved that, whatever comes next, the deception is finally over.

'Right, let's go and see what's happening in the garden, shall we?' DS Newman says.

The rest of us follow in his wake. Sweat trickles down my back despite the cold. I can't look at my parents. This is it – the moment I've been anticipating since I saw Cooper's body spreadeagled in my parents' decimated rose garden. The instinct that overtook me that day to protect them at all costs is as strong in me today as it was then. Here it is. It's time. I will take the blame. I'll tell them that I did it all, that my parents knew nothing about it.

I'm still trying to find the words as we round the side of the house. The security light clicks on, revealing the two guys from the other day, whey-face and flat cap. They are sweaty with exertion, each with a garden spade. I look down. They have dug at least six feet down and there's a huge heap of soil piled up beside the patio. But there is no body.

'We didn't find anything,' flat cap says to Beryl, eyeing the police suspiciously.

'No!' She darts forward, crouches down and lowers herself into the hole, clawing and scrabbling at the ground.

'Where is he?' she screams up at me, her raw pain like a knife to my heart. 'Where is my boy?'

I'm unable to answer – I'm as baffled as she is. I risk a look at Mum and Dad. I may not know them the way they know each other – like sculptors intimately acquainted with every curve and sharp edge of their creations – but it's clear to me that they are not in the least surprised.

'Mrs Hamilton.' Newman crouches down and extends a hand. 'Let me help you out.'

She ignores him and stays on her knees in the mud.

'What have you done with my boy?' She wails, looking straight at me. She knows. It doesn't matter if we get away with it, if his body (wherever it is) is never found, if Neville Smith is convicted of his murder. She knows. She will always know. And worse, so will I. While Cooper Brownlow was simply the lowlife scum who exploited and mistreated my parents, I could partially reconcile myself to what Dad did and what I have done in helping him and Mum cover it up. But today has shown me another Cooper, a Cooper who may have been flawed but was this woman's son, her baby. I'll never be able to unsee that, or the hurt and pain we have caused her.

'Why don't you take your parents inside?' Newman says to me. 'We'll sort this lot out and be in touch soon.'

I tear my eyes away from Beryl's anguished face.

'Good idea. Come on, Mum. Dad.'

'What happened to the roses?' DC Blake says idly.

The three of us stop in our tracks as if she'd held up a gun.

'What?' I say.

'Over there.' She gestures towards the mangled rose garden, just visible in the edges of the area illuminated by the security light.

'Blight,' my mother says confidently, no trace of uncertainty. 'We had to remove all the diseased bits and prune them right down. They'll be back later in the spring.'

'What a shame,' Newman says impatiently. 'Now come along, Mrs Hamilton, let's get you out of there.'

'Shall I go inside with them, sarge?' Blake is watching us, her eyes like two glassy marbles.

'No, that won't be necessary,' Newman says with a touch of reproof. 'We can come back in the morning, when everyone's rested.'

Mum and Dad follow me meekly inside, Esther Blake's cool stare following us as we go. As the door closes behind us, I fold my arms and face them. I very rarely swear in front of them but the words fly out before I have a chance to edit them.

'Which one of you is going to tell me what the fuck is going on?'

Chapter 46

'We changed our minds,' Mum says as if she's talking about painting the hall jasmine white instead of elephant's breath.

'When? What did you do?'

I look from one to the other. Dad gives a helpless shrug.

'That night,' she says, as if it should be obvious. 'When you went off and left Dad and I to clear everything up.'

'I had to go and get Zach.'

'You were gone for hours, Penny.'

'I . . . well, I fell asleep. I didn't mean to.'

'Quite,' she says. 'Dad and I decided that under the patio wasn't the best place for him after all – it felt too obvious. So, as I said, we changed our minds.'

'Where is he then?' I can hardly comprehend what I'm hearing.

'We thought originally that it would be best if you didn't know, and I believe that's still the case. It's safer for you to know as little as possible. We're very grateful for all you've done, but this is our mess and our responsibility.'

'We were trying to protect you,' Dad says. 'We should never have got you involved in the first place.'

'But I am involved! I'm massively implicated in the whole thing! I can't believe you've been lying to me all this time!'

'What difference does it make?' says Mum. 'It's all done and dusted now. What's happened here tonight has made that woman look thoroughly unhinged, so any further accusations she throws at us will be water off a duck's back. The police will never take her seriously. It's really worked out quite well.'

'Quite well? Quite well? Is that what you think? What is wrong with you? How can you be so cold? Did you see her out there in that hole? She's devastated. Her life has been destroyed – and we did that. It's our fault. And we get to walk away without any consequences. Do you think that's right?' If I could go back to that night, I'd call the police without a second's hesitation, the moment I saw Cooper's body sprawled on the ground. I'd take responsibility for it myself.

'What's the alternative?' Mum says, her eyes blazing. 'I spend the rest of my life in prison? What would that achieve? I'm seventy-five years old. I don't want to live whatever time I have left locked up with a load of criminals. How do you think I'd cope in there? What's done is done. When you get to our age, you understand how precious and short life is. Everyone dies. Bad things happen. They happen to everyone. You know that – look at Caitlin, dying before she reached fifty. Look at your sisters who never got to experience the world. Do you know what it's like to go through labour, to give birth, knowing that your baby is dead? Of course you don't, but I can tell you there is no pain like it. I made a mistake, but I'm not a danger to anyone. I'm not going to do it again. And what about all the good we've done? All the students that Dad inspired to achieve wonderful things. All the women I helped get away from their abusive partners, to understand their own worth, that there was a better life out there for them than the miserable ones they were leading. Isn't that worth something? What would it achieve, sending me to prison? Nothing. And what's more, a dangerous man is off the streets. He would have killed someone sooner or later, either directly or through supplying them drugs. I've saved that person's life. Doesn't that count for anything?'

'You . . . *you* made a mistake?'

'Yes. That's what it was,' she says. 'A mistake. I don't see who it helps if I go to prison.'

'No, but . . .' A lump forms in my gullet and I swallow. 'Dad said it was him . . . you both did. You said Dad hit Cooper with the walking stick.'

It's as if I've chucked a bucket of freezing water over her. She'd got so caught up in her own passionate defence she didn't realise she was giving herself away.

'That was my idea,' Dad says quietly, taking her hand. 'You saw the state Mum was in after it happened. I thought at first that we were going to go to the police, and I couldn't bear to see your mother arrested. I'd spend ten lifetimes in prison to spare her that.'

'Oh, Dad, you shouldn't have.' But who am I to say that? If it comes to it, I'll lie to protect them both. I'd go to prison to spare either of them from spending their last years in captivity. But am I really prepared to do that, to abandon Zach when he needs me more than ever?

'So what are you going to do?' Mum asks softly. 'Are you seriously considering going to the police and telling them the truth? We'd all go to prison if it came out. Would you really leave Zach to fend for himself without any of us to support him? And for the sake of what? Who would it benefit? You need to make a choice, Penny, like we all do, every day. After Cooper died, I chose not to make the rest of my life, and your father's, and yours, unbearable. And yes, that means Cooper's mother won't ever get the truth of what happened to her son, and yes, we will have to live with the guilt about what we've done – and before you say anything, I do feel that guilt, believe you me. But this is what I've chosen. Now it's your turn. What do you choose, Penny?'

THREE MONTHS LATER

Chapter 47

The early July sun is warm on the back of my neck. I adjust the muslin cloth so it's shading Clara. She wriggles and snuffles in my arms, screwing up her old man's face.

'I think she's going to cry,' I say apprehensively. It's been years since I held a newborn. 'Shall I give her back to you, Elaine?'

Elaine, who is lying back in a deckchair, opens heavy eyes and raises her weary head.

'I'll take her,' Martin says, transferring her capably from my arms into his, one hand supporting her head.

'I don't recall you being this devoted or useful when Zach was a baby. If memory serves me correctly, you were mostly at work, only arriving home once Zach was safely bathed and in bed.'

'I guess he's changed, then,' Elaine says looking at him fondly. 'He's very hands-on, does more than his fair share of nappies and night wakings.'

Despite this smugness, I've surprised myself by becoming quite friendly with Elaine. After everything that happened in the winter, I realised that Mum was right. Life is short, and we have to make the best of things, to work with them as they are, rather than as we want them to be.

Caitlin barely comes to me at all these days. I don't miss her any less than I did but my life is beginning to reshape itself around the hole she left. Almost as surprising as my friendship with Elaine is how close I've become to Julie Woodford, and not just because she's now my boss. We go for drinks after work every Friday and often meet for coffee or a walk at the weekend too. I think she's on her way to becoming an everyday friend.

'Cooee!' Sue waves over the fence from her recliner in their back garden where she's been watching Philip mowing the lawn in neat stripes. They finally decided to take the leylandii down. Mum and Dad haven't stopped moaning about the invasion of their privacy since.

'How's the baby?' she calls, as Philip winds the cord of the lawn mower back round the handle.

'Adorable,' I call back without hesitation, because she is.

'And your aunt?'

'Fabulous, thanks,' I say, feeling generous. Why hold back on behalf of my imaginary aunt?

'Funny I never heard Sissy mention her before,' Sue says. There's no reason why Sue should be suspicious, and I'm pretty sure it's all a product of my guilty conscience, but I feel the need to convince her, and to get rid of this aunt once and for all.

'She's gone off on a world cruise for a year, actually.'

'A year! I never heard of such a thing!'

'Oh yeah, it looks amazing, a real home from home, but luxury,' I say, leaning into it.

'That must be costing her a pretty packet.'

'It is. Her late husband made a fortune from . . . er . . .' Where do people make their fortunes? 'From the gold mines.' Gold mines? Where did he live, nineteenth-century California?

'Oh, I see,' she says, frowning. 'Well, I'll let you get on.'

Hopefully that's put paid to that, although knowing Sue, she's probably off to diarise asking me about my aunt's return in a year's time. Perhaps poor Auntie will meet with a tragic, fatal accident on board.

Zach comes out of the back door and settles down on the patio in the other deckchair, next to Elaine.

'How's my little sister?' he says, one hand shading his eyes against the sun's glare.

Another revelation is how Zach has taken to Clara, having initially been so resistant to the concept of Martin becoming a father for the second time. He's doing so well since Martin found him a new therapist who, as well as specialising in addiction, really gets him. Finally settling on an anti-anxiety medication that works for him has made a big difference too, plus he's like a different person since we agreed to him not going back to university. He's always wanted to work in film production, and when an old friend of Elaine's relocated his post-production company from London to a local office, she was able to swing him an entry-level job. It's not brilliantly paid but he loves it, and it gives him enough to afford the very reasonable rent on Mum and Dad's basement annexe, neatly solving their debt problem and giving him some independence. I don't want to count my chickens – I know there's always a chance he could slip back into his old ways – but I'm hopeful. Our relationship is different now. I no longer see him through rose coloured glasses – as if he was the cherubic baby I once bounced on my knee. I've finally accepted that what he needs is to be held accountable for his actions, not endlessly excused and protected. We relate to each other as adults, in the same way I'm learning to do with Mum and Dad.

'She's perfect,' Martin says. 'Like her brother.'

'I think that's overstating it a bit, Dad,' Zach says, smiling.

'Here we go.' Mum comes limping out from the house. She's using a walking stick on a temporary basis, having twisted her ankle earlier in the week. Dad follows, laden down with a tray of tea things including a lopsided, triple-layered Victoria sponge, the result of his recently discovered passion for baking. Most of his creations taste delicious but his enormous hands mean they leave a little to be desired on the presentation front. He sets it all down on the ornate steel table, part of the furniture set they bought after they got the patio repaved in light grey porcelain.

We all pull up a matching chair and I pour the tea, handing it round to everyone except Martin, who's wary of spilling it on Clara's soft little head, and then go around again with slices of cake.

'Here's to family,' Mum says, raising her teacup towards the cloudless azure sky. 'And absent friends.' She looks at me and I know we're both thinking about Caitlin, and about my sisters who never got to see the sky. Now that the dust has settled, I've developed a new-found respect for my parents. Six months ago, I could only see them as an annoyance, a problem to be solved. These days I see them properly for who they are. They may be getting older, but they're still there, the same people they always were. Dad is still a strong, empathetic rock with a genius for teaching. Mum is still a firebrand with an iron-clad sense of social justice. There's no one in the world I'd rather have as my parents.

'I must say, Sissy, the roses are absolutely spectacular this year,' Elaine says, blowing on her tea, savouring the opportunity to drink it while it's still hot. 'You've done the most marvellous job considering you were almost starting again from scratch after . . . what happened.'

'Thank you, darling,' Mum says. 'We were lucky in that we were able to save some of the bushes, and we've bought lots of new ones. It would have been nice to have started them from seed, but who knows whether we would ever have got to see them come to fruition. It seemed more sensible, given our advancing years, to put in some established plants.'

'Don't be silly,' Elaine says. 'You'll outlive us all, Sissy.'

'The roses really are stunning,' Martin says. 'How did you get it all looking so good so quickly? Did you use some kind of magic fertiliser?'

If Clara hadn't chosen that moment to start screaming, I wouldn't have looked up and I would have missed the glance that passed between my parents. As it is, I catch the tail end of it and as I do, I remember reading somewhere that human corpses can be an effective fertiliser, transforming the earth into nutrient-rich soil. Suddenly I know exactly where they buried Cooper. I choke on my Victoria sponge, coughing out a spray of crumbs onto the patio.

'Are you alright, Pen?' Dad says. 'Do I need to perform the Heimlich manoeuvre?'

'I'm fine.' I wipe my eyes.

'What's that space there for?' Martin asks, pointing to an obvious gap between a bush abundant with pale pink, trailing roses and one dotted with deep red tea roses.

'There's a couple of bushes we've had our eye on down at the garden centre at Knoxheath,' Mum says. 'So we thought we'd leave a gap for them.'

'Did you go and see your friend this morning, Sissy?' Elaine asks. 'The one who had a fall – Linda, isn't it?'

'Oh yes, we did. She's out of hospital now, which is good, but her daughter's completely useless, won't help look after her at all.'

'Sarah's got a full-time job, Mum.' My mind is still racing over the fact that they buried Cooper under the rose garden he destroyed – the destruction of which was the final straw that goaded my mother into lifting that fox-handled walking stick and bringing it down on the back of his head. However, I can't let this one go by. I know Linda's daughter Sarah, a nice woman who actually does a lot for her mother. 'You can't expect her to chuck that in to look after her mum – how's she meant to pay her bills?'

'Well, she's got some sort of paid carer in, but it's not the same, is it?'

'At least Linda's got some help.'

'But this carer's hopeless – awful!' Mum warms to her theme. 'Leaves her in bed for hours, doesn't make the food when she's supposed to, spends all day talking on the phone and smoking in the garden.'

'Do you think Linda's a little confused? Maybe the carer has fed her, but she's forgotten? It could be the beginnings of dementia,' I suggest.

'Linda's fine, there's nothing wrong with her apart from a bruised hip. No, the problem is the carer, but Sarah point blank refuses to do anything about it. You can't let people get away with these kinds of things. Sometimes you have to take the law into your own hands.'

'Your mother's quite right,' Dad says, ever loyal.

Mum downs the last of her tea, brushes the crumbs off her lap and looks thoughtfully at the gap in the ground between the rose bushes.

'No point letting the grass grow under your feet,' she says. 'Something's got to be done about that carer. Linda needs help. I'll go round tomorrow.'

She stands to go back inside. As she stumps heavily away, I notice something I didn't earlier, and I realise that the location of Cooper's body wasn't the only thing they lied to me about. They also told me they'd buried the murder weapon, but the walking stick my mother is using is made of heavy oak, and topped with a silver fox head.

THE END

Acknowledgements

As ever, huge thanks are due to my fabulous agents Felicity Blunt and Rosie Pierce, especially for their invaluable help in the early stages of this book. Somebody very wise once said to me when I was looking for an agent that (amongst many other things, of course) your agent needs to be someone with whom you can celebrate the good stuff, but also someone who you can burst into tears on when things are not going so well. I definitely tested that out this time and you proved yourselves worthy!

Thank you to my new editor Phoebe Morgan for your insightful edits, and to the whole team at Hodder. I'm so excited to be working with you.

Big thanks to my father, Murray, for horticultural advice about roses and the vegetables you might expect to find growing in an allotment in winter (and for not laughing too much when I asked how Brussels sprouts grow).

I'm very grateful to Matt and Kristina for invaluable advice on everything landlord-related, especially the tenant horror stories (thankfully none quite as bad as Cooper).

To Graham Bartlett, much thanks for sage advice on police matters. As ever, I have stretched reality to fit my plot purposes and any inaccuracies or ludicrous 'that would never happen' moments are down to me alone.

To all my writing friends, especially the Ladykillers, who are there for the highs, the lows, the filth and everything in between. Special mention to local writer bestie Nicole Kennedy for unequivocal support, pastry provision and a brilliant collection of private club memberships.

As always, thank you to my best girls Claire, Natasha, Catherine, Jane, Naomi and Rachel – and never forgetting our beloved Hattie.

I owe a massive debt of gratitude to YOU – all the readers and bloggers who write reviews and tell their friends about my books and contact me to let me know they've enjoyed them. It means so much.

And finally to my home team: Charlie and Arthur, the best sons ever, and Jon, to whom this book is dedicated (finally), my biggest supporter and all-round wonderful man. Everything is better with you.

Read on for a glimpse at the gripping first chapter of
My Husband's Killer . . .

Chapter 1

Liz

Today is my husband's funeral, but my grief has been stolen from me by what I've just found in the pocket of his shorts. Instead of crying, I am burning with rage. I kneel on the floor, his weekend bag still open at my side, swallowing down nausea. I don't have time for this now. My children, Ethan and Josh, are downstairs looking younger than their eleven and nine years, upright and silent in their formal clothes. They are waiting for me to go down and make it OK for them. That's what I have to do every day for the rest of their lives – try and make it OK that their daddy has died. Andrew has gone. There's no one else who can help me.

I close my eyes and shove the shorts back into the bag. It will have to wait. I paint on a smile and try to make my footsteps sounds light and breezy as I run downstairs.

'Right, boys! Time to go.'

In the church, the boys sit either side of me, huddling in as close as they can possibly get, my arms enfolding them in the vain hope of providing some comfort. The vicar's voice echoes up to the rafters, sonorously reading out the eulogy I wrote, the eulogy I put my whole heart into. I sat up at the kitchen table late into the night, crafting every word, retrieving every memory I could, contacting his family and old friends to ensure I didn't leave out any vital facet. I don't hear a word. All I can think of is my hand meeting that small packet. When she has finished, my husband's best friend Owen stands and makes his way from the pew behind me to the lectern, a couple of sheets of A4 paper in his hand. He stands for a moment looking at the papers, clears his throat and begins.

'I knew Andrew for over thirty years, since our school days at Winchester College. I was a scholarship boy, out of my depth and petrified. The other boys were either indifferent to my plight, or minded to laugh at me. Andrew was different. He took me under his wing, and that was where I stayed. Until now.' His voice cracks and he takes a moment to compose himself. He tells a couple of anecdotes about their school days that raise a few gentle laughs, and then moves on to talk about Andrew meeting me.

'Liz and Andrew were a great match, and I watched as first love, and then fatherhood, transformed him.'

Ethan and Josh huddle in even tighter. I screw my eyes shut, unable to feel the way I want, and ought, to feel. What I found this morning prevents the uncomplicated tears of grief that should be falling. Fury rises in me, hot and uncontrollable. My anger is partly directed at Andrew, because it has thrown everything I thought I knew about him into total disarray. He wasn't perfect, sure, but who is? But I never once suspected this. My ire is mostly reserved, however, for someone else, because what I found indicates there must have been a someone else. I don't know who she is, but what I do know is that she is sitting here in this church.

We finish with a hymn to which I hardly bother to mouth along, having let the vicar choose it, and a final prayer committing Andrew's body, wherever it may be, to a God he had little belief in. Originally I had mooted a non-religious ceremony but Andrew's parents had objected, and as I didn't have any strong feelings either way a church service seemed the right thing to do.

The boys and I are the first to leave with Andrew's parents following behind, his mother wailing and clinging to her husband who has aged ten years in the last three months. Mourners – family, friends, colleagues, red-eyed but offering supportive smiles – reach out from the end of almost every row. There are three serious men and a woman who I think are work associates. A dark-haired young woman I don't recognise sits in the final row, stifling tears, rummaging in her bag for a tissue.

The air in the churchyard is humid and oppressive, the sky a peculiar dark grey tinged with orange. Water droplets cling to the leaves in the trees, occasionally giving up and splashing to the ground. His mother wanted him to be buried here, but the Tyrrhenian Sea has so far refused to give him up. Behind me, she begins to cry, her raw unfettered pain echoing around the churchyard. I am dry-eyed, consumed with jealousy at her straightforward misery. My friends Poppy, Saffie and Trina form a phalanx of support around me, a guard of honour as we walk to the car.

Afterwards, we gather in the village hall. The weather is still unpleasantly oppressive, but inside the hall the atmosphere is lighter now the worst bit is out of the way – or the worst bit for everybody else at least. For me, it's only the beginning.

I smell patchouli and herbal shampoo and before I know it, my best and oldest friend Poppy has enveloped me in a massive hug.

'I know I've said it a million times, Liz, but I am so sorry.'

I allow her to hold me, limp like a ragdoll in her arms, but I can't be comforted by her today. She releases me and steps back. She's dressed conservatively (for her) in a deep purple maxi dress and tan suede boots, her pink-streaked chestnut brown curls tamed into submission in a knot at the nape of her neck, a hammered silver pendant hanging almost to her waist.

'Thanks.' I'm aware I sound stilted but I hope she'll put it down to grief. 'Who are those lot, do you know?' I indicate a small group of men in mostly ill-fitting suits chatting quietly amongst themselves.

'They're the GreenEc lot,' Poppy says. 'God, I suppose I ought to go and schmooze them – sorry not schmooze . . . I didn't mean to make this sound like some sort of grim *networking* event.'

I smile despite myself. Andrew had had his doubts about going into business with Poppy, but when he'd been looking for a partner to set up a PR agency with fifteen years ago, she'd been the obvious candidate. Her personal life might be chaotic but at work she was dedicated and professional, an ideal fit to support his vision for a PR firm serving ecologically, ethically sound businesses. For him it was a gap in the market he was keen to fill, but for her it not only chimed with her green instincts but was a natural next step from working as an in-house PR for various eco-charities.

'It's fine,' I say now. 'Go and talk to them.'

'OK, I'll have a quick word. Back soon.' She gives me another hug, a brief one this time, and heads over to the group. The men's faces light up. They are the earnest types – all natural fibres and vegan shoes – for whom Poppy's alternative style and natural beauty are catnip.

When Andrew and I were first together we would lie entwined in bed, discussing which of each other's friends we found attractive. It sounds like a dangerous game (and probably would be at a later stage of a relationship) but back then we were so secure in our love and attraction for each other that it felt perfectly safe. Poppy never featured very high on Andrew's list, although in retrospect that may have been political on his part. Is it ever a good idea to tell your partner you fancy their best friend? But I believed him, and have never experienced a speck of mistrust over all the time they've been working together. Mind you, how many times have I heard that over the years? By the time you get to your mid-forties, you've witnessed a lot of relationship break-ups. For every one of my friends who saw it coming, there's another that was blindsided by a partner who behaved in a totally unexpected way, as if they'd been a different person to the one they seemed to be all along.

As Poppy passes Trina and Saffie, she gives them an almost imperceptible signal that indicates I've been left alone. As one, they descend on me like well-schooled dancers in a ballet, getting every step right. Saffie is as glamorous and elegant as ever. Her dark blonde hair falls in neat waves over the shoulders of the unfeasibly expensive navy trouser suit she's wearing over a cream silk blouse, demurely buttoned almost to the neck as befits a funeral. Trina's wearing a classic black shift dress that used to be fitted but is now loose around her hips and gapes under the arms. Her always-sharp cheekbones are more pronounced than ever under the wings of her pale blonde bob.

'All right, darling?' Saffie presses her cheek to mine and I breathe in a waft of her perfume, heady with jasmine. Trina gives me a brief hug, all angles and bones – she's definitely lost weight.

'Have you seen the boys?' I ask, aware that they've slipped from the orbit I've held them in so carefully all day.

'They're playing outside with Milo and Ben,' Saffie

says. 'Owen's watching them, don't worry.' I can sense how hard she's working to say her ex-husband's name in a neutral fashion, to not let their animosity spill into my husband's funeral. Of the two of them, it's Owen who has more right to be angry. Nine months ago, Saffie left him for Todd. Todd is an improbably good-looking, rich American with whom it transpired she'd been having an affair for some time, a betrayal of his best friend that Andrew – and I, if I'm honest – struggled to come to terms with.

'Julian's out there too,' Trina adds. 'He's setting up a cricket game with a stick and an old tennis ball they found in the bushes. Do you need wine? Food? Anything?'

'Nothing, thanks.'

A silence descends in which they regard me anxiously. They'll put it down to grief, but I know I'm being short with them and until this morning I would have said they don't deserve it. Along with Poppy, these women dropped everything to support me today, and over these last terrible three months. They came to the registrar with me when, having finally received confirmation of presumption of death, I went to register Andrew's death, unable to deal with it alone. They sat with me at the meeting with the vicar, helping me plan the service, knowing what I wanted without having to ask. They set up the projector for the montage of photos of Andrew I spent hours putting together as I wept uncontrollably at his innocent childhood face. But one of them has ruined everything.

'I could do with some fresh air,' I say, unable to stand here with them any longer. 'I'll go and check on the boys.'

I leave, not having to look back to know their faces are creased with concern.

Outside, Trina's husband Julian has set up a small suitcase as makeshift cricket stumps. He's calling out encouragement to my eldest, Ethan, who is preparing to bowl at his younger brother, Josh. Saffie and Owen's boys, Milo and Seb, crouch in the field, concentrating furiously. Owen is surveying the scene, his back to me, and I feel a throb of gratitude towards him. He's not only Andrew's friend, he's mine, too, and I'll be forever thankful for the energy he's putting in to make this an OK day for my children, a day which is so difficult for him personally. I give myself a mental pat on the back for encouraging my friends to bring their children today. It's so much better for the boys to be out here playing than sitting inside enduring a stream of well-meaning sympathy.

'Hey.' I touch Owen's elbow gently.

'Liz. Hi. Was it OK? My speech?'

'Yes, it was lovely. Thanks for doing it.'

'God, you're welcome. It was the least I could do. How have you been coping?'

That bloody question. I must have been asked it hundreds of times over the last three months and each time I've been at a loss as to how to answer. I usually fall back on clichés like 'as well as can be expected', which I think is what they want to hear. They certainly don't want the truth. They don't want to hear about the gaping hole that has opened up in my life, the shock and trauma of my husband being by my side for almost twenty-five years and now suddenly gone. Disappeared. They don't want to know how I sit on the sofa night after night, when the kids have gone to bed, staring in horror at the empty space at the other end where he used to sit. They don't want to know what a monumental effort it is to get up every morning, exhausted from a tormented night lying awake, and put on a mask of happiness for my grieving children who mustn't be allowed for a second to think that their mum is not OK. They don't want to hear about how telling my boys their daddy was dead was the worst thing I have ever had to do, or ever hope to do, in my life. How when I opened my mouth, I wished I could suspend time and let them have a few more moments of innocence before I shattered their lives and took it away for ever. How I can't bear that they have had to learn this lesson so young – that life is cruel and unpredictable, that things change and people can be taken from you in the blink of an eye.

Since my discovery this morning, I'm even more poorly equipped to answer the question.

'I'm OK,' I say, unable to muster anything more detailed.

'Of course you're not,' Owen says. 'How could you be? None of us are. But it's a million times worse for you.'

For the first time today, a sob almost escapes my lips.

'Hey.' Owen takes me in his arms, and for a second I allow myself to relax, my face in his shoulder.

'Do you think we knew him?' I say indistinctly into his shirt.

'What?' Owen draws back, hands on my shoulders.

'Do you think we really knew him? That's what I keep going over and over.'

He hesitates for a second before replying.

'Yes, I do.'

'You don't sound very sure.'

'I mean … to the extent that we know anybody. There's always a part of everyone that's hidden, that they keep for themselves, I think. Don't you?'

'I suppose so.'

'And that's OK. Just because you didn't know every single little thing about Andrew doesn't invalidate your relationship with him, doesn't mean it wasn't real.'

'Mm hmm.' I press my lips together to keep the words inside. I want so badly to share with someone what I found this morning. Would it be wrong to do it here, now? Owen was Andrew's best friend. If there was something going on, there's a chance he knows about it. Andrew let his guard down around Owen. Once, years ago, drunk and uncertain of Andrew following an argument at a party, I'd asked Owen if he thought Andrew really loved me. Owen said he knew he did, and then asked me if I loved him. When I said yes, Owen said, *There's your answer. You're meant to be together.* I take a breath, unsure whether I'm going to tell him what I found or not, and then Julian comes jogging over, and the moment is gone.

'So sorry, old girl.' Julian leans down, hair flopping over his forehead, to give me a kiss on the cheek. I didn't know people in real life said 'old girl' until I met him. I once heard him say – unironically – 'tally ho'. I loathed him on instinct when I first met him, assuming he would look down on me for my background, but actually he's never been anything but kind and rather sweet. 'Anything I can do, you only have to shout. Boys seem to bearing up OK.'

'Yes.' I watch Josh racing up the pitch as Milo runs for the ball. 'I worry they're coping too well on the outside – that they're not telling me how they really feel.'

'They'll be OK,' says Owen. 'But don't feel you're alone – let us support you.'

'Thanks.' I bite back tears again. 'I'd better go back in – let me know if the boys want me.'

I just about make it through to the end of the afternoon. Trina, Poppy and Saffie come back to my house, not wanting to leave me alone for the evening. Not 'our' house any more, unless you count the children who are in bed, exhausted after a day of seeing adults who are normally in full control of their emotions weeping and embracing. Enduring hugs and kisses from people they barely know. Coming to terms with their new lives, the one where they will always be those kids whose dad died.

We've all been drinking this afternoon, but the empty Prosecco bottles continue to accumulate on the kitchen worktop. A casual observer would think it a touching scene. A woman, widowed far too young at forty-five, surrounded by three other women, old friends, a group supremely at ease in each other's company. The kind of friends who can conjure up a shared joke with a single word, who can go for months without speaking and pick up exactly where they left off without drawing breath; who can count on the others to be there when the chips are down, to catch them when they fall. We all lived in London in our early twenties, and then one by one moved out to the same family-friendly commuter town of Haverbridge. Andrew and I were the first to go, twelve years ago when I was pregnant with Ethan, in search of green spaces and extra bedrooms. Owen and Saffie, also expecting their first child, followed shortly after. A couple of years later, Poppy was left homeless after yet another disastrous relationship and with Scarlet due to start secondary school, moving here was a no-brainer. Trina and Julian were the last to tire of London but eventually they did.

There were tears earlier, of course, but now there is laughter and shared reminiscences and stories. The conversation around the kitchen table ebbs and flows like the tide that washed Andrew away. I'm not saying much, but my friends understand. They give space to my grief, allow me to just be, present but apart from them. The very best of friends. They think they know everything about me, but they don't. None of them would guess in a million years what's going on inside my head, eating away at me – chewing me up and spitting me out.

They are my three oldest, dearest friends, and I would have been lost without them these past three months. They helped with the logistics of my husband disappearing abroad, presumed drowned. They liaised on my behalf with the Landell Trust, a charity that helps people whose loved ones have died overseas. They brought lasagnes and flowers and books and chocolate in those slow, quick, hazy days after we got home from Italy, days I can now scarcely remember. They took my boys – shell-shocked and dazed but still needing company and entertainment – on outings, giving me time to deal with the endless admin, or to do nothing at all but stare into space or cry on the sofa. They sat beside me today, holding my hand, in the church. They walked down the aisle with me so I didn't have to do it by myself. They tell me, over and over, that I am not alone. That although we're not related by blood, they are my family, and I theirs.

Part of me wishes I had never opened my husband's bag this morning, the one he took to Villa Rosa, the Italian villa where we spent his final weekend with these three women and their families. The place where he died. I hadn't been able to bring myself to touch it before, but this morning I was looking for his watch. I wanted to wear something of his at the funeral, and I couldn't wear his wedding ring because he was wearing it when he drowned. I forced myself to rummage through the bag, a brand new one he'd bought for the weekend away. The smell of him – washing powder and cologne and something indefinably him threatened to overwhelm me as I ran my shaking hands through the contents. His toothbrush was in there, and the things from the bedside table – his glasses, the book he was reading. Clean underwear he never got to wear. Someone must have packed this up in the aftermath. Or perhaps it was me and I've blocked it out. No watch, though. I felt something in the pocket of a pair of shorts that he'd worn on the last day of his life, before he changed into his evening wear. I slid my fingers in and they met a small slippery square packet. I thought perhaps it was a sweet, although Andrew didn't eat them. I certainly didn't feel any trepidation as I drew it out into the light. It was like a kick to the stomach. I was already hollowed out by grief and exhaustion and the overhanging dread of the day ahead, but this was something else entirely. Something that snatched the breath from my lungs, made me tremble all over and press my hand to my mouth, stifling the urge to vomit. I had a contraceptive coil fitted after Josh was born. Andrew and I hadn't used condoms since we were first together. So why did he have one in his pocket? In sick fascination, I turned the shiny wrapper over and over, as if that would make it into something other than the betrayal it represented.

I look from one to the other of the dear faces of my oldest friends, seated around my kitchen table. They are more careworn and lined than when we first met, but as familiar to me as my own. All I can think is: which one of you bitches was sleeping with my husband?

THREE COUPLES. ONE MURDER.
A HOLIDAY TO DIE FOR . . .

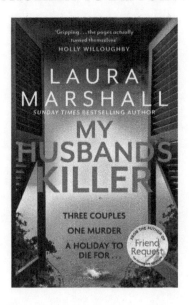

We arrived at a villa on the Amalfi Coast, ready to enjoy a sun-soaked weekend with our oldest friends - and one new face.

By the end of the weekend, my husband is found dead.

But how can I mourn him, when on the day of his funeral I discover he was having an affair? The only suspects are the women we went on holiday with. My oldest, closest friends. Do I really want to dig into my husband's secret? Do I really want to know who betrayed me?

And as I start to unravel their secrets . . . do I really believe his death was an accident?

The emotional, twisty mystery from number one bestselling author Laura Marshall is out now